The Blackthorn Legacy

Alan McIntyre

Copyright © 2012 Alan McIntyre

All rights reserved.

ISBN: 1508677913
ISBN-13: 978-1508677918

DEDICATION

Marie, the mother of invention

INTRODUCTION:

THE VISIT

THE sky above was an unbroken overcast of darkening grey. Martin Carey occasionally looked out his kitchen window at the changeable weather as he listened to his Citizen Band radio or CB to you and me. He had just finished eating his home cooked evening meal after another tiresome day at work.

His kitchen was a warm cosy room. It was a warm grey and the scene resembled a retro style photo of an unlighted kitchen in the descending dusk. Outside the cool September air had a bit of bite in it, however the flickering orange glow and accompanying heat from the fireplace insulated Martin from that weather outside.

Martin Carey was essentially a loner. He lived just outside the small rural village of Shayleigh. This was his second move and in his seven years as a home owner he had done so unaccompanied and all alone.

The village of Shayleigh was on the main road from the principle town of Fellowmore to nowhere in particular – and roads from it led to everywhere. The middle of nowhere is how some who happened to pass through the village described it and that's what endeared it to Martin. He spent his working hours in the boisterous environs of Fellowmore

The Blackthorn Legacy

and always looked forward every evening to coming home to the peace and quiet of his secluded house. The house was an old two bedroom farmhouse at the end of a cul-de-sac known as Ard Lane.

His kitchen window looked out to the West and on occasion the fiery sunsets would colour the room with strange magical colours and dark shadows. This particular evening though, the grey cloud cover concealed the sun's light show from sight, but it was there, somewhere. It was always there. The lower grey puffs that skirted over the horizon's uneven line looked as though they were carrying leftover orange and purple gases in their bases. Soon all of those colours would disappear for yet another one of his days.

The great ball of fire was on its way down behind the grey curtain would bring the day's heat with it. The dark end of the day would follow and daylight would be suffocated out until the following day when it would magically re-appear. Martin threw another log on the fire and watched as shadows of lifeless objects became energised and danced as though being conducted by the fire's jumping flares.

The jumbled conversations continued on the CB but none of it maintained Martin's interest. That happened from time to time. Boredom set in as the voices on the little black box were just of those faceless drivers travelling in lorries, describing the journeys they were making hither and tither throughout the country in their own code. His only other connection with the outside world, from this room, was his radio.

The monotony of the discussions let his mind wander and then he decided to get up from his comfy armchair and get a mug of water. He had recently bored a well in his back garden based solely on the decision implemented, by the Government's he hadn't elected to introduce water charges. Charges they had been agreed in the parliament, by those over-paid politicians, without public consultation, and were to be levied on the general public, with impunity. It was also

The Blackthorn Legacy

proposed that those with their own source of water would be exempt from the charge and this alone pushed Martin into at least investigating the possibility of boring his own well. After a week's exploration he decided to go for it. He believed that it was prudent to operate on the basis that the less the Government or Government agencies knew about him the better for him in the long-run. Now three weeks into his own water production and the taste was, well let's call it like it was. The water tasted a little bitter, or acidic. It was supposed to be tasteless. That said it still tasted that bit better than the stuff pumped through pipes by the Local Authority especially as it had all those additives included. Water should be to tongues what darkness is to eyes or silence is to ears.

He retrieved a mug, his favourite mug, from the press under the kitchen sink and turned on the cold tap. Water gushed out from the tall arching silver chrome tap, splashing into the sink and the jumping spray splashed up wetting his plain grey jumper. The tap jigged a little and then the water seemed to spontaneously stop flowing. It was however quickly followed by a gurgling noise, as if the tap itself was choking. Then as suddenly as all this had happened, the water began flowing again from the tap in a nice perfect crystal stream of clear drinking water. It looked like it could have been an opaque glass stem extending from the shiny and perfectly curved silver chromed tap, set at the back of the metal basin between the hot and cold knobs (also in chrome). The flow was just so perfect. It looked fabulous and inviting. There was obviously a problem, he thought with the pressure function in the installation out back. Martin neither knew nor understood very much about plumbing but he considered it a possibility that it might have been the water pump that was problematic. He would have to resolve this little glitch somehow, if there was in fact any trouble at all.

But that was for later.

He broke the liquid stream with his mug to obtain some of this beautifully crisp looking fluid. Martin raised the almost

The Blackthorn Legacy

full cup to his lips first tasting and then took a large gulp. He wiped his wet lips with the back of his hand and waited. The acidic taste was not as strong as it had been. He smiled a satisfying smile to himself and looked at his grinning reflection in the round free standing silver framed shaving mirror on the window board of the main kitchen window. On inspection he noticed some water droplets on the mirror glass and immediately plucked the hand towel hanging from the press handle by his knees and rubbed off the small liquid spots. Now he could see himself clearer. He tried a few different smiles and decided that the exaggerated beam, a snarl smile, was his favourite. Only he would ever see the funny side of it though.

The room itself was also spotlessly clean and everything had its place. He always preserved his kitchen in this condition, as in fact he did with all other rooms in his house too. The room was relatively small but was big enough for a single occupant. The only item that stood out was the Bankers' Lamp with a green glass shade that rested on a square fold away table in the left-hand corner near the side window; that looked out to the stony drive-way most of the way up from the lane. He rarely used the long tubular fluorescent light in the centre of the ceiling. Martin had theories about certain things and the use of those fluorescent bulbs and the harm they might cause was just one of those bugbears of his.

The site had been cut into what had once been a hilly field. Out the back of the site, beyond the barbed wire fence which separated his site from the other land, the field continued its slow incline towards a line of Beech trees and whitethorn bushes that created a natural break to the next group or separately owned pastures. On the right hand side of his site was a thick line of deciduous Poplar trees leading up to and converging with the Beech trees far up on the sloping field.

He heard a scraping noise at his white PVC white back door. It was a continuous sound of nails being scraped down. The scraping noise now strangely accompanied by a low

The Blackthorn Legacy

wailing din just outside his door. Approximately two inches of polymer and metal was all that was separating him from whatever was outside his house.

The hairs on his neck stood on end. He stood perfectly still in the darkness of his kitchen, alone, he hoped.

Silence.

The scraping sound accompanied again by the light scraping.

Continuous scraping.

Continuous wailing.

It was starting to get in under Martin's skin and a shiver passed up his back and down his arms.

He tiptoed to the kitchen window, peering out.

Nothing.

He stole out to the small back kitchen and turned on the light over the back-door and sneaked a look out the small window there.

Nothing.

Shit!

He closed his eyes, afraid. He opened them again and then he saw it.

A black cat.

His black cat. Relief passed over him in a warm wave. He had forgotten completely about Cat. He opened the back door and looked out. Cat, a simple name for his black feline friend, padded over to the doorway. The water dish was dry and there were no cat nuts left. No wonder it was trying to catch his attention. He picked up the old circular baking tin and placed it under the tap. A gush of silvery liquid gushed out forcefully and then stopped just as before.

Damn tap.

Water had splashed all around the sink and the worktop surface.

Stupid fucking tap. He'd have to clean up the film of water lying in small oval shaped puddles along the surface surrounding the sparklingly clean metal sink.

The Blackthorn Legacy

Having provided food and drink for Cat, he quenched the back light, cleaned his hands, mopped up the wetness and returned to the kitchen and sat quietly on the settee below the window that looked out on the stony driveway.

He sat there thinking for a good few moments, enjoying his own thoughts and the voice that spoke every so often from the back of his head. It only spoke words from time to time. It wasn't his own voice but it sounded very like it. He did know however, that whenever he had heard a recording of his speaking voice he didn't recognise it as his own. That voice could well be what his voice sounded to anyone else listening to him.

He was beginning to relax, getting the working day out of his head and about to do nothing.

As he sat on his settee under the side window beside his foldaway table contemplating his nothingness, he heard the sound of stones crunching underfoot outside. This was his very own alarm system. An unfailing system because it was impossible to avoid making that crunching sound on Martin's driveway basically because of the slope up from the lane. The slope made sure that every footstep had to be placed sure footedly causing the thick evenly laid load of chippings had to go somewhere. This caused friction and then noise - basic physics.

On hearing the multiple footsteps he pulled the cord on his Banker's Lamp and immediately saw two men in Garda uniforms walking up the sloped driveway from a parked squad car which looked almost as if it had been just abandoned across his gate. The uniformed men were approaching his front door. Seconds later came the rat-a-tat-tat sound of one of the men presumably knocking on the door.

Strange, he thought.

Half seven in the evening and he was having a visit from the law. He walked through the short hallway and reached for the front door knob and immediately felt the blood drain from his face as he slowly pulled in the heavy teak door. The

The Blackthorn Legacy

accompanying long drawn out squeaking sound made by the old hardly used hinges did nothing to improve the situation for him. The two well-built Gardaí stood side by side silently on the bare concrete doorstep which was slightly elevated from the crushed stone of the driveway. They stood silently with tough but concentrated looks on their otherwise expressionless faces.

"Hello", said Martin almost as a question.

"Sir, my name is Garda Sergeant Dunning and this is Garda Dunne. Would you mind turning on a light or can we come inside?" Dunning was an extremely serious looking man and his voice did nothing to change Martin's first impression of him.

"What's this about?" Martin was not about to allow them over the threshold without at least one good reason. This seemed to get Dunning going because even though he was standing on a level slightly below that of floor level he was still taller than Martin. Small Man Syndrome was the Garda's first impression and he was going to bring his superiority to bear.

"It's about the lifeless victim located at the top of this lane. Circumstances relating to the death are of a suspicious nature Mr..." Dunning opened his notebook and rifled through his notes until he came to where he needed. "Mr Carey. Martin Carey. That's you isn't it?" Martin nodded with a confused and bewildered expression on his face. He could see the sneering look grow across the Garda's face as the uniformed man continued, "we need to speak to you about this matter. We're canvassing all the houses on the lane and as there are only two..."

Martin heard no more as he gazed into the darkness that had replaced the fading daylight and engulfed the view from his doorstep. Then he saw it appearing before him as if in a hazy dream. There before his eyes was a large hilly meadow covered in long golden wild grass, blowing in the warm breeze. He could smell the fresh flora fragrance and the clean

The Blackthorn Legacy

and clear breeze. It was perfect. The trance was rudely interrupted by sharp voices.

"Mr Carey, Mr Martin Carey", the voices of the two Gardaí. Back to reality with a bang.

"Get your coat and keys Mr Carey; you're coming with us..."

CHAPTER ONE:

THE ROBBERY

THE feeling of freedom was immense. Martin Carey was just enjoying his first hours of freedom from his job as a week's annual leave had just commenced at five thirty that very Friday evening. Now five minutes later his pulse was racing as he walked down the busy Fellowmore street.

He worked hard in his profession as a speech and note writer for the top brass in the Department of Education. He was known as The Deceptakon within the walls of the Department. A name given to him by his co-workers but they never mentioned it in his presence. They realised how important he was to the office and deception was his game – a game he played well, for that team. It could have been the fear factor. He was one of the quiet ones they were the ones to be watched. His work was always of first rate quality and he put everything into it, no matter how unimportant or insignificant in the scheme of things it appeared to be. Each speech, each profile, each note was prepared and included all the relevant information. Often the material provided by Martin had more than that required but he believed it was better to have something and not need it than to want or need something not available.

Making the Minister and indeed the Government look good no matter what the situation that cropped up was his

The Blackthorn Legacy

job and boy did he excel at this. He could word a speech so well that even in the worst of public relations circumstances he could make it so that it appeared that his boss was bringing beneficial news to the listening masses. The notes he provided for media interviews were so masterful that the Minister or his officials could speak for minutes without actually saying anything or giving anything away. But it wasn't until later during the usual analysis by armchair and professional journalists that the lack of factual content would become apparent to those the Minister had faced.

He was that good.

Martin hated his job though. He was forever forced by his superiors to introduce so much red tape within the Governmental system that the Department he served was for all intents and purposes being held together by this same excessive regulation that was really only created to keep the political classes in their cosy jobs. In essence, he had to lie to remain in employment and his very job created the cotton wool that preserved his bosses' glossy and clean appearance. That appearance was only skin deep though, but then again there was always so much skin to penetrate in any case.

This removal of the heavy shell of deception for nine consecutive days of leave when he included the four weekend days was a fabulous sensation. The conning and the pretext associated with his job had been left behind, in the confines of prison cell type office space that he occupied for eight hours a day, five days a week. It was tiresome. That said the one thing he enjoyed was the silence of an individual space afforded him rather than the open plan area he was cut off from.

This man had no real vices to report except maybe holding short conversations with himself. He didn't smoke, or drink unless you include the time when he and his cousins approached the alter during mass one Easter weekend and requested the Blood of Christ. However, to say he never had smoked was incorrect. He had for about six months when his job almost got the better of him, but he had quit.

The Blackthorn Legacy

The boys were fairly certain that it was just a representation of blood and that it was just watered down wine. The argument between the boys beforehand had centred on Communion and the Blood of Christ. Why would a congregation of possibly the largest religious grouping – Christianity – focus their celebration on a form of cannibalism?

It didn't make sense, did it?

Anyway the three cousins decided that the priest's chalice held only wine. And so they queued for a drink, pretending it was for religious reasons. On the way back to his seat, Martin made so many faces; the others did well to hold in their laughter. He had hated the taste of it and decided at that time, aged seventeen that he would stay clear of alcohol. Drugs were certainly off the table. From that day on, Martin had become an all-round teetotaller.

But it wasn't just this aspect of his life that singled him out from those around him. He knew his current work colleagues thought of him as strange, but that didn't bother him. He much preferred to be wrapped up in the solitude of his office than the noise and all that went with fifty people working together on a large open floor. He didn't need people talking rubbish around him when he had the comfort of the voices in his own head. He could control those anyway, if and when required.

No, sitting out among those people was not his idea of enjoyment.

In fact, it was fair to say that Martin Carey had been a different character up until it all changed eighteen months before, when the Gardaí called to his house, and possibly even just prior to it.

Up until the incident.

*****

To be honest Martin was always a little different. He was an only child. His parents, Pat and Mary Carey, ran a little

The Blackthorn Legacy

convenience store in Dungeandan, a small town about twenty miles from Fellowmore. It was a busy store with a community feel about it. There were three shops in the town, but whenever someone said they were going to the shop, it was almost always Carey's.

The living space over the shop was small but cosy and it had its advantages for the young Martin. Because the shop opened until 10pm on week nights, he was allowed stay up until it was closed and had been readied for following day's business. Martin helped out as best he could, but he very rarely came out front, mainly because of his timidity, but he did put in his fair share of toil.

One Friday night after closing up, the Carey family settled down to watch television. Minerals and popcorn were shared between them.

Soon after they were all settled in front of the television, Pat thought he had heard a noise downstairs. He opened the sitting room door to the landing which led to the staircase which would bring him down to the shop floor.

He opened the door and immediately closed it, leaning his back against it.

"Hide", he ordered Mary and Martin is loud whisper. His face was a mix of emotions – fear and distraught, mostly.

"There's someone coming up here, hide, quickly."

Mary froze on the chair she had been sitting on. Martin however, sprang into action, running into his bedroom which was directly opposite the door his father was now guarding with his life. The little boy left his door slightly ajar, so he could see what was happening. His mother was still on the armchair, rooted to the spot. Martin had thought she was brave, not realising that fear had in fact superglued her to the chair.

Voices, shouting voices, muffled shouting voices were outside the sitting room door. Repeated banging on the door. The shouting became roaring and within only a minute of banging on the door. Then it was squeezed opened, even with his father's weight against it. Three men, dressed in dark

The Blackthorn Legacy

clothes and wearing women's tights over their heads eventually pushed in passed Pat Carey. All three were armed. One with a shotgun and the other two had tool handles. One of them looked like a pick axe handle he had seen before somewhere.

Without doubt, these men would have no problem in using and force they had to. The first man in through the door grabbed Pat Carey and threw him on the chair he had just gotten up from.

The man with the shotgun raised the recoil pad to his shoulder and pointed the barrels at Mary Carey's head and looked at the woman's husband threateningly.

"Where's your fucking money?" One of the men with the wooden handles demanded.

Pat mumbled something inaudible. Fear had taken hold. His mouth felt as dry as cotton wool just out of a package and now that he was trying to talk, it felt as though his mouth was full of the stuff.

Bang. The hoodlum who had made the money demand raised his pick axe handle high over his head and brought the implement down on Pat's thigh with all the power he had in his arms. The scream from Pat terrified his hiding son. Young Martin, hiding in his bedroom barely managed to keep in the scream that had being building up in his throat. He covered his mouth, closed his eyes tight and tried to think of the jumping sheep that calmed him at night and allowed him to find sleep.

"Money, motherfucker. Where is it? You got it here. Get it out now." The punisher with the pick axe handler was speaking through the tights that clung closely to his face, making it difficult to understand, especially under such stressful conditions. "He'll fucking shoot your missus if you don't spill it out now, Pat", he continued, pointing at his wife. That was the scariest part for Pat Carey. Not the fact that he could be beaten to death for not being able to talk, but that the faceless thug standing over him knew him by name.

"I...I...ehh...I don't...can't...get..."

The Blackthorn Legacy

Wallop. The other leg got the same treatment. This time there was a distinct cracking sound. Pat howled in agony. This time it was unbearable. The pain, the blue and white specks passed across his line of vision and when he closed his eyes, the specks were there too. He was unable to talk. Unable to think straight. All he could think about was his son hiding close by. He doubled over in pain on the armchair. He almost lost his breath in the wail he had let out and then soon after, he was reduced to inconsolable sobs. Mary looked over at her husband, tears streaming down her pale face and they were now falling onto her blouse and the wetness was expanding on the material.

"In – the – safe." Talking through her sobbing was difficult, almost impossible but she couldn't watch her husband suffering anymore. The man administering the beating stared over at her.

"Does she always talk out of turn, Pat? You should do something about that. I wouldn't let my woman show me up like that." He paused a second and the scariest smile broke across the man's face through the tights. "Where the fuck is the safe, bitch?" The sarcasm and something else was cutting. "Do you want to see your Pat getting another lesson? I'll make it simple for you. I'll be Simon and Simon says tell me where the fucking safe is. Do you understand that?" Mary nodded quickly a couple of times. Some of the shouting man's spit had managed to get through the material of the tight and it landed on her chin. Just ignore it now, she coaxed herself. She pointed at the door behind the television which was now showing a quiz programme. The answers in that quiz were probably easier than those that were being put to the Careys that night.

"It's." she coughed and cried a little more. She regained her composure because she knew she had to, for her family's sake. "It's in the press under the sink."

"The code?" Shouting behind the door in the kitchen.

Oh no, she panicked. Her mind went completely blank. All she could think about was their safety. She looked up without

The Blackthorn Legacy

moving her head, in an attempt to get her memory to restart.

"What's the fucking code? Someone's gonna get it if I don't hear a code coming from your mouth by the time I count down from five." He banged the tool handle of the arm of the chair Pat was seated in. The man was still writhing in agonising pain, silently. He was in a world of pain. The arm the tool handle hit, splintered, such was the power put into the action by the thug. Mary jumped with fear at the sound of the bang.

"Five."

She tried to think, but the harder she tried, the further the answer moved into the dark unused part of her brain.

"Four."

Mary closed her eyes, squeezing out tears at the corners of her eyes. Warm, salty tears. Think, she shouted at herself in her own mind.

"Three."

Jesus Christ. The fear of torture was now far greater than the fear of being robbed. Her mind was now blanker than it had been at the start of the maniac's count. All she could see in her mind was a dark murkiness. A thick fog, preventing her from seeing the safe's code which she knew was just beyond that syrupy mist.

"Two." "Time's runnin' out missus. You better start getting that code out, before I get my dick out. Some fun we gonna have then." He laughed like a lunatic, a raving mad lunatic.

She was terrified, but it was that extra horror that seemed to clear the fog in her mind and there up ahead in her unclogging consciousness, in red neon type lights was the code. She had found it, somehow. Oh God, she thought, just say it out.

"One. Ok missus, that's it. Time's up."

"No, no, I got it. I know the code. I can tell – tell you what – it – is." She had begun to weep again.

"Well what the hell is it?" The exasperation that had not been in the torturing brute's voice before was now in

The Blackthorn Legacy

evidence. He wanted it bad, so bad. They had just come for the money, but the punishment he had meted out seemed to have been a bonus for him, if not all of these three ruffians. Mary took a deep breath and looked up into her brain, her cortex brain function, to see the numbers she had found there moments earlier.

"Twenty two, oh seven, seven one." A heavy sigh of something was let out of her lungs as if it had been expelled. The gang member who had already gone into the kitchen to locate the safe had gone quiet.

"Did you catch that Sea...shit. Did you catch that?" The use of names was a no, no. He had almost given away the names of one of his partners in crime. He knew he had messed up. The partner with the gun shot a glance across at him. It wasn't clear to Mary what was in that look, but she knew it wasn't good.

"Yep", came the reply from the kitchen. The mistake had also been noticed by him and the single word response had been enough to let his partner know what he thought of the stupidity of the blunder.

The shotgun holding gangster was moving around the room and accidentally kicked a half full glass of mineral, spilling it in the well-worn carpet. A third glass and accompanying popcorn. He looked around the room and reckoned that there had to have been a third person, maybe a child in the room. He looked at the distraught couple, almost feeling sorry for them – but managing to fight it off. He saw the room with the door standing ajar.

"Hey guys" he said with a panicked twinge in his voice.

"What", shouted his partner, not taking his eyes off of Mary.

"I think I heard a noise. A sound."

Mary's already pale face went grey in the second. She sneaked a glance over at Martin's bedroom. Shotgun man had seen it.

"What noise? I heard nothing."

The Blackthorn Legacy

He looked at the terrified woman wriggling in the chair opposite him.

"Please, no", begged Mary. "Please don't." She broke out into a full wail, a gut wrenching wail.

"Nothing, I heard nothing. I just thought, is all." He could see the despair in Mary's face. They had come for the money – that's all.

The man in the kitchen burst into the small sitting room with a black bin-bag, with whatever had been in the safe hanging in the bottom of the bag, shaping it. It looked like an inverted mushroom like the photograph taken after the Hydrogen bombs dropped on those Japanese cities in 1945.

"Come on, let's go." The shot gun man wanted to get out as quickly as possible, before his partners found out what he believed he knew. The perspiration on his forehead was not being allowed to run freely under the tights and was gathering around his eyebrows, ready to drop and sting his eyes.

The brute stood looking over at the shot gun man and shook his head. "We can't go yet. They know Sean's name. They gotta be dealt with. We can't leave like this."

"Surely you're not going to..."

"We gotta. What's the point in taking all this money if we have to give it back to the cops?" The man who had emptied the safe was with his pick axe handle had sided with his similarly tooled up pal.

"Shit."

The punisher stared at the back of Pat's head. Pat was still doubled over in pain. The thigh bone of his right leg had splintered and he had almost passed out with the pain. Thud. The pick axe handle came down with unbelievable force on the back of Pat's head. The sound of timber splitting bone is horrendous, but the sound of smashing bone is sickening. So much so, Mary fainted. This made it easier for the man to land a killer blow on her. The strength of the blow had pushed Pat's head down further than it was naturally intended to go, snapping his spinal cord. His head dangled in

The Blackthorn Legacy

an unusual angle. Moving freely but sickeningly. His pain was gone, along with his life.

Eight year old Martin saw the execution of his father through the slit of light between the slightly ajar door and its frame. As bad as it was witnessing it the sound was far more sickening and he quietly vomited on the carpet of his room. His mother suffered an atrociously similar end.

The memories of this night were pushed back to the back of Martin's mind, into an envelope, and posted to a dark place, never to be re-opened. However, even though he placed the robbery and murder of his parents away, to wipe from his memory, it still go some way to shaping him.

*****

Describing Martin as a changed character, from that of the Martin before the Garda visit, might lead you to believe that he had laughed and joked with his colleagues back before this time. No, this did not happen, but he had mixed with the others at work on occasion back then. Whereas now he waited until the corridor his office was located on was completely quiet and empty before he ventured out the door. This walkway was a long and narrow carpeted hallway relying completely on artificial lighting. The dark green flooring did absolutely nothing to help carry the lamination, and the dull grey wallpaper was equally boring and exactly as it sounded – dreary. There were eight individual offices on this hallway – four on each side. Seven of the eight dark pine doors mostly remained open during working hours. Martin's being the only one that was consistently closed. His was the last door on the right before the corridor led into the open plan area.

Prior to the incident, Martin met and 'mixed' with others in the kitchen area on the ground floor. Now he was never seen and the bosses contacted him by phone and e-mail. The incident had what his colleagues referred to as, a detrimental effect on his well-being. His human being.

The Blackthorn Legacy

Back then, the night the Gardaí called to his house, he had spent seventy two hours in the Garda Station under suspicion of murder. Everybody who knew Martin Carey knew he wasn't capable of such a terrible deed especially when the victim's body was discovered in such a terribly mutilated condition, that it had never been identified and the case was still in the unsolved pile in some holding room in the Garda Station. There was nothing to go on. In the morgue was the torso and legs of a male body, lying there, missing its head, both hands and feet. Identification was nigh on impossible.

That was the scary part. The unknown killer could still be out there.

CHAPTER TWO:

THE HANDKERCHIEF

ALTHOUGH the sensation of freedom ran through his whole body it created just a momentary high. It was something like a version of the hit that a drug addict would have felt after shooting up. The initial high was gone now that he returned to reality. He had to get to Duigan's Camp Shop to get a few things for his week off. It was up the far end of the main street of Fellowmore. He could see the overhanging sign up ahead, maybe three hundred meters further up the street.

The thoroughfare was thronged with people. He met some surly looking faces attached to unmannerly bodies. There were unwritten rules in pavement walking, rules that were generally obeyed up until people became lazy and self-important in recent years. Rules like – stepping aside for on-coming path users if they have heavy bags or for those who are pushing a buggy. It was for the most part common sense, but someone seemed to have cancelled all those rules – without informing Martin what the new ones were, if there were any. He felt like he was walking against a Tsunami of nobodies, most of who believed they were a somebody.

Clipidy Clipidy Clop was the relentless sound of all the footsteps around him. Hard shoes, high heels and trainers. Mixed with that was the constant sound of motor engines passing up and down the street. On occasion others joined

The Blackthorn Legacy

the march, coming out from shops with shopping bags in their hands. Martin was invisible in the crowd. The Average Joe in conservative clothing, grey coat and denim jeans, undetectably walking amongst the crowd who in most cases seemed to be in a hurry to get to somewhere else.

Up ahead he noticed a curve in the horde of walkers. He had an idea what it might have been but waited to see for himself. There it was, one of the Government's spies or as others stupidly called them – beggars.

Martin had noticed this anomaly some months back. These people rested on the street side on the pavement on rugs or cardboard boxes. They always appeared to him to be relatively comfortable. The real chink in the plan was that they always had paper cups, camel brown in colour with a design of thin white lines thinning as they moved down the brown coloured cup from top to bottom. They were always the same.

Always.

The cups they used were like those provided by coffee shops for take-away drinks. Two things that didn't add up in Martin's mind though, were that one; those cups used by the beggars were never available in any coffee shop he'd ever been in and two; who would let a beggar into their coffee shop. He was sure that these people were gathering information for the Government and nobody else was able to see it. It was brilliant – but he wasn't falling for it, no sir-ee.

He gave the woman kneeling on the multi-coloured rug, holding the camel brown coffee cup out, a wide berth while hiding his face, turning his head from the woman, without trying to make it look too obvious that he was concealing himself. If the Government wanted information on him they were going to have to work for it.

He was coming up to a junction. The crowd was beginning to bunch together. The ones ahead were stopped waiting for the pedestrian traffic light to turn green. Martin walked on looking on the ground. He knew there was a manhole cover up ahead somewhere and possibly in his line of walking.

The Blackthorn Legacy

Martin never stepped on manhole covers.
Never.
So much foot traffic every hour of every day on these metal plates and he was supposed to believe that one day they wouldn't collapse under him. He wasn't heavy, far from it in fact, but it could happen to anyone. What really hammered this home for him was the case where some woman who sued several County Councils over injuries she had suffered due to faultily placed manhole covers and she had fallen into the holes. It is true that this was insurance fraud on her part. However at least three different judges had agreed with her, therefore agreeing that it was possible that it could happen. Martin wasn't falling into any hole in the street. Not if he could help it. That was for certain.

Then, from the group of legs just ahead the rectangular cover appeared. It was long but narrow and he was approaching one of the narrow ends. He changed his step length, almost skipping and then slowed to step over the dark grey metallic rectangle caked with years of muck, dirt and dead rust coloured leaves. He stopped and as he was about to make the long step over the metal cover, he was hit from behind. His agility helped him step forward and land with each foot either side of the cover and then began a tirade.

"Watch where you're going, you idiot." A very well dressed woman, maybe in her late thirties, her wavy blonde hair hung loosely down her back. She was dressed in a professional looking navy suit of one kind or another, carrying a dark business style carry bag over her right shoulder, away from Martin. Her long legged pants and jacket were set off very well by the crisp snow white blouse. Her black high heeled shoes gave the impression that this was a tough woman, as did what came from her mouth.

"This is a bloody path for people to get from one place to another and not some playground. Grow up. Idiot."

She pulled out a cloth handkerchief from her left jacket pocket and began to rub her clothes as if to convey the notion

The Blackthorn Legacy

that she was getting rid of any mark, or dirt, he may have left on the navy suit material. On pulling out the handkerchief she managed to inadvertently remove a three and half inch by two inch white card from the same pocket. It fluttered to the ground, landing behind where she now stood. The act of rubbing the dirt from her clothes ended and she looked over at Martin with distain and then continued her progression to the traffic lights. Martin went to the card, through the sea of legs and picked it up and examined it. The card, a business card, belonged to a Deirdre King, Solicitor, working for a local law firm called *Legal, Wrights*. The small photo in the top corner was of the person who had just verbally attacked him. He placed the card in his hip pocket. It was time for him to continue his own walk to Duigan's Camp Shop.

CHAPTER THREE:

THE HUMPY DUNPHYS

NIGHT was coming in early cross the sky as it tended to do in March. As the light disappeared it brought any heat in the air with it. Martin was driving home from Fellowmore. He had his low beam lights on and the shaded cones of illumination were almost properly visible in the not dark but equally not lighted atmosphere. This was worst time of the day to be driving on the roads. He had met a couple of cars driven by dumb drivers who had not bothered with any lights. If he had a mobile phone he would have called them in, but alas he didn't own one. Like in the early days, he would be located if something important occurred but more importantly, he could remain anonymous and alone when he didn't want to be contacted.

He was approaching Shayleigh and as per usual all the traffic was coming or going through the village – not stopping. Very few of those passing through did any business there. It was just a place on the road that broke the boredom of travelling. A public house and two small shops were all that marked it out as a place inhabited by people.

The village had a larger population than would be expected from just passing through it on the way to wherever they may have been heading. According to the most recent national

The Blackthorn Legacy

census it had a recorded populace of one thousand and seventy nine.

Martin passed Foreman's shop and then made a left turn off the main road onto a secondary road. Hidden from the view of so many passers-by was the church, school and mini-market shop, also run by the same family. They had a monopoly on shopping in Shayleigh, but they were local and so it was just accepted by the villagers. Martin continued for another mile on the windy narrowing road. Green ditches on either side of the road hadn't been cut at that time so any driver or road user who may have suffered from Claustrophobia may have had problems using this particular thoroughfare. Individual leafy branches from the wild ditches reached out to the road and in windy weather it often appeared as if the growth was reaching out to get a hold of those passing by.

His lights were more useful now as the darkness was spreading across the countryside and he could make out the potholes on the road and avoid them where possible. Secondary roads such as this particular one were hardly ever resurfaced by the Council, but instead individual holes were filled from time to time. He could make out the intermittent dark tarmac blotches on the old well used stone road, where this work had been carried out from time to time.

Just up ahead was the turn to Ard Lane. There were two relatively new bungalows of modern design on the road just before the turn. Then the old house just down from the corner which was lived in by the two crabby old sisters.

The Dunphy sisters.

The Humpy Dunphys.

They certainly knew how to complain and boy did they let you know if they were unhappy about something. It seemed that whinging about anything is what kept the two seventy something sisters alive. The Humpy Dunphys is how they were known in the village. The light over the front door was lighted and shedding some illumination on the weed covered concrete walkway. It definitely resembled a house from some

The Blackthorn Legacy

children's fairy-tale story. They would most definitely have been the baddies.

From bad to worse on the lane. On the right-hand was a heavily weeded recessed gateway. The gate itself was hardly visible, so high and thick was the overgrowth. This was where the body of the victim (headless, handless and footless) had been located some eighteen month previously. The murder investigation that had seen Martin in interrogation for three days before he had been released without charge. And no apology for the mistake made by the law either. That was a sore point – for the Gardaí, because the case was still unsolved and for Martin because of the treatment he had believed he had been unfairly subjected to.

There were many faces to this lane. Although it was only just about two kilometres in length it had many different parts and stories. The laneway itself was an uneven dusty roadway composed of clay with broken stone, forming the most part. The driving surface was divided in two by a green fringe of grass and weeds down the centre where motor wheels never crossed. It was like a continuous centre line supplied by Mother Nature herself.

The first kilometre of the lane was a straight run although there was a noticeable incline just after the Humpy Dunphy's house. The car lights shone on an old stone wall at end of the straight. In the dark on approach the old wall appeared like battlements of an old historic castle building. When up close it became clear that the shape and outline of the wall was due to disrepair. The wall was the boundary for an old dilapidated farmhouse which now lay in ruins. All three of the small front windows frames were gone and weeds and ivy grew out of the spaces and were met by nettles and weeds from the outside. A large timber board lay across what had been the front door. The grey building was a sad sight in daylight, but in the hours of darkness it seemed to have a completely different shape about it. It was like a nocturnal concrete being – coming to life after daylight had departed.

The Blackthorn Legacy

Martin twisted the steering wheel and followed the lane to the left and almost immediately again to the right. This was the highest point of the lane.

During the hours of daylight to the right a dormant volcano could be seen clearly from that point. It was the only volcano of its kind in the world as it was located in boggy ground and was in a depression. Because of where it was situated, it appeared to be not as high as it officially measured. It had been dormant for thousands of years and was now nothing more than a mountain. It was called Slieve Lea. Its shape and colour were something to behold. They were postcard perfect for anyone who cared to visit the area, which wasn't really expected, and rarely happened in any case.

The grey mountain had a jagged outline all the way to its base where it darkened considerably as it reached the ground. The dark grey volcanic rock at the base of the mountain lay exposed for the centuries since the hot lava had last gushed from the mountain top. Surrounding the base of Slieve Lea was the picturesque sepia brown boggy terrain interrupted only by the naturally growing green ferns.

Martin's car continued the journey down the lane as the road descended towards its end and, of course, his house. It was much darker here under the cover of intermingling branches of tall Beech trees on either side of the lane. As he came to his house the roadway evened out somewhat but the Beech trees interspersed with wild growing brambled bushes blocked his view of the mountain entirely from his house. The line of growth also obstructed the view of the land as it fell away downwards from the road while it equally it rose to the left. His house was on the left.

He turned in the gateless gateway and could feel and hear the driveway stones moving and creating a crunching, scraping noise below the car tyres.

The house was a forty year old building with a familiar look to it. Anybody who had ever perused the Bungalow Bliss book of house designs would have seen this house and many

The Blackthorn Legacy

others like it throughout the country. It was a simple looking hip-roofed structure. The front of the house incorporated a recessed front door in its own porch flanked by equal sized windows – the left one a sitting room and the right a bedroom. A window on the left side of the house – looking out to the driveway – belonged to the kitchen. The exterior wall was a white pebble dash finish. The plinth and window sills were a buttercup colour as were the window reveals and the recessed front door. It was a dated look but that's what Martin liked about it.

Martin stopped his car and got out. Here he had made a change to the original layout of the driveway for himself. He had constructed a concrete wall from the back corner of the house across the thirty foot driveway to the high Beech trees flanking the site to the left. This was built to stop people from driving around to the back of his house. He needn't have bothered building it because he very rarely had visitors anyway. In the centre of the wall was a gate made of narrow lateral timber planks. It was wide enough for a car or lorry to pass through when opened wide. Each morning Martin locked the gate when leaving the house and opened and re-locked on his return each evening once he had parking his car at the back-door.

When he had finally parked the car for the evening he got out, pocketed his keys, and walked to the pump-house. The recently erected building was for all the world like a miniature house. It was approximately seven feet tall at the highest point of the A shaped roof and six feet square. Plastered professionally in a nap finish it looked elegant in the spacious back lawn area. A lick of paint would be applied in the summer. That was Martin's plan in any case. The entrance door, wooden and painted jet black, was at the gable end facing him. He removed his set of keys from his pocket and unlocked the padlock keeping the pump-house protected from whoever it was that might be after him or his belongings. The door opened out to him and he pulled the hanging string to light up the space. Outside the door he

The Blackthorn Legacy

noticed that some of the grass around the shed had turned a burnt orange colour. It had formed a kind of border around the entire structure.

He looked at the internal workings and from what he could see everything seemed fine. Not that he knew much about mechanical workings, but nothing appeared to be out of place.

That was a relief.

The problem of pressurised water spurts from the cold tap in the kitchen had happened again. From Martin's relative experience (which was very little) the pump seemed to be in good order.

Martin re-locked the pump-house door and then looked around. The darkening evening sky was now a navy grey colour and the evening breeze had picked up. Light grey fluffs were visible in the same sky looking like the rough edges of some of the dark clouds. The grey fluffs were moving and changing shape as they did so like some sort of unknown code being sent to the lookers on, on the ground.

Once he was inside his house Martin locked his back-door. The only sound to be heard was the ticking analogue clock in the kitchen. He had purchased it in a second hand shop earlier in the year. It hung over the fireplace. The notches that marked the numbers had a luminous green coating, as were the two large hands.

The back kitchen, which he had to pass through to get to the kitchen area, contained all his white goods and there he opened the fridge. It was as if a block of light fell from the white box on to the floor in the darkness. He removed the two litre plastic carton of milk and filled the kettle with water in the tap at the small sink there and then closed the fridge door when he had prepared everything to make a mug of coffee. The tap only gurgled once and then flowed freely.

The plan for the evening was to turn on the radio, sit and drink his coffee and plan how he would spend his next few days off. He walked into the kitchen and he was met with the increasing *tick tock* sound of the clock. He could see the time on the clock as the only properly visible objects were the incandescent markings on the clock face. He also noticed the lingering smell of fresh paint that still hovered in the room's still air. The tired old colours needed the upgrade that was for sure. The dull grey colour had been annoying him and the new soft peach brought a bit of life to the otherwise lifeless room. The new wall colour brought out the best in the white skirting board and pine wooden floor. He walked to the kitchen window and looked into the reflecting glass of the shaving mirror. The rest of the house's interior was pretty much as it was when he acquired it a couple of years ago. No phone sockets.

"Nice job eh?" He was leaning up on the counter beside the sink, peering into the shaving mirror. There was no reply from the dark reflection. Was it looking back at him? It was hard to tell.

"I'm really happy with it. I hope you like it because you're going to be seeing it all day."

Still no reply.

CHAPTER FOUR:

SPLINTERS OF WOOD

THREE young men, all dresses in shell suits and football jerseys, made their way through the ferns and up the steep incline through thick grass and weeds. Following a fight with the undergrowth they eventually cut through a slight opening in some thorny brambles and then they were up onto the laneway. Jay O'Carroll or Jok as he was known to his friends and also by those whom he had stolen from, beaten or just had generally treated appallingly was leading the other two – Stan Duffy and Tommy Smith.

The lads, all in their early twenties had been in trouble of some sort with the law over the last number of years. Duffy and Smith were followers. They just did what they were told. Jok was a leader. He had already done a stint in jail for aggravated assault nearly two years back. He had also been found with some white powder on his person, but this had been knocked down to having for his personal use rather than for distribution. Most likely he would have served the same sentence for both illegalities, but at least his record would not show any drug related crime. The truth was he was never going to change. The other two had a chance however, but they were just too afraid to make up their own minds. Jok made everything sound so great. He always told them what he had heard on the inside. His line was if you're

The Blackthorn Legacy

not living on the edge then you're taking up too much room. He didn't have a clue what it meant, but it sounded cool.

Jok had gotten his hands on some good coke and he needed a good quiet place for the three of them to do it. Somewhere quiet and away from prying eyes. All the regular places were now known to the do-gooders and that made sure he had to find somewhere else. He had done some recon, found a suitable place and now they were nearly here. At the crest of the killing climb he pointed to the house, dark and most likely empty.

"This is it boys. We can get our coke on here."

"You sure about this Jok?" asked an unsure Duffy.

"Course I'm fucking sure. I cased it out myself. Look at it. The damn place it empty. Always is."

"It looks too good to be true." Smith's voice was a little shaky. He was trying to be the perfect follower, but he was also a little unsure. It looked to be in good condition. Someone must have been keeping it up.

"We're not going to get somewhere, anywhere better than this. Come on, what are you two waiting for. The long grass they had traipsed through had been holding thick moisture and the evening dew had added to it. Their white footwear and lower tracksuit bottoms were wet. That didn't matter so much to them when they were expecting to be high in a matter of minutes.

They crossed the lane and through the gateless gateway. Trudging slowly up the loose chippings, making noise underfoot as they made their way to a wall, split only by a six foot wide wooden gate.

Inside the house Martin was still at the kitchen window facing the round shaving mirror.

"Did you hear something?" he asked his own image. "I did", he continued, "And I don't like it one little bit." He went to a drawer near the sink and grabbed a carving knife and quietly made his way outside. He could hear the footsteps now and the voices of the three youths advancing. He moved silently into a position opposite the timber gate that split the

The Blackthorn Legacy

concrete wall he had erected to stop people such as these coming in. He stood with his heels to the concrete kerbs that divided the lawn from the driveway.

"Get off my land", he shouted from behind the gate.

"What the...I thought you said this was empty." Stan Duffy was having second thoughts. "We should go, Jok."

"I'm going nowhere."

"I'm warning you, I'm armed. Leave me alone. I'll call the..." Martin was growing in confidence. He was a little unsure of himself, but he was going to defend what was his.

"Shut the fuck up old man. I'll go where I want. You want me to leave come out here and make me. Fucking coward, hidin' behind a Goddamn gate."

Smith looked at Duffy, both of them with fear and confusion etched on their faces. "Jok, come on. Let's go while we have a chance to get out. He hasn't seen us yet, come on." Duffy pulled Jok's sleeve. Jok immediately pulled it away and stared threateningly at his pal.

"Nobody tells me what to do. You hear that old man. I do what I want." He began walking towards the gate and rattled it with menace. "Open the fucking gate."

"I implore you not to come in here. I cannot be blamed for what will happen to you if you do. Please stay away. Go away. I'm going inside to call the..."

"I ain't leaving 'til I get in there and you better believe it old man. You can threaten me all ya want. I fucking heard worse and done worse. Open the fucking gate. Now!" The plain and rough bog accent that Martin despised was plain to hear.

"Come on Jok, let's go. We didn't come here for this. Let's go." Smith was anxious to get away. Duffy was equally uncomfortable and fear had started to build in his lower belly.

Jok rocked the gate, grabbing hold of the top frame, pushing and pulling the gate for all he was worth. A sheen of perspiration appeared across his forehead after just a minute

The Blackthorn Legacy

of this work. He stopped and looked around at Duffy and Smith.

"Get over here. Now! Break this fucking gate in."

"But Jok..." Stan began but Jok interjected by slapping him across the top of his head with his opened hand.

"I'm not leaving 'til I get in there. You hear me? Nobody, nobody gets the better of me. Now start hitting it with your shoulders. Put the work in and make the gate go in."

After two or three minutes of banging off the gate, splinters of wood began coming away and low creaking sounds were coming from some of the timber lattes.

Snap.

One of the timbers broke. The others around it were loose. Some were warped.

"We're nearly in. He's going to pay." Jok's crazy facial expression informed the other two that they had better do what he asked.

All three were in a lather of sweat in the cool March air.

"Stop!" Jok was leading again rather than ordering. "We can finish this off easily enough now."

Smith wiped his perspiring brow with the sleeve of his navy shell suit top. Duffy was bent over, his extended arms holding him in place as he rested them on his lower thighs.

Jok turned sideways, raised his foot and kicked at one of the gate's planks with the sole of his white runners. The definite sound of a tearing crack in the wooden board he had connected with. It was ready to give way. The sound of the weakening timber drove him on and his frenzied attack on the gate began to frighten Duffy and Smith. Within two minutes there was a hole big enough for him to climb through. He looked up at the other two as he began climbing through. His hair was wringing around the edges and his face was red with all the exertion.

"Come on." He waved his arm in a follow me motion. He stepped through the hole he had just made and stared threateningly at Martin Carey who was standing at the back lawn kerb, some twenty feet from the gate. Martin still had

The Blackthorn Legacy

the black handled carving knife in his right hand although he didn't look as though he was about to use it. It was dangling in his hand by his right leg, harmlessly.

The three of them were in through the gate and Jok stood ahead of his two pals staring at Martin. There was intent in those crazy eyes.

Those dark crazy eyes.

"Do you know who I am old man?" asked Jok of Martin. He just shook his head.

"I'm the man you never say no to, that's me. That's who I am. You just pissed me off, old man."

Martin just looked back almost apologetically but said nothing. He dropped his eyes to the chippings on the ground around him.

"Look at me when I'm talking to you motherfucker. Are you dissin' me?"

Martin looked back but not really understanding the question.

"Are you going to use that big bastard of a knife?" Jok was sneering Martin now.

Martin looked down at his right hand and then put the knife down on the driveway at his feet.

Stan Duffy put his hand on Jok's shoulder and leaned in to him. "Come on, man. This poor guy is afraid. Let's just go."

"Let's just go?" shouted Jok; "he's seen our faces now. No, he's going to pay for this", he continued. He removed a switchblade from his right front pocket and flicked a button at the top end of the handle. A large, sharp looking blade sprung out. Then a crazy expression appeared on his face again and then he sneered at Martin and said, "That ain't a knife, this is a knife." He cackled at his own joke.

"What do you say to that old man?"

Martin was now staring straight at Jok, into his eyes. He lowered his forehead while he still remained looking at the man who had just smashed his gate. The look became a glare.

"Do you feel the way you hate, or do you hate the way you feel." Martin's voice had gone an octave lower. Duffy and Smith felt a change in the atmosphere. Something had definitely changed and the man whose driveway they were on had something to do with it. Whatever it was, it drove Jok to run at Martin with his switchblade out like a bayonette at the end of his arm.

Martin hadn't being paying attention for the last moment. He was caught up in the vision of the golden meadow, long grass, sweet smell, gentle slope up ahead of him and then the sight of high trees on his right hand side. His dream was crudely interrupted by the sound of an ear-piercing, high-pitched hollering voice and then he saw who it belonged to. The leader with the knife.

CHAPTER FIVE:

REPORTERS WITH CREDENTIALS

THE lights were blasting blue and red streaks through the darkness near the gateway and in the driveway of Martin Carey's house. Five vehicles in all, two squad cars, two ambulances and a dark blue unmarked Garda car were there. The two ambulances had been allowed up to the yellow *Crime Scene* tape, which was marking the area where unauthorised persons were not permitted to go beyond.

The flashing lights and blaring sirens had created quite a stir in the community when they had sped through the village, attracting rubberneckers and busy bodies to the location. Among the group of on-lookers standing around at the gateway were the usual local reporters, waiting for news that would undoubtedly make the front page headlines for their respective papers.

Two of the Garda officers were put standing at the house's gateway, prohibiting any prospective on-lookers from entering the site. This was a crime scene and would be treated as any other crime scene anywhere else.

Some on-lookers had come prepared for a long stay. They were armed with flasks and sandwiches. Professional, experienced on-lookers. The interest in others' problems was much more fun to talk about. Once those people had a part of the story, the remainder would be their own version and

The Blackthorn Legacy

exaggeration played a large part in stories such as these as they progressed.

There was a palpable air of anticipation hanging effortlessly in the cool crisp air. The excitable, growing crowd had been there now for over an hour since the Garda cars and ambulances had gathered at the scene and both the professional and amateur news vultures that lingered outside and around the gate felt that news of some sort was imminent.

Events such as these rarely occurred in Shayleigh but when they did, the news - be it true or otherwise - spread like wildfire. In recent years, the use of Smart phones, tablets etcetera ensured that large crowds gathered at scenes such as these.

The misfortune of some brought joy, prying eyes and occasionally excitement to baying crowds.

The waiting, anticipating crowd began to move towards the gate as they saw two ununiformed men walk down the sloped driveway towards them. The two officers at the gate who were maintaining the scene had their work cut out for them in containing the moving mob, but they just about managed to do so.

Detectives Mason and Walsh reached the site entrance and scanned the growing crowd. There must have been thirty or forty people there now. The detectives seemed a little surprised at the numbers standing before them in groups, like sheep. Both men were in their late thirties and both were dressed in plain clothes. Mason was tall and thin with narrow hips and long legs. His blonde crew cut hair made him look like a Swedish high jumper. Walsh was a little shorter and not in as good a shape physically as his partner but it looked like he was the bad cop of the partnership. His creased face framed by thick wavy brown hair gave him a hardened look. His broad shoulders and wide body did nothing to improve one's first impression of the man. He often said nothing but if looks could talk, there would be a lot said.

The Blackthorn Legacy

Both men looked at each other as the growling crowd, baying for information moved forward in waves at the sight of the two men coming forward. The disbelief in the crowd size had definitely surprised them. The officers at the gate were finding it more difficult to supress the weight of the swarming people and this bulk was greater than normal because of the weight of anticipation pushing them along.

Walsh stepped forward, almost losing his step on the lose chippings underfoot. He moved and stood behind the two officers who, it must be said, had been doing a Trojan job holding back the surge. He raised his arms above his head and his black quilted unzipped jacket spread across his chest. The interior yellow lining became visible as did the Smith & Wesson holstered in his shoulder belt. The night breeze rose momentarily, tossing his hair giving him the look of a lunatic seen on all those films about asylums. Some of the front row crowd noticed the firearm and became a little less persistent in pushing forward. His appearance also put a little fear in the minds of those shouting and pushing moments earlier. A whisper began funnelled back and the shoving eased a little. The number of reporters had grown and squeezed to the front, popping out between shoulders of some of those retreating ever so slightly from the front. The pressure on the two holding officers had eased considerably. Talking and whispering amongst the crowd continued but it was incomprehensible to the four Gardaí standing at the gate.

Mason strode forward, tapping Walsh on the shoulder. The more aggressive man stepped aside, never once taking his eye from the crowd. The bulldog had done his job. Walsh looked out at the crowd and then picked a spot in the dark trees across from where he stood, just above the head of the furthest out hanger-on. He began addressing the highly strung assembly standing before him.

"As you have probably realised by now, the Gardaí were called to this house earlier this evening to assess an incident. An investigation is still currently underway. The State Pathologist and the Crime Scene Team have been informed

The Blackthorn Legacy

and they will be on site tomorrow to carry out their own investigations. As of yet there is nothing substantial to report and we would advise you all to go home. That's all, thank you".

Mason was about to turn when a barrage of questions were fired at him. The shouts and screams of what had been an expectant crowd became intense. This is not what they waited here for, he knew that. They wanted answers. But the response was unexpected. Arms were waving at him looking for a chance to throw a question his way. There was a definite sense of dissatisfaction out there and the last thing the Gardaí wanted was an uprising of any sort. Mason looked over at Walsh who just stared back blankly at him, shrugging his shoulders. Mason didn't know what to do.

This was awkward.

He had come out to give this horde an update. He thought they would have been satisfied with that. But they wanted more; they wanted information and not just some speech that passed over the real information. If they wanted that, he realised they could have just as easily stayed at home. This crowd could become a mob and then an angry horde and before long, well he didn't want to contemplate what would be next. He had to do something. He retook his spot where he had given his speech from and raised his hands.

"Ok, ok, ok, I'll take a few questions, but from the press first and then..."

This still wasn't what the boisterous crowd wanted at all. They wanted to see into the scene. They wanted to know what had happened. The menace that was forming in the crowd was now tangible. They were acting as a single unit, all seeking the same thing. Walsh stepped forward again and reached to the back of his trouser belt. He pulled out his Taser stun gun.

"Anyone who tries to get past these two officers' gets a dose of this", Walsh shouted threateningly.

"You can't do that", came a response from an anonymous man in the crowd.

The Blackthorn Legacy

"Just try me", Walsh shot back.

"We all know what you're capable of Detective Walsh", said a butty man in his mid-twenties, head shaved, wearing a hoody under a leather jacket was standing three quarters way back in the crowd stared directly at Walsh. His name was Jimmy Jones. Mr Jones had had a couple of run-ins with the Gardaí over the years. Mostly menial stuff, but a law breaker all the same. He had brought a complaint to Walsh's Superintendent regarding an alleged incident. He claimed that he had been assaulted by the detective for *'no apparent reason'*. The case was dismissed after an internal investigation was instigated and information from other witnesses were collated and presented to the Superintendent. It had been noted during the internal review however, that a number of others over the years threatened to report the same detective for roughing them up but, for one reason or another (everyone knew the reason) the statements were never submitted.

Walsh searched the faces in the crowd and eventually found Jones glaring back at him.

"This is neither the time nor the place Jones. Are you looking for trouble?"

"I probably wouldn't have to stray too far to find it, would I detective. I'm not afraid of you, or your threats. I would advise you to concentrate on your job, for once anyway." The confidence in Jones' voice was entirely evident. Walsh's ego took a whack when he scanned the crowd and saw the smiling faces and heard the tittering at the back.

Walsh made as if he was going down to show Jimmy Jones who was boss, but Mason caught him. He leaned over and whispered into the raging man's ear. Whatever he said somewhat soothed his partner's temper, quenching his emotional sensitivity at that particular time.

With all this bickering and shouting between the two men, the crowd seemed to dissolve into a mumbling bunch of stragglers.

The Blackthorn Legacy

"Just let Detective Mason answer a couple of the questions. Only a few mind." There was still an edge to Walsh's voice but it had been softened a little.

The majority of the forty strong crowds seemed to accept the plan to be able to make some queries and find out something. Something happens in your community where the law is called surely you had the right to know what for, was etched across many of the forty something faces in the crowd. One or two of them mumbled disagreement and one walked away waving his hands and arms all over the place, eventually throwing an empty beer bottle into the ditch on the opposite side of the road. He almost followed it in to the ditch; his balance had deteriorated so much. Bottles of warm beer could do that to a man.

Mason faced the disgruntled group and in some cases fearful crowd members. The fear was in most cases for themselves. They didn't want any such trouble as had appeared to have gone on down this lane, on their own doorsteps. One of the reporters raised his hand.

"Yes", said Mason pointing at the journalist.

"Detective Mason, you said earlier in your piece that the State Pathologist have been informed of the incident here tonight. Does that not infer that a serious crime, maybe even murder has been committed here?"

Members of the group began shouting their agreement with the question, aiming their ire at the cops. Mason considered the questioner for a moment ignoring the calls and cackling, and then answered the question.

"You will also note that I said that both those offices will be sending people to assess the situation. I never said anything about murder or serious crime nor did I mean to infer this. You will have to accept the information I gave you as being all that is actually known at this particular time."

"Are you covering up something Detective?" One of the other reporters decided to get in on it.

The Blackthorn Legacy

"Who gave you permission to shout up a question?" Walsh was losing it again, it appeared. The reporter sunk back and lowered his head, averting his eyes to the ground.

"It's ok Detective" said Mason, "I'll take the question", he continued. The reporter looked back up at Mason, a sense of relief visible on his face. "Look people, I can only tell you what I know. Anything else is just rumour and so on. I'm not going to do that." He paused, looking at the obvious doubt and suspicion perceptible in the crowd as the noise level began to rise again. "I'll tell you all that I can. I'll take contact numbers from reporters with credentials and contact you personally as developments occur. You will be able to keep the public up to date. That's all I can do."

The reporters struggled to the gateway and each of them handed cards and ID to the officers who had been blocking the entrance to the house. The reporter who asked the first question looked up at Mason as he turned to leave and pointed up at him.

"I'll hold you to that."

The crowd of confused people looked around not understanding what just happened. They should have been given news. The sound had reduced for the first time since the detectives had come out to meet them. The volume button had been moved down a level, a few levels and suddenly the crowd was reduced to just a bunch of moaners.

One of them turned and left giving the Gardaí the finger and so some of the others followed sheepishly. A few lingered and looked as though they were in for the long haul.

There was more movement up in the driveway as the ambulance crews mounted their vehicles, started them up and began their return to the depots, empty.

A cream tarpaulin was being erected along the length of the wall where the gate had been smashed in by the three youths. It was mounted on a wire connected to the house on the right and a lower sturdy branch on one of the Beech trees. When this had been completed the few hangers-on decided it was time to move on.

The Blackthorn Legacy

Nothing to see here.

Mason and Walsh were walking back up the sloped driveway in silence and Mason stopped and looked down at the uniformed officers who had done such a sterling job in maintaining the peace to the extent they had.

"Guys, you were brilliant tonight. Great job, under the circumstances. I'll have you replaced here soon. Thanks".

The officers both felt a warm buzz. It wasn't often that they were complimented for doing a good job. Mason continued his walk up the stony surface, bending under the yellow crime scene tape and made his way towards the tarpaulin into the stiffening cold breeze which was coming down the hill at the rear of the site from a North Westerly direction. He saw Walsh up ahead of him, squeezing through the hole in the gate that had been created by the attackers earlier in the evening and lifting the tarpaulin and disappear totally from view as it dropped behind him.

It looked as though he had disappeared into another world.

On reaching the wall and the gate with the man-made cavity, the cool wind seemed to have dissolved into nothing. The canvas sheeting up ahead was acting as a blocker. Of course its primary task was to obstruct the view of the particular crime scene, but now it was double jobbing.

The remaining uniformed Gardaí were also leaving the scene. The shift change was on.

Once around the back of the house Mason felt a strange sensation in his bones. Three beige ten foot square evidence covers stood out in the dark, in a triangular shape. The point of the triangle was aiming away from where he now stood. He unknowingly kicked a cardboard box on the ground and realised it was a box of blue booties. They had been instructed that these had to be worn to protect the ground but looking at the chippings that covered the driveway it was impossible to see how anything could be gained here from wearing these stupid things. But then again he got paid to obey the rules and not to make them.

The Blackthorn Legacy

Mason put on the blue booties and began walking slowly towards the beige pop-up scene preservers. It was pitch black out in the country. He was amazed at the difference street lights made. The detective found it difficult to make out anything properly in the darkness. If he lived out here he supposed his eyes would quickly become accustomed to such gloom. Not right now though.

He removed a torch from an inside pocket of his warm jacket and pointed the thin white beam along the base of the nearest tent and saw a small yellow evidence marker labelled 1. He searched around and eventually discovered a further marker up ahead near the kerb that separated the back lawn from the driveway. It was marked 2. This one was away from any of the beige pop-up units. It seemed strange that should be only two such markers, but then the whole case had a smell of strange about it.

The breeze was gaining in power still and, was becoming more a wind, a cold wind. The thwacking sound of the bare branches and twigs created by them banging off each other in the otherwise dark silent landscape was unnerving. These wooden extremities belonged to trees that detached this site from the surrounding fields.

The black clouds in the Northern sky were moving in the strong wind and they looked like a think nylon material passing over a large stage light as the moon made an attempt to be seen through the murky haziness in the sky. Rain was probably not that far off. As the old people used say, there was a drop on the wind. Mason never really felt that floating drop the wind supposedly carried, but the thick shady clouds that obscured any view of the stars above, probably meant that rain was coming. Even one of those weather forecasters on TV would have even predicted the weather standing where Mason was positioned right then, he said quietly to himself.

He heard a knock on glass and looked immediately around, on guard, only to see Walsh at the back kitchen window motioning him to come in.

The Blackthorn Legacy

His senses came alive all of a sudden and then the sound of chewing and scraping came into earshot and he stopped in his tracks and swung around his torch to where he thought the sound was coming from. He flashed it over to the right and then back, skimming over a dark shape. Moving the torch slowly back in the direction he believed he might have seen something, he was met with two moving reflective green discs, each the size of a ten cent coin, hanging about eight inches from the ground. The discs seemed to be changing shape or size or both. Short black threads moved in circles just in from the edges of the green flat circular shapes in a frightening yet hypnotic fashion.

It took Mason a couple of seconds for him to realise he was staring into a pair of cats eyes. The jet black feline was sitting over a bloodied animal, lying in an impossible position, ripped to shreds. The cat had no right to have killed an animal the size it now sat over. It was eating its victim in the dark, at the far end of the house, hoping to remain in the dark shadows. Martin Carey's house had what seemed to be two rooms and a toilet beyond the back kitchen block which jutted out from the main rectangular shape of the original building. It was most likely an after- thought.

The small cat hissed ferociously in Mason's direction, its large teeth were dripping enormous red droplets. It lowered its head as if in an attack mode, bringing its muscled shoulders forward. The sheen of the cat's coat illustrating its muscularity, even in the darkness.

Mason extinguished his torch but light from somewhere still persisted. Where was it coming from? He looked around, always keeping the cat in his peripheral vision and realised where luminosity radiated from. It was the full moon glistening in the Northern sky that seemed to have pulled away the clouds so it could take centre stage on the sky's dark canvas. It shone on the ground almost like the main beam shining on the cast of a huge stage show. The cat stared unblinkingly at Mason, striking fear into the detective, who began moving slowly towards the back door to enter the

The Blackthorn Legacy

house. Cat maintained its stare while still remaining motionless. Mason reached the back door and shuffled in, back first, not turning away from his watcher. As he entered and closed the door behind him Cat returned to eating what remained of the animal it had torn apart.

Was it a dog?

Just get inside, he told himself nervously before he had closed the door out fully.

CHAPTER SIX:

BIG BROTHER

MASON closed the backdoor. He took a deep breath to help regain some composure and also to calm his shaken nerves. A moment later he stepped through the small dark back kitchen, into the dimly lit kitchen. The Banker's Lamp in the corner was the source of the poor illumination.

He entered the quiet room and could immediately sense the tension that hung in the air. Walsh was standing in the centre of the room, facing a strange looking man who was seated to the left of the middle of the old settee. It was situated below the window from where he saw everything and everybody who paid him or his site a visit. The number of people who had ever actually made that call, he could have possibly recorded on the back of a stamp.

Martin Carey looked afraid yet upset. His head was slightly dipped and his hands were balled up in tight fists and were resting on his thighs. His fists were so tight in fact that his knuckles were an off-white colour. His body was also rigid and only moved as he inhaled slow deep breaths and exhaled them quickly each time. Mason looked at him for a second and stared at Walsh and then back at Martin Carey. The face of the house owner was scrunched up so that he appeared to be having trouble with something but behind this facial

The Blackthorn Legacy

expression, breaking through, there was a fear. Mason was beginning to wonder if his partner had done something.

"What's up?" asked Mason of his partner tersely.

"Look at him, he's just sitting there doing nothing until I walk over and touch something and then he just...Watch this." Detective Walsh stepped towards the table, a round pine coloured wooden board standing on four simple darker coloured wooden legs. Four old style chairs were neatly pushed in under the table, each with decorative cushions on the seats attached to the backs of the wooden chairs where they were tied into position with snow white linen strings. Walsh put his hand on the chair nearest to him at that time and was about to pull it out when he pointed at Carey. Martin had bent his head and placed the palms of his hands over his ears and his fingers were lying close to his crown. He began rocking backward and forward gently and breathing a little more loudly as he puffed out each breath.

Mason took a slow step towards Martin and leaned down a little.

"Are you ok Mr Carey?"

"I don't want him touching my stuff. I keep this house spotlessly clean, every day. I don't want..."

Mason looked back at Walsh and nodded at him, directing him away from the chair. Walsh acted like the bold child at the back of the class who had been breaking the little rules, the ones that didn't matter so much. The ones that were there to be broken, asking to be broken. He stepped back to the wall facing the settee that Martin Carey occupied.

"It's ok now Mr Carey, my partner has moved away. Can I get you a drink of something, water, tea, anything?"

No response for a moment. Then Martin looked up at the two detectives and eyed both of them. His dark eyes framed by black bags underneath, dark eyebrows above and shadows across the left side of his face caused by the obstruction of the dim light over his right shoulder.

"Why are you here with all your people? I didn't call you."

Mason and Walsh exchanged glances of disbelief.

The Blackthorn Legacy

"There are three dead bodies lying out on your driveway Mr Carey. A call was received at our station, a call from someone in a state of distress. We were informed of the situation and posted out here. We arrived and we found three dead bodies."

"Oh yeah, them. I forgot about that. I must have pushed it to the back of my mind. I don't know what happened out there." Carey's interest in the whole event seemed minimal at this stage.

"You put the call in Carey." Walsh was starting to get a little edgy.

"Oh yeah", countered Carey, "Tell me how I called. I don't have a bloody phone, no mobile, no landline, nothing. Figure that out first." Martin Carey was becoming less hospitable with each passing moment. Visitors in his house, visitors he hadn't even invited – two groups in one evening.

It was unheard of.

Detective Edward Walsh didn't take too kindly to being treated in such a manner. He patted the chest area of his warm jacket, pulling the zip halfway down. Reaching inside he removed an old style Parker Pen and began pressing the clicker, releasing the nib, retreating it back up the navy pen barrel. He did this a number of times and it was obvious, especially in the short lull in conversation that the sound was annoying his partner. Mason turned to look at his partner, frowning first. "Can you stop that Ed? I'm trying to take some notes. That annoying clicking noise is nothing short of irritating." He spoke like a disappointed parent might to a silly adolescent. Walsh looked at him, his unhappiness was extremely visible. If looks could kill there would have been another death to account for. Walsh leaned back against the wall, resting his elbow on the short shelf that held a radio and a glass containing pens and nick knacks. The detective played with the glass with his pen for a moment, just to calm himself down.

"I've lost my train of thought", Said Mason, looking down at his notes. "Here we are", he continued, "So you don't have

The Blackthorn Legacy

a phone?" Mason asked this with a touch of scepticism in his voice.

"I don't want or need a phone detective. I don't want one because Big Brother is everywhere. Everything you say on your phone is recorded by the providers. And I don't need that, because I just don't. If someone wants me and it's urgent they'll get me." The sound of *there you go take it or leave it* that could easily have become *I told you so* was so clear in Martin's tone. It also felt to Mason like he was being given a lesson on the disadvantages of technology and that he should think more about his phone usage.

"Who the fuck phoned it in then?" Walsh's temper was fraying. He could feel the blood pumping fast through his veins and this might only mean one thing – trouble. Ed Walsh was inclined to do this and on one occasion and it had almost gotten him in trouble before. He wanted cases to finish with the first interview no matter how that was achieved. Patience wasn't a virtue he could claim to have in his back pocket. When patience was being handed out he was probably hiding behind a big door.

Mason looked back at him, staring at him. Willing him to shut up. He turned with his professional expression back in tact towards the astounded Mr Carey.

"Let's just concentrate on the scene outside for a moment Mr Carey. Do you mind if I call you Martin?"

Martin shook his head. He actually preferred it. It made him feel a little more at ease.

"Ok then." Mason removed a small notepad and pen from a pocket inside his jacket.

"Do you have a cat Martin?"

"What?"

"A cat? Do you have one? Like, a pet cat?"

"Yeah, why? Is he in trouble?"

"No need to get smart with me Mr Carey. I was just wondering. I saw one out back, eating something. I was just curious."

"He's company for me."

The Blackthorn Legacy

"What happened this evening out there?" Mason snapped his wrist as he pointed ferociously outside to the crime scene with his plastic see-through blue pen.

Martin intertwined his fingers and was now looking down at his open palms. He stared for a moment and then quickly brought up his head to face Detective Mason who was pointing at one of the wooden kitchen chairs asking with his eyes if could pull it out and sit on it.

"Go ahead. I just like to keep everything in its proper place."

Mason pulled out the chair. He pulled it to him dragging the back legs on the timber floor.

Ffffffffffft.

Then he sat down and was almost level, face to face with Carey, except that Mason was still about four inches taller than Martin and some of that difference in height was in evidence even as they were both seated. To be fair, the wooden chair was a little higher than the settee in any case.

"Back to my question. What happened out there this evening?

Martin looked back at his hands again and started rotating his thumbs around each other. His eyes looked dark again as he peered back up at the detective.

"Did you see what they did to my gate? That main one, the one who did all the mouthing wanted to harm me. I knew he did, it was in his voice. He was saying something about...I don't know. He wanted to get in to my house to smoke or something."

Mason looked around at Walsh who just nodded and slapped his right fist into his left palm in satisfaction and a mad smile appeared in his face.

"You got them Martin Carey. You got them. Yeah, you took them out."

"What is he talking about?" Martin's face turned pale, almost transparently so."

"Ignore my partner for the moment Martin. What happened next?"

The Blackthorn Legacy

"You saw it yourself what happened next. The three of them, well the leader and the other two under his instruction broke my gate. They got in and then he, the leader, he pulled out a flick knife and spoke threateningly to me, at me."

"I saw another knife out there. It's marked as a...It doesn't matter why, but is that your knife, the other one out there?"

"I guess it is, yes."

"Did you use it?"

"No, I put it down as soon as they confronted me. What use was it going to be to me against three of them? One of them was just pure evil. No I laid it down, to try and calm everything down."

"Then what?"

"Nothing."

"What the hell? Nothing? There are three fucking dead bodies lying out in your driveway, and all you can say is nothing?" Walsh's patience was wearing again.

"If you would prefer I'd lie, I can change my story." Martin's contentment had grown as had his patience. It was strange. First he had been like Gloria Gaynor, afraid, but instead of becoming petrified, he had calmed. Maybe it was the telling of his side of this story that made him feel somewhat better. Or maybe it was just seeing Detective Walsh squirm. It could have been that. It was funny seeing him lose his temper, trying to show his masculinity or something else maybe.

"Look Martin, my job is an easy one, in theory. I just have to get to the truth. I need your help to do this. Just tell us what you know happened from the time the three...youths broke in your gate. Start from where you left down your knife. The real story." Mason was trying to ease the truth from his interviewee. The good cop bad cop thing was definitely not going to work with Martin Carey. Especially with his partner's frequent interludes. That was patently obvious here.

Martin looked down at his hands again. His fingers were still intertwined, resting on his thighs. There was a certain

The Blackthorn Legacy

kind of vulnerability about it. He looked alone – as he certainly was – for the first time since the questioning had begun.

"I had left my knife down and still the verbal attack continued and still the leader continued his inching forward towards me with intent. He...I was in his way, even though I was of no threat to him." Martin took in a gulp of air and held it and let it out slowly this time.

"Take your time Martin. Take your time." Mason could see that this was difficult for him.

"I remember staring at him, the leader guy. Really staring at him and could feel rage building up inside me. I could feel my blood bubbling in my veins. I was mad. I wanted to..." He stopped.

"What? You wanted to what? Kill him?" Walsh was at it again.

"Yes, I wanted to kill him, but it wasn't in me, but I really wanted to all the same. Then all I remember was a blinding flash somewhere from behind me. Over my left shoulder maybe."

He paused.

"Then the next thing I remember was the flood of coloured lights, red and blue, flashing, invading my house. People I hadn't invited storming my land. Now here we are."

"That's it? That's all you have? Are you on drugs? He's gotta be checked for drugs Mason."

Mason sat back on his chair. He stared at the man sitting before him. The man who just poured out this half arsed story about a flash of light doing –. Doing what exactly?

"Is that it Martin?"

"It's all I know. That's what you asked, isn't it? It's all I know." Martin Carey collapsed into the settee, spent. Mason finished scribbling on his little pad and just gaped at the man before him who seemed completely depleted. The story he had just told appeared to have taken it all out of him. Was it true? Was there a blinding flash of light? He shook his head.

The Blackthorn Legacy

Stop talking nonsense, he thought. But it's what the man before him certainly seemed to believe, he could see that.

"Do you believe this shit, man?" Walsh obviously didn't buy it. "What about the other one? The unsolved one? This fucker was taken in for questioning then too. Coincidence? I don't think so", he continued in his harsh voice that seemed to rise in strength with each passing second. His face was reddening, most likely in rage.

Mason sat silently for a moment tapping the end of his pen on the cover of the closed notepad as he considered this. He leaned forward again. His left elbow on his left thigh, making a hollow in his trouser leg. He rested his chin on the heel of his left hand and cupped his fingers over his mouth. He was in full thought mode now as he stared out the small kitchen window over Carey's head. He took a deep breath and looked intently at Martin.

"What happened that night Martin? It does seem strange that you could be somehow mixed up in these two incidences. I don't believe in coincidences, I'm a detective, that's how I'm programmed."

Martin was still crumpled in the settee and slowly he returned to a sitting position on the edge of the settee and looked Mason directly in the eye.

"Detective, I was brought in for questioning that night, as you call it, because I didn't have an alibi. I was treated like a criminal for almost three days because I fitted into someone's plan for a win." He made inverted commas with his fingers as he said *win*. "All they had was that I didn't have an alibi", he continued in a flat direct voice. "A man was found dead at the top of this lane completely mutilated. No head, no hands and no feet. Do you seriously think that I am capable of carrying out something like that, or why I would even try? Is that what this has come to now? You don't have an alibi so you must be guilty. There are people living twenty miles away that don't have alibis and nobody else seems to have been treated like I was. That absolutely sickens me. What I told your people before...it's all I knew." Martin sat

The Blackthorn Legacy

there shaking. He even frightened himself with how intense he had been during that speech. Red blotches appeared on his pale cheeks.

"I'm sorry Martin, but I had to ask. It's my job to investigate." He looked back at Walsh who seemed anything but convinced that what had just come from Martin Carey's mouth was genuine. Sure he sounded genuine, but anyone fighting for their lives will do what they have to, to survive.

"Let's just take what we have for now detective. It's all we have. It's all we know." He blinked and shook his own head violently from side to side trying to clear his mind. They were exactly the words Carey had uttered twice during his interview. *It's all I know.* Was there something in this air? Could there have been...*Stop it Michael Mason.* His dead mother's voice. She often steadied the ship for him. Detectives sometimes needed outside help.

"Are you alright Mason?" Walsh interrupted his thoughts and brought him back to reality, whatever that was.

"I'm fine." A strong vocal reply even if his mind wasn't fully behind it yet. He stood up from the chair and with that Martin sat back up straight again, looking at the detective.

"The chair?"

Martin nodded. Mason pushed it back in to the table. The chair's legs screeched as if in opposition to the move but slid in easily all the same.

"You'll have to come with us Mr Carey" said Detective Mason.

"You can't stay here tonight, this is still a crime scene", he continued in a robotic sounding voice. One he had used on numerous occasions at other crime scenes.

"Are you arresting me? What did I do?"

"You're not under arrest".

"Yet", interjected Walsh

Mason stared at his partner and then turned back to Martin and continued his explanation. "But as you seem to have nowhere else to go, we will put you in a Holding Room

The Blackthorn Legacy

for tonight, or at least until our forensic guys and the State Pathologist's office have examined the scene outside."

"Holding Room, don't you mean a Holding Cell?" asked Martin.

"Whatever you prefer. It's still the same room." Matter of fact reply from Mason.

"What's in it? What's in the Holding Room, then?" Both detectives ignored the question.

"We'll need to take a look around the rest of your house Mr Carey." Mason was back in full detective mode again. "It's precautionary. We need to be certain that the house is safe and clear and of course for us to finalise this segment of the investigation."

"This segment of the investigation? Am *I* under investigation?" Martin wasn't sure if he was a suspect in what the detectives were calling a crime scene. "Am I a suspect?" There he said it out loud.

"You're catching on quickly." The sarcasm in Walsh's voice was very clear as he turned and walked out the kitchen door into the hallway.

The brown and black square linoleum floor tiles gave the hallway an old-fashioned feel and the mushroom brown painted wall did very little to make it a memorable space, but then again it was the hallway of a bachelor's house who had very few visitors.

To the right of the doorway was an old radiator heated by the back-boiler system in the fireplace. The fire hadn't been lit so the space was cold. The hallway itself was small. Straight ahead out of the kitchen where three white plain doors all slightly ajar. To the right were the front door and on either wall facing each other were two more doors, both slightly ajar also. Walsh pushed open the door on his right first and stepped in. He turned on the centre light and stood aghast on the door saddle. His mouth agape and at last he managed to get his voice back.

"Christ almighty."

The Blackthorn Legacy

Mason rushed out to him and after seeing the expression on his partners face, brushed passed him in to the sitting room. On the end wall opposite the men was a book case. Floor to ceiling and wall to wall, it was completely full of books. Books of all types' size and colour. It looked like a ready-made library. In front of it was a small coffee table that seemed dwarfed in comparison to the shelved monstrosity built into the room. Underneath the table was a blue box. In fact it was a timber box with blue material which had been machine stapled onto it. It looked like an old sewing machine but Mason knew what it was because his parents had one up in the attic. It was an old style record player.

He had liked using their player at home when he was younger and his father would take it down once in a while to play some of his records. That crackle sound as he put the needle down in the groove. Oh it was a beautiful sound. But yes, it was rarely used back then because they all listened mostly to cassette tapes and later CD's.

A stack of old LP's were neatly piled beside the player on the plain but shining wooden floor.

Another old style settee in this room was situated under the room's only window directly across from the clean and virtually unused fireplace. And that was all the decoration that existed between the buttercup yellow walls and large teak book display.

Mason stood back from the door and stared in at the room. He had always wanted a room like this.

A room for himself.

"Can you believe this shit?" Walsh stared in at the room but only saw the large built-in book shelf. What a waste of time, effort and space that was, he thought. Who the hell would even read books now? The internet had all the answers to everything. Everybody knew that, because that's what the internet said.

Mason hardly heard his partner's rhetorical question. He was caught up in the moment.

The Blackthorn Legacy

Martin Carey joined the men at the sitting room doorway and saw the differing facial expressions. The look of awe and appreciation on Mason's and disgust on Walsh's.

"What is this shit?" Walsh had no other way of asking the reasoning behind such a room, such a misuse of a good space.

Martin just smiled at Walsh, a knowing smile, a smile that Walsh realised Carey was glowering down on him from a height. From his own self-made pedestal. The invisible one he put himself up on. That would have to change, and would. Ed Walsh would do everything in his power to see to it.

"Nobody reads books anymore. For God's sake, man. The internet has changed the way the world is lived in. My wife, my ex-wife, has that many books on her nine inch tablet. Who the hell...? What's all this even for? Who...?" He made a clicking sound with his tongue as if to magnify his point and then looked away with his hands in the air the way a teacher might if a pupil was not able to understand to most simple maths problem.

"I consider myself to be like a man with unquantifiable riches. His thirst for more wealth is like my thirst for knowledge in that the more I acquire, the more I want." He stood looking at Walsh, arms folded across his chest, chin up and the look of calculation on his pale face. He knew this would madden the detective. Mason drew himself away from the room and switched off the light.

"Back into the kitchen Mr Carey", he directed. It changed now from Mr Carey to Martin now back to Mr Carey again. Martin returned to his seat on the settee and waited while both the detectives searched the remainder of the house, three bedrooms and a bathroom. Nothing to be found there.

Walsh returned to the kitchen first and looked bullyingly at Martin, pointing towards him but at nothing really as he gave the orders. "Grab your shit together, we're leaving in two."

The Blackthorn Legacy

Martin could feel the uneasiness in his head and stomach as that animal detective shouted at him. Then it came again. The dream or a version of it.

It was he, himself walking through the long golden grass in the meadow. He knew it was himself. There he was brushing his hand over the top of the long golden blades and pulling the golden heads, dispersing the seeds in the warm breeze. The tall green ditch on his right was full of nests, but it was quiet, too quiet. He was walking towards and up the slope in the meadow. He reached the top and there before him was a trough or dip. It was a steeper walk down the other side.

"...Now!" Walsh was barking out orders again.

Mason returned to the kitchen to see Martin standing up from the settee, looking dazed and confused and blushing, his self-esteem had taken a bashing from the bellowing detective for the last couple of moments.

"Are you alright Martin?" asked Mason, with concern in his voice. Martin had noticed the change again, even in the haze of reality he was now living in. Mason was calling him Martin again. Martin shook his head to rid his mind of the confusing dreamy feeling.

"I'm ok detective. I'll just get my coat and keys."

Mason put his hand in his jacket pocket and pulled out a pair of blue booties and handed them to Martin. "You'll need to wear these", he said almost apologetically. He turned to face his partner who has removing his own blue footwear covers from a pocket.

"What?" asked Walsh in a high pitched voice as if he had no idea what Mason was getting at. The lead detective shook his head in disbelief, annoyance and disappointment.

*Sort it out Michael Mason. Sort it all out...*His mother's voice in his head again. He stopped where he was, balancing on his right foot as he attempted to place the second footie over the other one. He was perfectly still, motionless and the blood seemed to have drained from his face. Martin had a side on view of this and he knew something had happened. Had he seen the golden meadow as well? Was he walking

The Blackthorn Legacy

through the long grass on a warm day just, Martin wondered? He hoped he had, because then he wouldn't feel so alone.

"What are you waiting for?" Walsh was less concerned and the lack of anxiety was plain to hear in his gruff voice. Mason woke from his own daze and wobbled and almost lost his balance, hopping on his right foot towards Martin, then realising he could put his left foot on the floor. Mason looked at Martin as if asking for permission, pulled out one of the wooden chairs from the kitchen table and sat down to don the footie. He rose immediately as if to demonstrate he was fine and shoved the chair back into its rightful place – almost.

"Right, let's go." Mason's voice was a little quirky; he had been a little affected by his mother's intervention, twice in one evening. Only Martin picked up on it because Walsh was only interested in himself and how strong and pushy and in control he had felt.

Martin Carey stood up, looking down at his stupid footwear. The booties looked like oversized plastic slippers on his own shoes. They were just covering the first two lace holes, puckering because of the elastic within. The sound the synthetic covers made as he began to move across the wooden floor both felt and sounded weird. He walked to the table and put the chair Mason had moved moments earlier back into the position he liked it to be in, then they walked outside and the back door was locked.

CHAPTER SEVEN:

EVIDENCE COVERS

THE Northerly wind from earlier had dissipated but the static air was still stony cold. The sky overhead was now completely clear and it was dotted with twinkling diamonds for as far as they could see. Some of the sparkling lights were bigger and brighter than others. Mason couldn't believe what he saw above him. Not an hour or so ago he felt or more correctly, assumed that rain was on its way. The clouds above him then had all but said it. This evening just got stranger and stranger. He just couldn't believe the change in the overhead conditions.

Martin looked up at the clear pitch black sky and marvelled at all those planets and shiny rocks floating around in the unending deep space up there. In the Eastern sky, looking over his house, he could see what he always thought resembled a simple join-the-dots game. By drawing the imaginary lines that joined the sparkling points he could make a saucepan. Of course it was more commonly known as the Big Dipper. The only other constellation he knew how to find was to the South – Orion. He could only ever make out the Belt however.

Straight ahead where the mysterious dark horizon line came in contact with the black sky, there was an uneven smudge of light; brighter on the horizon line and losing it's

The Blackthorn Legacy

intensity as it rose into the ether. That refraction was no doubt caused by the lights of Fellowmore where they were to go to.

On their right the moon was a bright yellow light, hovering in the sky partly blocked now by the bare silhouetted branches looking like long arthritic fingers pointing upwards, moving in the slight breeze as if trying to pull down the black cloth that had covered the sky. Any leaves that had covered these cold bony branches had long since been blown to wherever leaves finally came to rest after the late autumn and early winter winds took them. The cold pastel light was casting long strange shadows here and there.

No sign of the cat but something that was impossible to make out was lying there where Mason had seen it and was threatened by it earlier. Whatever was there was very small and shapeless, probably bones and fatty remains.

The entire surroundings were completely soundless, eerily so. As they began to walk, the sound of plastic booties on the chippings seemed to be magnified in the surrounding sound of nothingness. The artificial slippers seemed to cause the men to walk as if on egg shells, trying not to break the surface underfoot when in fact they were trying not to allow the sharp chippings to pierce holes in the thin plastic coating. It was funny, funny peculiar. They were like cartoon characters sneaking across the big screen. After about ten steps Mason realised how foolish they actually looked. He stopped walking and looked at the other two who also stopped behind him, with inquisitive expressions on their cold faces.

"What now?" asked the clearly peeved Walsh. Mason looked at him and then at Martin Carey before staring down at his hilariously dressed feet.

"We are expected to wear these ridiculous booties. We are not going to affect anything at this scene. How can we, the stones we are walking on will be moved every time someone walks across them and we can be sure there will be a lot of foot traffic over the next day or two?" He looked at Martin

The Blackthorn Legacy

and continued, "Martin questioned the need for them for that very reason earlier. I'm removing mine now. Anyway the sound is freaking me out. It's like the sound of rustling stuff all around me."

"The first bit if sense spoken this evening", said Walsh and immediately bent down to get rid of his own. He nodded at Martin who did likewise, with delight. When they were finished they all stood for a moment and together felt as if something had improved even though they had really only removed fancy plastic bags from their shoes. It's the small things, thought Martin as he looked around.

He could however feel the chill of the night air as it seemed to wrap its cold fingers around him, causing him to uncontrollably shudder for a split second.

"Come on, let's go", ordered Mason. He too had felt the biting air as it tried to get into his bones. He pulled his warm jacket in closer around his body.

"Wait", said Walsh, "I want to see what's been investigated. To see what this creep did to these three dicks", he continued, looking at Martin as he spoke to his partner.

"Leave is Walsh; let's just get in out of this cold." Walsh considered this for just a short moment and then walked to the front of the beige ten foot pop-up evidence covers. He moved quickly, fishing out his mobile phone and turning on the flashlight app. The expanding cone shaped bright beam from the phone was pretty impressive. Walsh got to the tent-like cover and bowed down to reach the zip at the base of the cover's front. He pulled it up, taking two attempts with the zip sticking in its metal teeth on the first attempt.

Mason and Martin were moving from foot to foot in the ever increasing cold, watching Walsh as he looked into the tent-like feature.

"Oh shit. Jesus Christ."

The sound of disgust in his voice startled the other two and brought them over to him to see what he had seen, what had caused him to react the way he had. To see what had revolted him.

The Blackthorn Legacy

As they got to him he was pulling out his head. His phone had dropped to the stony driveway. Mason picked it up and looked at his partner who had gone a white shade of pale. The phone light in his face may have exaggerated the paleness, but he had been affected by the sight, that was for sure.

Mason pulled back the flap to see for himself what had unnerved his hard-man partner. He was shining the phone light at his feet and wanted to bring the light up slowly so as not to suffer the same fright as Walsh.

Jay O'Carroll was lying motionlessly, as expected, on the chippings. He was on his back and facing up. His legs were out completely straight, symmetrically but at an angle that would be tiresome. That confirmed it in Mason's mind, there definitely was no way this guy was playing dead, he was gone. His life had been taken from him. Jok's two hands were joined over his head making it look like the all-seeing eye. But it was looking at his face that produced the queasy feeling deep in Mason's stomach. It looked as though his facial skin had been pulled tight from the back of his head. The over-stretching appeared to have triggered the peeling of some of the epidermis on his nose. A crusty dark red scab had formed over the inch long break in the skin. A couple of maroon tear like lines were traced down his face on either cheek. His eye balls seemed to be too large to have been contained in their sockets. Someone had gone to town on him.

Mason pulled away from the tent quickly and ran over to the row of Beech trees along Carey's driveway, his cheeks bulging and barely making it to the cover; he vomited up the contents of his stomach. The dry retching sound afterwards was hard for the other two to bear, although they each pretended not to hear it. All Mason could think about was his mother's voice in his head and how she hadn't been there passing on her *special* advice. Typical, she only seemed to intervene on silly occasions. He wiped his chin and nose with

The Blackthorn Legacy

one of the booties he had taken from his feet just moments earlier. Both his vomit and dignity removed at once.

CHAPTER EIGHT:

THE KIOSK

THE twenty minute car journey back to Fellowmore was a silent one. Martin had wondered what had caused the detectives to react the way they had after peering into the evidence tents. He knew better than to enquire.

Martin stared out the window in the back seat of the car all the way into town. He altered his focus from time to time so that sometimes he gazed at his own transparent reflection in the glass and then out at the darkened passing flora and fauna that appeared so much differently at this time of the day than it did in daylight. He felt as if he could just as easily have been in another town, country or maybe even planet.

There were murmurs and whispering sounds in his head, somewhere at the back, but he had heard that sort of thing before. He had grown used to the voices in his head – the quiet ones anyway.

They pulled into the Garda Station and drove around the back to the Garda car park. The building was relatively new – maybe ten years old. The outer walls were an Ochre colour. The window frames and doors were a black uPVC. Some of the windows were throwing out soft yellow light into the night air. As Martin considered the big structure, he struggled to believe that it remained open for business all day every day. Funny business.

The Blackthorn Legacy

There were a few spaces left in the car park, but it was probably never full. Or at least it shouldn't have been if it was designed properly. Just beyond where they parked was a six foot high palisade fence with a matching gateway behind which was where cars were held by the Gardaí. Cars without insurance, stolen etc. were stored there. It was like a big showroom for second-hand cars of every ilk and condition. The entire area was secluded from the outside by a large dreary grey brick wall which had never been plastered. Strong overhead halogen lights and the dome shaped CCTV cameras made sure it was difficult for chancers to break in unnoticed under cover of darkness.

All three of them got out of the car simultaneously. The three car doors were banged closed making three individual banging sounds, two of which were almost at once and the third a little after. The echo in the enclosed space of the car park was a weird sound. It sounded as if the airwaves had been bent and had created a warbled reverberating sound.

They walked in to the station still without a single word being spoken between them. Mason's face was grey. The pallid colour was obviously a combined result of tiredness, sickness and presumably the horror that he had seemingly witnessed in that pop-up tent back at Martin's house. There were still marks of sick on his face. The bootie hadn't done much to clean him up. It looked like he cared little how he appeared just then.

The back entrance door could only be opened using a swipe card and Walsh did the honours. He looked only slightly better than his partner but his face was clean.

"I'm going to the toilet" said Mason, directed at no one in particular but Walsh just grunted agreement and nodded in his partner's direction. He grabbed Martin under the oxter and forcefully pushed him through the swinging double doors just inside the small lobby area.

"I want a word with you detective." Mason's voice was so weak it was almost a mumble but there was meaning in it.

The Blackthorn Legacy

Walsh walked on and it was difficult to fathom if he had in fact heard what Mason had said.

He proceeded in, continuing to shove Martin onwards and down the long hallway which was illuminated by recessed florescent lights sitting up in the tiled suspended ceiling. Halfway down the corridor one of the bulbs was flickering incessantly and randomly. On its last legs. The bright blinking artificial light reflected on the recently waxed marmoleum floor covering. It was as though Morse code signals were being transmitted to no one in particular. Long flashes, short flashes, no light and so on. Although it seemed spotless there and then, Martin was willing to guess that if he ran an ultraviolet light along the same surface, spots would be found. Evidence of crimes, unsolved crime in a Garda Station. How ironic. No public building appeared as clean as this one was, he thought through the discomfort being forced on him by Detective Walsh.

Martin felt a little exposed in the empty hallway. There were no doorways to duck into. It was strange to see a place that was more than likely was normally full of energy, to be so quiet right now. The ricocheting sound of their footsteps off the walls in the narrow walking space was also making him feel a little uncomfortable. That and of course the strong hand of Detective Walsh tightly gripping his upper arm.

They came to the flickering light and Martin noticed a dark shadow on his left and then realised it was an unlit corridor leading somewhere into complete darkness. He could just make out an open doorway about halfway down on the left. He didn't get much time to figure out what it could have been because of the shoving from behind. They had only passed three doors thus far, all of which all were closed tight.

Then suddenly as if out of nowhere they came upon a naturally coloured wooden frame surrounding two foot square of unbreakable glass. The glass had a perfectly circular hole in its centre and other smaller holes surrounding it. It looked like the glass maker wasn't much of an artist. If he had attempted to create a floral design, he had

The Blackthorn Legacy

failed miserably. If it was supposed to be the sun with circular rays emanating from the central circle, it was also very poor. Below the window frame was a metallic drawer system, where items could be passed in and out without the person behind the glass being exposed to any kind of harm or danger.

The position was unmanned so Walsh pressed the button of the bell on the counter. The sign on the left of the glass, which had been hand written in black marker of an A4 white sheet, read *Push the Bell for Service*. The bell resembled the kind you would probably see on the frame of an average dwelling house front door. It was a black rectangular cuboid shape with a circular white button on top and in the centre.

A tired and bored looking individual dressed in a Garda uniform came to the kiosk and produced a practiced smile. He was in his mid-forties, somewhere around the same age as Martin. A rotund man with a small chubby round face. That was the fairest way of saying it. His second and third chins looked to be balancing on his shirt collar but were ready to fall out over, probably in the next few months they would. His cheeks were red. Vein lines were visible in the redness suggesting he enjoyed a tipple, regularly.

The Garda looked as though he knew the man approaching, the one holding Martin Carey.

"Detective Walsh. To what do I owe this honour?" There was more sarcasm than humour in his droll monotone voice.

"Very funny Joey, ha ha ha." It was obvious from the tone of Walsh's childish type reply that the remark did hurt Walsh's ego. "I need to put this guy in Holding 1" he continued. Joey reached under the counter and retrieved a form. It was a three page document with the Garda insignia on the centre top with the Fellowmore address underneath. This particular form was supposed to be completed by the officer who wanted the use of the Holding Cells. Walsh pulled the handle on his side and stared into the metal drawer. A look of disgust crawled across his face and then he moved close to the speaking holes in the glass.

The Blackthorn Legacy

"Can't this wait until tomorrow, man? I'm off duty now and I don't have the energy to fill out your admin shit." He let go of Martin's arm and checked the time on his wrist watch. "Just put him in the cell, Joey. His name is Martin Carey and we have him in for..." He paused and looked at Martin. "For questioning. He was going to break him. He resumed his begging tone some more. "Come on, I'm beat right now. I'll fill that paperwork out tomorrow. I'm back in at eleven tomorrow morning. That's only twelve hours from now. Come on, Joey, you know me." He looked like he was nearly ready to cry. It was all an act of course but needs must.

"Martin Carey?"

"Yeah."

Joey noted something on a sheet and then looked back up at Walsh.

"Ok, here's the deal then, detective. I'll allow you to use the Holding Cell and I'll record your man's name."

"Great, Joey. I owe you one."

"But..."

"What?"

"You've got to deliver your prisoner to the cell. Do your own dirty work. I ain't doin' it. Or everything associated with it."

"Gimme the keys." Walsh growled at Joey through the glass and picked the keys from the drawer. He looked at Joey over his shoulder as he walked towards the dark corridor they had just passed moments earlier.

"I hope you didn't beat that one too." There was sarcasm and something else in Joey's voice.

Walsh just ignored the jibe and looked somewhere in the direction of the Garda and said "Tell Mason I've gone home and I'll see him tomorrow. Can you even do that much?"

"Don't get smart with me detective, I'm doing you a favour that could just as easily be overturned. Don't you forget that." As Walsh walked further down the corridor Joey mumbled something under his breath that wasn't too

The Blackthorn Legacy

complimentary. Joey could threaten as good as the best of them it seemed. Walsh patted his chest with his free hand. Nothing. He searched all his pockets. Still nothing. "Shit", He muttered more to himself but also in Carey's direction.

They turned down the dark hallway and Martin was beginning to lose his temper and he could feel the bad tingling sensation running through his stomach and up towards his throat. He waited for the acidy bile to erupt from the depths of his gullet as he was commandeered down the corridor. The acidy liquid remained where it was. The sharp sour taste associated with rising bile did however remain there.

They reached the junction and turned right onto the unlit passageway they had passed earlier. The flickering light was still at it.

Martin then began to feel something running through his veins. Was it ice? It was cold whatever it was. There was certain clarity of thought pulsing through his brain now. He was beginning to feel the need to give the ape detective, who was pushing him through the Garda Station, a piece of his own medicine. He felt it, something shadowy, invisible but hovering – it was all around him now.

Walsh felt something too. He felt the darkness wrap itself around him. Then the sensation of black arms lightly touching his own arms and back. It was difficult not to feel some fear. The flickering bulb on the main hall was affecting the quality of available light to them as they continued further down. It was as though they were walking away from a silent thunder storm. Something was brewing. His imagination was running wild. He thought the walls of the corridor surrounding him were taking shape. Arms were protruding through the concrete, bending it into the shapes of human extremities, all trying to catch him. It felt as though the growing darkness was trying to cover him, to suffocate him. His breathing became erratic, sharp intakes of air as he tried to stave off the smothering sensation. He loosened his grip on Martin's arm.

The Blackthorn Legacy

Martin Carey was beginning to feel somewhat more powerful. However, that was easy to say coming from such a low base of security, but he could sense a change in the atmosphere. He could hear the quick inhalations of his imprisoner. He was still however being shoved down a corridor but Walsh's strength had definitely diminished noticeably in the last few seconds. Martin was beginning to think that Walsh had intended bringing him down the dark hallway to hand out his own form of punishment. And that now he was having second thoughts. A strange change, he said, considering how he had been treated by the detective up to then. And also considering how he heard the other heavy set Garda talk to him. Had heard him ask Walsh if he had beaten him yet?

After about sixty steps they reached a doorway, where the door itself was slightly ajar. This was the doorway he had noticed on his way to the kiosk. The handle was on the right side of the door, was away from them and so he could read the lettering on the open door. HOLDING ROOM 1 it revealed. It looked like it had a letterbox three quarter way up but Carey realised within a split second of seeing it that that was where items such as food, post and so on were handed in to whoever happened to be residing in there.

Walsh hauled the door fully open pulling the chrome plated bow handle that was securely screwed in place. He was looking over his shoulder anxiously, as if expecting to see someone or something that had followed them down the dark hallway.

Nothing.

All was clear as far as he could see, and looking back to where they had come from, it was easier see because he was seeing with the aid of the light from the main corridor.

The door which for all intents and purposes was a blocker or people retainer was a strong looking fitting. It was approximately a two inch thick wall on hinges. Painted Cobalt blue, which gave it the depressing look that was obviously being sought by those who put it there in the first

The Blackthorn Legacy

place? Who imagined ever going to a prison cell of any sort and being overcome with delight at seeing the lovely high sheen bright red door – no, that was not how it happened.

Walsh let go of Martin's arm for only the second time since they had entered the building and this time it was only to push him in to the back, into the dark cell's gloomy interior.

"Lights out at eleven", Walsh looked at his watch and then continued, "Looks like you're out of luck, and it's after eleven." There was something else in his voice though. Martin sensed anxiety of some sort.

The door slammed shut and the sound of a large key turning in the lever lock looking for purchase should have been a soul destroying sound for Martin, but it wasn't. It took Walsh a full minute to get the lock in place. There were several one way foul mouthed assaults on the lock. Heavy puffing. There was definitely a tremble in Walsh's voice, Martin thought. And the detective's breathing was definitely erratic. Then just as he locked the door Martin could hear Walsh mumbling to himself and then he heard the man running away from the door. The thought of the squatty man trying to run entertained Martin Carey for a moment. That only lasted a very short time. The pain in his arm, where it had been held tightly for some time by the waste of a detective, stole his complete attention for the following few moments.

Nothing you can do about this right now, he told himself. Just get on with what you have. He took a deep breath and exhaled slowly with puffy cheeks. That felt better already, a little better.

For the first time this evening he was alone in his own room. Albeit a small room. The cell was fifty six square foot in size. That sounds bigger than it is, let me tell you. That cell was seven feet wide and eight foot long. It contained an aluminium toilet bowl, aluminium wash hand basin and a wooden bench that doubled as a seat and bed. Martin's eyes had become accustomed to the darkness with the assistance of the pale light peeping in through a small high window. He

The Blackthorn Legacy

sat on the bench and looked up to his right at the small window which was secured with upright metal bars.

He continued to stare up and a strange smile crossed his lips. The window was about eighteen inches long and six inches high. Who did they keep in these cells that could possibly escape through such a small hole? Were security bars really required?

The day's activities were catching up on him and his body clock told him in no uncertain terms through aches and heavy eyelids that it was time for him to sleep. The evening had certainly taken it out of him. Something had happened at his house earlier in the evening. Something. What was it that had occurred? No matter, he thought, he was now going to get a well-earned sleep in a Garda cell, only because he was a victim of circumstance. He pulled out the blankets that had been folded neatly on the bench and made his own bed and lay in it.

One thing that he had learned that night was that the Department of Justice had to pull something out of the bag regarding Walsh. They had to show how they would be able to make a detective out of an asshole and that would be a trick, he said to himself, inside his own head.

He lay down on the temporary bed. This was great, the quiet, being alone.

Sleep came quickly.

So did his dream.

CHAPTER NINE:

RAHADUFF

HE was standing on an old well-worn grassy track. He knew he had been there before but for the life of him he couldn't remember when or for that matter where the hell he was. The countryside was bathed in warm sunshine. On his right was a big chunk of stone that was certainly out of place. It was a weathered block of limestone covered in moss and lichens. There was something carved into the face of the rock. He took a closer look. RAHADUFF. What the hell was that? He looked around him again. He had been here before. He racked his brain but nothing came. He took a step forward and all of a sudden he was back in the golden meadow.

He was on the summit of the hill. The seeds of the golden grass were blowing in the warm breeze. His nose was beginning to itch.

Bloody hay fever.

He walked down the far side of the slope and soon reached the bottom. There was that metallic smell again. Maybe it wasn't metallic, but...

Then he saw something up ahead. It looked like it was a handle of some sort leaning up against a rock, a shaped rock over to his left. As he moved towards it he heard the unmistakeable sound of trickling water. It took his attention from the wooden handle. He followed the sound through the

The Blackthorn Legacy

long grass. There was nothing visible ahead that resembled a natural waterway.

He took a few more steps and almost lost his footing when he reached the banks of the babbling stream. The sound of the gushing water was so very soothing. Martin knelt down by the water's side and pulled away some of the grass that protected the stream from view. Oh, the sparkling, clear water. He dipped his hands into the cool water and splashed his face. Then a message, from somewhere. It came straight into his brain. Where the hell had it come from? Why would anyone say that to him? What had he done to get such praise? The message that came to him said, *well done, now let's clear it up*. It wasn't actually said to him, there was no voice, and it was just lodged there in his head. Hanging there, like an audio sign.

Who was watching him? He was out in a big wide open space but he felt claustrophobic all of a sudden. The air was thinner. He didn't want to be here anymore. He needed to get away from this madness. Messages in his head. It was becoming more difficult to breathe in the deteriorating air quality. He needed more air. He took in bigger breaths.

Not enough oxygen. Everything around him had stopped. The entire field looked just like it was a photograph. A moment in time.

He awoke in a jolt. He sat up on the bench. His clothes were drenched in perspiration. He swung his legs out over the side of the made-up bed. Droplets of sweat rolled down his face. He was still shaking. He was breathing quickly, trying to get the necessary amount of oxygen into his lungs. Deep breaths in and then blowing out the air with puffed out cheeks. That positively felt better.

The dream was still clear in his mind. He could remember every part of it. It didn't mean anything to him, even though he felt he had been there before. Could it in fact be called a night mare? Was it just a weird dream? There had to be something to it. It was like a continuation of his previous day dreams.

The Blackthorn Legacy

He looked at his watch. The luminous hands indicated the time. It was still early in the night. He didn't feel like falling asleep for a while yet. He looked up to his right and saw that the pale light that had been falling in before, through the small barred window, up high was now gone. He was in total darkness.

CHAPTER TEN:

REMEMBERING THE DREAM

BANG BANG BANG.

Martin was bent over. He had dozed off sitting on the bench. Sleeping was not an option if those hallucinations were going to continue. The clarity of that night's one was a little unnerving, even for him. Not knowing what any of it meant was also somewhat disturbing given its lucidity. His eyes were caked together and rubbing them with the backs of his hands was not really helping all that much. He needed to yawn to create the liquid from his tear ducts that would soften the sleeping glue holding his lids closed shut.

BANG BANG BANG.

There it was again, or was that the first time. Had he already heard that noise? Where was it coming from, that noise? Where the hell was he anyway? His eyelids peeled open and then it all came back to him. It was bright outside and the natural light shone in through the one available window.

The pain in his back and more precisely his spine was very uncomfortable. What did he expect? Falling asleep in a seated position, and the weight of his head leaning forward, his chin resting on his chest, arching his back. It was bound to have some sort of affect.

BANG BANG BANG

It was loud knocking on the cell door.

The Blackthorn Legacy

"Martin Carey, are you in there? Are you alright in there?"

Martin looked up at the tiny window high in the wall. He shook his head in disbelief. All it did was let in a limited amount of light. Did whoever that was on the other side of the door really think I got out through that space, he asked himself?

"Yes, I'm here and I'm ok."

"I'm going to open the flap and push through a tray with food on it, ok?"

"Fine."

"Detectives Walsh and Mason will be back on duty in an hour or so. You'll have to remain in there at least until then."

The flap opened, making a slapping sound as it did and a metal flap on his side of the letterbox style hole formed a shelf, allowing the black non-slip serving tray the other Garda pushing in, to balance there. Martin got up off the bench and walked over to the door, took the tray from the shelf and peeking out through the rectangular hole. He found himself looking into the eyes of an old tired looking man. He was wearing a Garda shirt. The black rings under his eyes suggested the man was working the night shift for several nights but was unable to sleep properly through the hours of daylight.

The shelf was pulled away and the flap closed shut hurriedly and fast footsteps followed.

Martin looked down at the tray. Four slices of toast on a paper plate, steaming tea in a polystyrene cup. That was it. Really appetising, he thought with a touch of sarcasm in his own head voice. Still, it looked edible. He walked the five steps back to the centre of the bench and placed the tray down on it. He looked at his watch. Five past nine.

Another hour in here.

Great.

The excitement was overwhelming

Well, done, now let's clear it up.

It was the voice in his head, the same one from the dream. Except then he felt it, rather than hearing it. He re-ran that

The Blackthorn Legacy

part of the dream. It was like fast forwarding a DVD and then stopping on the scene he wanted. There he was kneeling down by the stream. He splashed water up in his face and then that message *well done, now let's clear it up*.

What had he done that the message, now a voice, felt it needed to compliment him.

And the sign at the beginning of the dream. What or where was Rahaduff. If he had heard of such a place that would have been something, but to come to him out of the blue, somewhere he thought he recognised but couldn't quite put his finger on it.

The discomfort on his upper arm returned. It wasn't as bad as the previous night but it had become a pulsing sensation. It was like an invisible mechanical arm pushed a blunt needle onto the flesh for a second in time and then removed it. Then it repeated the needle-work placing it on the flesh and so on. It was there, it was gone, it was there, and it was gone. Repeatedly.

Detective Walsh needs to be taught a lesson. The voice again. The same one that had complimented him. What did it mean?

"What do you want?" Martin stood up off the bench as if that would make it easier to spot the owner of the voice, even though it was from his own brain.

You know he has to learn from his mistakes, we all do. Martin put his hands over his ears and scrunched up his face as if in physical pain. He wasn't thinking clearly at all. The voice was in his head already. Covering his ears was just maintaining it in there.

"What do you want from me?" Martin was shouting now and writhing around the small cell.

It's your job to teach those who disobey the laws – social and legal. They must be shown the errors of their ways. Or else made an example of. Watch Almo Stace.

"How do you expect me to do that? What or who the hell is or was Almo Stace?"

The Blackthorn Legacy

The power of water, Martin, but you knew that already, didn't you? I think you already know Almo Stace.

"Why me?"

No answer.

He was now almost hysterical. He was almost at the point of crying, but just not yet.

The walls of the small cell were closing in around him, or was it just his imagination. Claustrophobia was beginning to get hold just like it did in his dream just hours earlier. His breaths were becoming more laboured. The room definitely seemed to be smaller. Shadows appeared in places where they hadn't been. They seemed to be forming shapes of...He didn't know what. Martin's thought process was scrambled. Was it down to lack of oxygen? Was his brain not getting enough? The shadows on the closing in walls looked as though they had formed arms and hands and were looking for him, searching him out. Maybe this is how it feels to be losing your mind, he thought.

Managing to rip his eyes from the vision of the shadows on the walls of his ever decreasing cell, he glanced over at the bench.

There were the tea and toast still untouched on the black easy clean tray. He managed to struggle over and dug in. Anything to take his mind off, well off his mind. The cool tea and even colder toast certainly could do that.

The Blackthorn Legacy

CHAPTER ELEVEN:

DARK INTERVIEW ROOM

THE cell door catch was unlocked with relative ease unlike the effort put in by Detective Walsh the previous night. Garda Joey stood there like a jailer with a bunch of keys on a ring in his left hand. He pulled open the Cobalt green cell door, standing back a little. The man was over-weight, there was no two ways about it, and he was almost bursting out of his uniform.

Martin stood inside the cell. To the Garda with the keychain the prisoner was a forlorn looking sight, a sight for sore eyes, maybe, whatever that meant. One of those meaningless sayings, Joey thought to himself.

"Mr Carey, will you follow me, please!"

It wasn't a question, but an instruction and Martin had discovered the previous night just how sharp Joey's tongue could be. He stepped over to the bench and picked up the black tray, now holding an empty Styrofoam cup and crumb sprinkled paper plate.

"Never mind that, mate, someone else'll see to it. Come with me." Joey seemed much calmer this morning. Martin forced a smile in Joey's direction which as it happened went completely unnoticed by the uniformed man who only seemed interested in getting the prisoner up the hallway.

Martin walked to his, what could only be described as, qualified freedom. As he exited the dark cell to the brighter

The Blackthorn Legacy

corridor he could hear muffled, yet strong voices. Kata-Kata Kata-Kata was the sound Joey's tough soled shoes made under his slow and heavy but deliberate footsteps. The sound made on the hard shiny ceramic tiled floor was sort of in time with jangling keys he held. It sounded like a child's attempt at playing the drums. The slow bass drum and constant cymbal, slightly but not totally out of rhythm

Raised voices.

Voices Martin recognised.

Detectives Mason and Walsh were having words – with each other. As Martin walked the hallway back towards the main corridor, from where he had come the previous night, the voices became clearer.

"You can see the results for yourself, they're fairly conclusive." Mason's voice was strong but level. He wasn't losing his temper but his mind was made up on whatever it was they were discussing.

"Bullshit. You know he did it, I know he did it. He's a fucking psycho. I can feel it, I felt it last night. I don't trust him one bit. He's bloody guilty." Walsh was also adamant about what he felt. Martin was listening while trying to pretend as he strolled in front of Joey that he wasn't. He was pretty sure now that they were discussing his very case.

"You can't just go accusing people of crimes without hard evidence. You have a hunch, that's fine. It's noted, but without any kind of evidence it's just a...a...useless guess."

Martin in the accompaniment of Joey, still travelling up the darker corridor, heard the distinct sound of a cardboard file slapping off a flat surface.

"Shit."

"That's right Ed: you're pulling me into the Quicksand now too. This stuff with Jimmy Jones. He's making a complaint to the Super. (The Super was the name used by all the staff when talking about the Superintendent). Another one. You got lucky the last time. I'm putting in for a new partner. I'm not going down that slippery slope with you."

"You f...you cowardly..."

The Blackthorn Legacy

Joey and Martin turned the corner on to the main corridor. The approaching kata-kata kata-kata jingle jangle sound shut the two men up immediately. They didn't want to have their disagreement aired out in the open – but that was too late. The proverbial horse had bolted.

The two detectives watched Joey and Martin approach their position near the kiosk window where they both stood. They looked like the kids at the back of the classroom who had been found copying the big test. Their faces had turned bright red – blushing with embarrassment without them realising it. Surely their heated discussion hadn't been heard, or so they hoped. Mason bent down sheepishly and picked up the buff coloured thin file lying between his feet and Walsh's. It was a thin file with only a couple of sheets of paper poking their corners out from between the covers.

Joey walked up to them with Martin by his side.

"Your prisoner, Detectives". He was washing his hands of the entire incident and he made no attempt to hide his feelings. The three men watched as Joey walked away and in through a door before he appeared again the other side of the perforated glass panel at the kiosk.

Mason walked up to the window.

"Joey, can I have Mr Carey's personal effects please?"

Joey stared at him incredulously.

"Ask your partner. The Incredible Sulk probably has it all. He locked up your prisoner. Don't bring me into this sh...stuff." Mason turned around to Walsh who was in the middle of a staring match with Martin Carey.

"Detective." No move from Walsh

"Detective." A little louder this time but still there was no response. Walsh wasn't giving in. That's one thing he didn't do. Giving in was for the weak, is what he always preached. Continuously. Annoyingly. Mason walked between the two men to break the contest.

"Where's his effects, his stuff? Have you got the envelope?" Mason asked.

The Blackthorn Legacy

"What?" Walsh couldn't believe the question. He wasn't part of administrative structure. That was the job for those who preferred to shine the seats with their backsides. He got the criminals in and solved real crimes. "That's not my job. He looks after all that shit. Ask him", said Walsh pointing demonstratively at Joey who was perched behind the safety of the glass.

"I heard that." Joey pressed his plump face against the glass. "I left the whole matter to you partner, Detective Mason. I told him I would have nothing to do with it and just gave him the keys. What he did was his business" he continued, dismissively. Mason turned slowly, purposefully and stared directly into the reddening face of his partner. Walsh realised he had messed up, and like the boy who had been found copying the answers to the big test, he dropped his head. His chin rested on his chest. He was sorry, only because he had been found out. Only because he wasn't good enough to hide or cover up his mistake. He wasn't supposed to be doing paperwork. That was for...And in usual Walsh style, he glanced over at the kiosk window and rushed at it.

"You dick", he shouted. This wasn't his fault. It was never his fault. How was he to have known? He never did such menial work. He looked back at Mason.

"It's not my job". It sounded like he was trying to convince himself that he was right. Mason looked disgusted but shrugged it off looking at Martin Carey who was standing there motionless and silently. Walsh was about to speak again but decided better of it. He waited until two uniformed officers passed by them on their way up the corridor.

The flickering lightbulb was still at it, but it didn't appear to have the same effect as it did the night before. One or two of the office doors were now open, allowing grey daylight to spread out into the corridor. Artificial lighting was still required however, but not as necessary as during the hours of darkness. Martin watched the bulb igniting and quenching randomly as it had the night before and surmised that its

The Blackthorn Legacy

effect had been lessened by the effect of the daylight that sneaked in from wherever it could.

Mason moved to the kiosk window. It was obvious he was grating his back teeth. The stretching sinew lines on his lower jaw gave it away. The detective wanted to keep his mouth shut. The less he said right then he knew, would be better for both him and his partner.

"Are any of the Interview Rooms vacant Joey?" He tried to sound normal, but his voice crackled a little. He was upset. It was obvious he liked his job and that he followed the rules that had been set down for him and all of the others working there and were expected to follow. He just seemed to him that he was cleaning up after Walsh every time. Every bloody time.

"Number two around the corner is open detective."

"Thanks. Can I get one of those release forms?" He looked over at Martin, the quietest prisoner he had ever seen. Not a word from him so far. No complaints about being brought in there the night before either. He then looked at Walsh. "This paperwork needs to be taken care of. Is it below your pay grade to do that much?"

"I was tired, ok? We all make mistakes. Build a fucking bridge and get over it." The metal drawer opened under the kiosk window and Mason went over to retrieve the necessary forms. "Let's go, Interview Room two then."

A barely audible phone ringing sound could be heard in Joey's room as the three men made their way towards the interview room. A door opened behind the men as they walked up the corridor and Joey appeared in the doorway.

"Detective Walsh?" Walsh turned around to see the happy face of Joey. "The Super would like a word with you, now." The happiness in Joey's voice had spread to his voice.

"Go" said Mason, "I can take care of this. You're probably in enough sh..trouble without making it worse. Go!" he said. There was a little touch of sadness in his voice. As much as he loathed others cutting corners to get results, he also disliked officers getting in trouble. Stick together, is what he was told from the time he had began working in Fellowmore.

"It's Jimmy Jones again. It's gotta be." The rage was visible in his face again. The shoe on the other foot made Martin smile internally. It was more a laugh than a smile. It made him happy, but he was able to contain his pleasure totally within. Nobody else would have guessed how he felt from his expression, the same sullen expression that was on his face since departing the dark, dreary, nightmare cell. The cell that created nightmares.

The two men entered the interview room and Mason directed Martin Carey where to sit. It was a 100 square feet windowless room. The walls were painted dark brown, matching the colour of the floor covering. The only light came from recessed florescent light units in the ceiling, casting light directly on the Formica table and the four plastic charcoal chairs, like spotlights. The chairs were evenly divided by the table – two each side.

A simple room. There was an electronic recording device also in the ceiling, beside a small dome shaped CCTV camera. The device was about the size of an old DVD player, hanging from four thin cylindrical pipes.

Mason began writing on the first of the two stapled sheets he had brought with him. Martin was still regarding the room and had come back to the table he was now sitting at, observing Detective Mason. The chair he was sitting on was unstable. An old trick in this investigating room. The back right leg of the chair he was directed to was cut a little short. This was to make the interviewee uncomfortable so that he or she would be concentrating on their balance rather than creating a cock and bull story. Sometimes it worked, sometimes it didn't, but it was better to have than to not have. Martin tried the chair beside him and found it to be steady. This would be for his representative should he require one. The chair that rocked. That sounded like a musical or something, maybe like the film about the boat.

The Blackthorn Legacy

He stared at Mason who had been hunched silently over the desk as he continued to fill out the form. Martin strained his eyes to see across the table. Reading the large lettering upside down at the top of the sheet the detective was filling in from where he was, was not as difficult as he thought it might have been. DETAINEE RELEASE FORM (F1.1). He tested himself further and glanced down the headings already completed by the detective in clear printed writing. Name. That was fine. Address. No, there was an incorrect address inserted, he noticed. That had to be fixed. He had to tell him. He built up the courage.

"Sorry, Detective Mason, I think you have noted my home address incorrectly there. I live in Ard Lane and not whatever it is you have recorded there."

"Sorry, Mr Carey, it's correct. Rahaduff. That's the official name of the area you live in. Ard Lane is the local name for it. I know it's generally more popular, but it's not the official name." A very matter of fact reply and immediately he went then back to writing.

Darkness came across Martin's vision. There was nothing else in the room.

Rahaduff.

That was the sign in his dream or nightmare the night before. Suddenly it felt as if a hand had got a hold of the soft tissue of his stomach and was now squeezing it like a face cloth.

He felt sick.

Maybe his nightmare was a vision after all. That was scaring the bejaysus out of him. Droplets of perspiration appeared on his forehead.

The nightmare or vision was still crystal clear in his mind.

The stone sign indicating he was that he was in or at Rahaduff in his vision. It was crystal clear, yet he'd never heard of the place. Then to make things a little more peculiar, the detective told him he lived in Rahaduff.

Was it all just a vision? The long grass, the hill, the stream, the voice in his head, the metallic smell? Oh and the

The Blackthorn Legacy

diminishing air quality resulting his inability to catch his breath, not to forget that.

He began to shake, first his fingers. Then his arms, his shoulders. It lasted only seconds, but it replaced whatever energy he had with nothingness.

The dark interview room began closing in on him. The walls were approaching, from all four sides. The air was being squeezed out. The small shadows on the floor around him created by the table, chairs and the two men seemed to be dancing as if...as if what? Why were they stirring at all? He tried to cough and but throat seemed to be constricting with the lack of air available to him. Mason though continued to write unaffected. Martin began coughing, a choking cough, an acute unexpected reflex. He closed his eyes and could see a kaleidoscope of colours on the inside of his eyelids as the episode continued.

Just as suddenly as the attack had come, it subsided. He opened his eyes, almost afraid of what he might see. There before him was Mason, looking concerned mouthing something to Martin in a muffled voice. It seemed like the sound he had heard as a young boy when he and some other boys played with the central cardboard tube from the used up toilet rolls. It was an echoed noise, yet indistinct.

He sat there as this bizarre event played out for several seconds. It seemed like an eternity of time had passed. Everything stopped and he realised that all around him had returned to how it was when he first entered. Mason's voice became clear again.

"Are you ok Mr Carey, do you want a drink of water?"

"I'm fine, thanks. It was just something. It's nothing."

"You're sure?" Mason wasn't sure that Martin was telling the truth. It was obvious from his tone.

"I'm fine detective. It's over now." He coughed a single dry cough but that was it.

"Ok then, I'm nearly finished now. I'll need to clear a few things with you and then you'll be free to leave. Ok?"

The Blackthorn Legacy

Martin nodded, indicating he had grasped what had been said to him. Mason continued reading and filling in blanks of the form. He finished as much as he could and looked up at the pale faced Martin sitting opposite him.

"I've a few questions for you Mr Carey. These are standard enough and should be easily answered. Ok?"

Martin nodded again. He was unable to speak, his throat had suddenly dried up and he was unable to loosen it himself even by swallowing saliva repeatedly. It felt like he was trying to wet the driest part of the Sahara in the driest season.

"Can I get that drink of water now, please", he croaked.

"Sure thing." The croaky reply forced the detective into action. He rose from the table and stepped outside the door for a couple of moments and returned with a transparent plastic cup three quarters full with clear water. Martin raised the cup and gulped down the water. Although he complained of the bitter and overall appalling taste of the water pumped into the piped arteries throughout the area by the Local Authority, he still enjoyed the cool, moist feeling as it wet the dry gorge at the back of his mouth and lubricated his voice box.

"Is that better Mr Carey? Are you ok now?"

"Yes, thanks." The liquid had brought the colour back to his cheeks and in turn improved his being. He was able to clear his throat properly and it felt good.

"Ok then, these questions. Are you on any prescription drugs?"

"No." Definitively no. He hadn't been sick in years.

"Have you recently ingested or smoked any drugs that have not been prescribed.

"No." This was an emphatic response. He was almost disgusted to have been asked such a question. Mason sensed the feeling in the answer.

"I'm sorry Mr Carey, these are the questions on this form and I just have to fill in the answers. Obviously only the ones

The Blackthorn Legacy

I don't already know the answers to. Please just concentrate on the answers and not what you perceive them to be. Ok?"

Martin nodded again.

"Do you still work at the Department of Education?"

"Yes." To anyone else, more awake, or interested, would have recognised the boredom in Martin's voice relating to his place of work. The form filling was almost completed. Mason looked up from the page considering his interviewee and rehashed the talk he must have given at least a thousand times previous to this particular morning.

"I'll need a contact number from you. You'll need to remain in the area, insofar as you should not leave the country. We may need to talk to about this particular case at a later date. So, can you provide me with a contact number please?"

There a nervous pause. Mason stared at Martin as he balled up his hands on the table, uncomfortably. Then he answered the question.

"I don't have a phone."

"What? A landline number then?" The incredulous tone in the detective voice was impossible to ignore. If there was a way of measuring a thing, it would have been off the scale. Someone without a mobile phone in this day and age, Mason was flabbergasted.

"No sir, I don't own one of those either." Martin's voice was low, as if he wanted to keep a secret between himself and the shocked man sitting opposite him. "I don't believe in communicating with people in what is claimed to be a confidential manner, only for others, unnamed others I would like to add, a clandestine organisation reporting to our own and other governmental agencies. No sir. But if you must contact me, I'll be back in work on Monday week where I have a work phone. Do you want that number?"

He provided the number to the still visibly shocked detective who then signed the form and asked for Martin's signature also. He stared at the two pages front and back and then looked up at Martin.

The Blackthorn Legacy

"That's it Mr Carey. You are free to leave."

Martin sat there motionlessly waiting for news on how he would be getting home.

"Oh yes, I'm sorry, you'll have to make your own way home Mr Carey. I am sorry." The second apology was as if he had been joking about it while in fact, he was actually employing a recent policy change. Martin rose and slowly left the room, glancing back at the detective, who seemed to be just coming round from the shock of the non-existence of a phone in the life of Mr Martin Carey. Mason nodded almost embarrassed. The door closed and he was alone.

He's not a sheep Michael Carey. You should be more like that young man. Make a decision for yourself once in a while.

Mason's mother's voice was beginning to annoy him, although he had heard the same sermon from her twenty and more years previously.

The door burst open and Walsh walked in looking rather pleased with himself. Mason wasn't sure if he was pleased or upset. The two feelings were very close on the human emotions radar. Maybe he was experiencing both at once. Yes that was it. He was pleased because Walsh's presence would almost certainly ensure his dead mother's interfering voice would stay away, and upset because the partner he wanted to be rid of looked happy and that undoubtedly meant one thing.

"Thanks for knocking on the door, Ed." Walsh chose to disregard the lame shot across his bow.

"We're staying together, you and me." Walsh's voice was like that of child unwrapping gifts on Christmas morning and finding exactly what he had asked for. "The Super wants us to stay on this case. He said that we are the two halves of a perfect detective. Your ability to ask the right questions and to meticulously record our movements. And my ability to get information from those normally unwilling to provide it. He told me that the Jimmy Jones problem will be dealt with by him himself."

The Blackthorn Legacy

Mason was unmoved. He had heard everything Walsh had said but he wasn't listening. He was still thinking about Carey and his phone situation.

"Are you alright Mason? Look, I'm sorry for fucking up last night. But you know me and paperwork."

"He doesn't have a phone." Mason was thinking out loud, staring into nothingness.

"What?"

"Carey, he doesn't have a phone. You and me searched his house last night. Did you see any phone sockets?"

"What?" Walsh was lost. He was so caught up in his own delight; he wasn't interested in anything else.

"Carey, Martin Carey, last night. We checked his house; did you find or see a phone or any phone sockets?" Mason's eyes were no longer glazed over. He was in the zone, the detecting zone. Walsh looked at him and then looked up at the ceiling as if seeking some sort of divine intervention. He followed the visible cracks in the ceiling tiles surrounding the recessed light fittings, with his eyes. After a moment of searching the crevices brain he looked back at his partner.

"No, not that I remember, why?"

Mason had that disturbed look on his face again.

"Something doesn't add up, that's what. I think Carey was set up, he had to have been." Walsh was about to burst into his speech about all sorts and about how he wanted to sort out Martin Carey. Mason recognised the look and continued. "He doesn't have a phone line, ok?"

Walsh nodded visibly unconvinced.

"The call that was received in the station that ultimately sent us out there was received from a landline out there in Rahaduff."

"Where?" The place name confused Walsh. He didn't remember being in such a place.

"Ard Lane, where we were last night." He was getting annoyed now with his partner. How the hell could Walsh not have heard or understood what he just said. Was he stupid as well as dangerous, he thought to himself.

The Blackthorn Legacy

Walsh looked a little worried now. Was his partner having a break-down? He looked fine, but confusing the name of the place where they were with Raha – something or other.

The large fluorescent lights flickered and went out for a second. The room was completely black. The two men jumped a little but neither wanted to let the other know that they were anxious in the darkness. Especially after what they had seen last night. That body, that head, disfigured the way it was. The lights flashed again and returned to full beams, glowing down on the table, casting those shadows again.

"Did they not pay the bill?" Walsh was half serious in his open question. Mason ignored the remark and looked back down at notes he had made.

"How do you think the killer carried out these murders? There were no marks found on the bodies. All three of them had the skin pulled tight at the back of their heads…You saw the reports too." The picture of the dead O'Carroll lying in the evidence tent was still clearly set in his mind. Like a photograph hanging there in a darkroom from a thin line of wire, drip drying. It was so clear in his mind's eye.

The skin ripped at tip of his nose and a crusty scab already formed over the break in the skin.

He coughed a little.

Walsh covered his face and rubbed his open hands up and down his face quickly and looked at Mason. He had felt a sickening rise of something from his stomach the night before but he had managed to hold onto it. He realised Mason was revisiting the scene again. Anyway, he knew *he* was right about this case. He was certain Carey had done it.

"Look, I don't know, maybe he drugged them or some shit. All I know is that I think Carey had a lot to do with it."

"No drugs in their system except a trace of crack two of them had ingested a couple of days previously. They weren't moved to where they were located from another scene – evidence shows that as does the medical report." Mason placed his elbows on the table before him and rested his forehead on the heels of his hands for a moment and then

The Blackthorn Legacy

slowly looked up at Walsh. "This is going to be bigger than we thought, Ed. This could be huge."

Walsh was astounded. How long had it been since his partner had called him by his first name. They usually called each other by their surnames, a kind of unwritten rule.

Mason rose from his chair. He walked over to Walsh and put his arm around his shoulder.

"Let's go Ed, let's get some coffee and you can tell me all about your chat with the Super."

Walsh was taken by surprise by this complete change in his partner. He liked it but it did unsettle him a little. The two men walked out of Interview Room Two. Mason pressed the switch, quenching the lights.

The door closed behind them as the spring lever pushed it out. Inside the lights flickered again and the letters *JJ* were being scrawled on the wall by a non-existent writer. Then, **needs to be gone**, was scrawled in the same uneven writing.

The Blackthorn Legacy

CHAPTER TWELVE:

ALMO STACE

MARTIN sat in the rear of the taxi as it travelled back to Shayleigh, back to his house. The sky had scummed over with cumulonimbus clouds which could only mean one thing. The weather was going to change, for the worse.

He hated public transport; it normally meant having to talk nonsense to people he had not already nor probably would, meet again. All that small talk about this and that and in the end it would lead to what some called uncomfortable silences. To avoid falling into the dreaded uncomfortable silence trap, Martin used it as a starting point. Don't talk to anyone and then you won't get caught, he always told himself. An easy rule to follow.

This taxi driver who even introduced himself as Akos from somewhere in Eastern Europe. He wanted nothing more than to talk. Martin was ready to break his rule, but the strength came from somewhere. It washed over him, telling him to just give monosyllabic answers. He stared out the window, watching the fields and ditches pass him by as they got to the outskirts of Fellowmore, heading out of town.

The journey down Ard Lane was no different to the rest of the trip. Martin had listening to the driver complain about the condition of the roadway they were travelling on and how the County Council and of course the Government were at

The Blackthorn Legacy

fault for the failure to fund public roads. Not to mention the burden of the expected water charges. Martin just listened at the back as the driver droned on and on, almost continually talking without taking a breath. He himself had taken charge of the water charge situation. His well would take care of that. This one way word traffic was better however than the questioning that had been directed his way at the beginning of the relatively short journey.

They reached his gate and after making the due payment, Martin walked up the slope to his house. It was all his own again. The yellow crime scene tape was gone as were the tarpaulin and the evidence tents. The only thing that remained the same was the hole in his gate. The bile rose in his throat as he approached the damaged entrance. Now he was going to have to repair this...this destruction.

More will have to be done Marty, and you know it. You know what you have to do. Almo Stace. That voice in his head again. It was a cool, dark, inviting yet annoying voice. It certainly had loads of push behind it. Why did the voice call him Marty? Nobody called him that, not even his parents. They were dead now, but when they were here with him on this earth did they call him Marty. Only one person, his friend...his name escaped Martin. It shouldn't have been too difficult to recall the name of the single comrade he'd had up to this point of his life. That voice, it was in the part of his brain he just couldn't do anything about. It was like one of those ear worm tunes. It always stuck in his head and it couldn't be removed no matter how hard he tried. The more he tried to remove it from memory, the stronger it seemed to get. Just forget about it Marty, he said to himself. Marty?

Never mind, he said waving his hand before his face, swatting away the thoughts.

He opened the gate and closed it again behind him and made his way slowly around to his back door. Cat was waiting for him. His little companion, his shiny black coat, gracefully made his way to the door, following closely behind Martin. Cat sat their while Martin delved into his jacket

The Blackthorn Legacy

pockets for his keys. The white triangular shaped fur just below his small cuddly face made it look like Cat was wearing a tuxedo.

Searching in his coat pockets he eventually felt the cold of the nickel plated brass blades.

Then something else.

A rectangular piece of card.

He pulled both items out of his jacket pocket. The card was of more interest even though his main reason for being at his back door was to gain entry. It was the business card belonging to Deirdre King, the solicitor from the previous day. That bitch who had verbally abused him on the street the previous day.

Deirdre King. Why did that name mean something to him? *(Almo Stace)*

Never mind, probably just his mind playing tricks with his...mind, he thought.

It was time to get in and get something to eat. He had only realised as he swung in the door how hungry he actually was. He also needed to use the toilet.

After half an hour inside, the fire was lit and he had had a good feed. He felt relatively well within himself but he needed some sleep. His interrupted slumber in the cell wasn't much to write home about. The fire had begun to take hold, so he piled it up with timber and briquettes. He could never have imagined looking forward to a sleep at three in the afternoon before, but needs must, as the old cliché went. He also feared it with the prospect of another nightmare. Or was it a day mare if you have it in the afternoon.

The Blackthorn Legacy

CHAPTER THIRTEEN:

YES, LIGHT WAS STRONG, BUT NOT AS POWERFUL AS THE DARKNESS

HE awoke from his deep dreamless sleep in complete darkness. Martin opened his eyes wide to make sure that he hadn't lost his sight during his hours of sub consciousness. He still wasn't sure where he was. It felt like his mind was doing cartwheels inside his head and he was in a state of confusion, most likely caused by the change to his normal routine.

He glanced around nervously, as some reality began to make its way to his eyes. A cool shudder trickled down his spine. The sombre portrait of Che Guevara hanging on the wall opposite, was staring straight at him. Did he know something? It felt as though there may have been someone else in the room, or somewhere, watching him. That cool shudder again. El Che would keep him safe, wouldn't he? Did the man in the framed picture know why Martin's bedroom door was closed, or had he in fact closed it himself? Was it the *other* in the room? Was there an *other* in this room? He lay back on the bed covers where he had fallen asleep but with his pillow wrapped around his face to keep from seeing what he didn't want to see – an *other*. Although he temporarily blinded himself he listened intently for any unusual sounds.

The Blackthorn Legacy

A creak up high.
Was it the ceiling or was it in the attic.
There it was again.
Creeeeak. Then right over his head was a single low singular bang and a muffled flushing sound. What would an *other* actually look like? Would it be the physical form of that pushy voice in the untouchable part of his brain?
Suddenly calmness drifted over him. He realised that the sounds he had heard were coming from the attic. They were all part of the new water system. He should have known that from the beginning but his over-active imagination had gotten a hold of him and wouldn't let go.
He removed the pillow from his face and only then realised he had been holding his breath.
His eyes started to become accustomed to the murkiness as did his mind. He felt a silliness begin to creep in now. Afraid of the dark in his own house, in his own bedroom? What an idiot, he thought to himself. He looked around the room and marvelled at how the darkness reached into every crevice and corner. It was the complete antithesis of light. There was a certain heaviness about darkness. It filled and covered everything it came into contact with. He reached over to his bedside locker and turned on the small lamp. A pale but bright creamy yellow radiated from the fitting. It filled the room. It had an incomprehensible strength in it. *The light shines in the darkness and the darkness has not overcome it.* Something he had remembered from Religion Class in school. It was a quotation from John Chapter 1 as far as he could remember. An uplifting thought. But that's all it was – a thought. He looked around the artificially lit room. There were still some dark patches – shadows – where the light had been unable to reach. Yes, light was strong, but not as powerful as the darkness.
The old analogue double bell alarm clock he had inherited years before, stood on the locker facing him, telling him the time. The white but greying face of the clock always seemed to have a look about it, a no-nonsense look. It was twenty

The Blackthorn Legacy

past seven on Saturday evening. He had slept for almost five hours. What was most important about his slumber was that he had slept uninterrupted, without any bad dreams. The field with the...he pushed the thought of it back in his mind. He didn't want to think about that right then. Martin swung his feet onto the soft thick creamy shaggy rug where he had left his shoes. He was feeling peckish again; the sleep had obviously taken it out of him. It was hard for him to understand how doing almost nothing could create an appetite, but that's just what happened. He remade his bed and tidied up the room to its original perfection.

After feeding his hunger, Martin decided it was time to do some research. He went into his sitting room to where his little library had been belittled by Detective Walsh the previous evening. He wanted to carry out his own investigation and find out what he could about Rahaduff. Was it real, was it made up or was it just an old name to be found only on ancient Ordnance Survey Maps? If he managed to locate information he was then going to find out what he could about understanding dreams and what certain actions suggest or if it was just part of the human psyche that had never been properly or scientifically probed or scrutinised. Maybe there was a perfectly good reason why he had had those dreams and gone into those trances.

He had also left the business card on the table. The Gardaí wanted him to stay around. He felt like he was being treated like a suspect and that maybe it would be no harm lawyering up.

That was for Monday morning however. Now it was time to delve into the books.

The Blackthorn Legacy

CHAPTER FOURTEEN:

JJ NEEDS TO BE GONE

SUNDAY morning was normally quiet in the Garda Station in Fellowmore and this morning was no different. It was the usual business the night before with the regular number of visitors brought in to discuss the trouble they were creating out in the streets of the town while under the influence of alcohol. The six cells in the station were almost always occupied with idiots who believed that had transformed into superheroes during the ingestion of liquor on a night out.

There were some regular visitors and then there were the trouble makers who took advantage of situations and ended up in the interview rooms. It was Joey's job, or whoever was on duty on Sunday morning to ensure that the questioning rooms were up to standard – clean and shiny after the busiest night of the week. It really didn't take much. A few stray pieces of litter and such like.

He opened the door of his room, the kiosk, and walked out into the corridor. He glanced up and down. To his left the flickering bulb was being replaced by one of the officers, Colm Carney, known to workmates as Chili. It was funny to start with, everyone calling him Chili Colm Carney but it soon wore thin but Chili stuck. At least the removal of that flickering bulb would be one less headache, literally.

He walked down the corridor, armed with a black bin bag in one hand and a clean looking dry cloth with an aerosol

The Blackthorn Legacy

cleaning spray in the other. Although the interview rooms were numbered one to four, they didn't follow one another that way on the corridor for some unknown and inexplicable reason. The furthest away was room four and that was fine, but then the next rooms were one, three and two in that order. Figure that one out.

The process was usually a relatively quick one. This particular Sunday morning had begun reasonably characteristically. He entered Interview Room Four and turned on the light. After three flashes the bulbs lit up the centre of the room. He made a face and raised his hand to his nose. What was the overpowering smell, he asked himself. He glanced around the room and then saw it. A brown paper bag with dark brown see-through markings, crumpled up in lying on the ground in the far corner where one of the interviewees had obviously brought in or was given greasy fast food of some sort or other. Seeing the bag ignited the switch in his brain that allowed the lobe in that muscle to put the picture and smell together and to realise what it was. The pong of fast-food hung heavily in the air. Not a nice scent early in the morning. It was such a strong stench that he felt he would be forced to cut it out of the atmosphere. He stopped and dreamed of himself at home creating a new machine that could destroy wretched smells from the air without leaving an odour of its own. He dismissed the idea immediately, considering it an impossibility.

Gingerly he picked up the brown bag using only the bare tips of his fingers and threw it into his own black bag. He wanted to be sure that he wouldn't catch anything from the bag. It could happen, he convinced himself. The smelly culprit had been caught in the Interview Room.

"No way out for you, mofo".

Joey got a little carried away during this drab job but his imagination kept him going. All that was left now was to spray the table with his aerosol and wipe it clean with the cloth and then he was onto the next room.

The Blackthorn Legacy

By the time he got to room two he, was beginning to lose interest. He opened the door, switched on the light and glanced around the floor.

Empty.

The cleanest room of the four. Joey sprayed the table with his aerosol and wiped the table clean. Great, it was over. He peeped at his watch. Only another half hour left and he was off for three days. That feeling put a pep, albeit a small pep, in his step. Joey walked to the door and was about to turn off the light, looking back into the room when he saw something written on the wall. Not written, scrawled on the wall. Investigation was not his thing but he walked right up to it to study and maybe examine the scrawl. From the doorway it resembled some of that cave writing he'd seen on those television documentaries. What did they call those old Egyptian markings? Hieroglyphics, yes that was it.

Joey recognised the words as he closed in on the writing.

JJ was written (scrawled) and then underneath it the words, **needs to be gone**. Who the hell? What the hell? He stared at it for a moment not really sure what to think.

Was JJ a person? Shit. Did he know them? He got into a bit of a tizzy, shaking all over. He could feel the first bead of sweat forming on his forehead and about to begin its journey down his pudgy face. Then it hit him. Joey knew what needed to be done. He frantically rummaged in his pants pockets, both of them, and dug out his Smart phone. His hands were all sweaty and he let it fall to the floor. The excitement inside him was so great he bent down to pick up the device. Some threads in the seam on the seat of his pants stretched –audibly.

That didn't matter. Joey pressed the on-screen button to bring up the phone's camera. He aimed it at the wall and took a picture of the scrawled writing. He brought the screen up closer to his face to examine the photo. It was perfection itself.

This was an investigation *he* was going to be running – all by himself. He left the doorway and began moving quickly

The Blackthorn Legacy

towards his kiosk. It was quicker than he had moved in years and his lungs were feeling it. It was only a hundred yards from Interview Room Four to his work station and when he got there his chest was burning up inside. His wheezy breaths sounded like that of a dying man. Each a sharp rattle in his diaphragm finishing each time with a little whistle. He was bent over, leaning his hands on his knees trying to recover from the first activity he'd had in some time. His rapidly heaving shapeless chest was taking as much of his energy as the slow jog had. Dark patches of perspiration were forming down the centre of his back and in his armpits. Droplets of perspiration were forming on his face with more regularity now that he was cooling down. A small pool of sweat had formed on the floor at his feet.

No matter, he was going to persevere because he had a job to do.

Finally his breath regulated and he was able to stand upright once more and he entered his kiosk. He rushed over to his computer and searched the database that contained the names of all those brought in for questioning in the last twenty four hours. Wiping his brow with his sleeve only made the persisting droplets of sweat worse. Everybody knew that eyebrows had a single job – to ensure that sweat did not roll into one's eyes. By rubbing and disturbing those short hairs only allowed the liquid secreted from the sweat glands to move easily down one's face and of course into their eyes. Why then did he rub his forehead with his sleeve? He figured out his mistake within moments of brushing his brow.

His eyes were burning from the sweat as it steadily rolled down towards his eyes. He leaned over the computer, feeling that sitting down was going to waste valuable searching time. He knew that every second was important.

After getting into the database he required, he entered a search command and input JJ.

Nothing.

The Blackthorn Legacy

He stood up, hands on hips. He was extremely displeased with the response. His hands were now down by his side as he continually made and opened fists with them as he tried to concentrate. Where else would he even try to look? Then as if a bulb had lit up and exploded over his head, cartoon style, he returned to the keyboard. This search was a little more complicated. But he'd done a few favours in his time (for co-workers and others) and he knew how to circumvent some of the required information fields to get to his destination without leaving a trail of data crumbs that would lead right back to him.

Once again he entered JJ into the search box he'd brought up on screen. He waited as the processing unit did its work, hunting down the information he sought out and all the information that was magically attached to it by computer programmers. The information available flashed up on screen. Joey stared dumbfounded at the results. There were two separate entries. One six months previously and another, the day before. Mr James 'Jimmy' Jones. He had submitted a report of unprofessional conduct concerning Detective E Walsh.

"Shit." The surprise on Joey's face disappeared and was instantaneously replaced with a look of glee. His smile spread from ear to ear, like that of a hyena that had just fed on something else's kill.

"You'll be hearing from me Detective Walsh", he said to himself in a sly low voice, "But not from me directly", he continued.

There was noise outside and he looked at his watch. His shift was over. He had the next three days off and during that time he was going to put a plan together on how to bring down Walsh. That man needed to be brought down a peg or two, he told himself. The door opened and Joey jumped into action. He saved the information on screen into his own personal folder and just clicked from the off-limits screen he had been using.

The Blackthorn Legacy

His colleague sneaked up behind him, glancing over his shoulder, just missing the show. Joey turned around and walked into Garda Dalton, not realising he was so close, startling him.

"What's up?" asked Dalton.

"Nothing", replied Joey. The reply sounded very unconvincing in his own head, but it seemed to placate Dalton. "I'm off", he continued still suffering a little from the mini shock. Dalton stared at him, shaking his head in some sort of disapproval or disbelief. It didn't matter because Joey wasn't staying to find out. The quicker he was out the less that would be made of it. That was the logic in his scrambled head at least.

He walked out onto the corridor and stood in the middle of the floor watching as business began continued as usual. People were moving up and down the corridor, unaware of what had just happened in the kiosk. The safest place to commit a crime was in the Garda Station. He smiled again, this time with pure satisfaction.

Joey took a step forward but slipped, flailing like Bambi on ice but miraculously recovering his balance. He looked down at the floor and only then realising it was his own sweat on the sleek floor that had almost brought him down. The break from work was really required now because his heart was not going to be able to cope with any more shocks.

On the way out the door he glanced up at the noticeboard. The up to date work rota hung there from a brass thumb tack on the pine framed cork noticeboard. Mason and Walsh were off until Thursday.

He smiled as he left the building for the car park and his car. Things were going to improve no end, he predicted to himself.

The Blackthorn Legacy

CHAPTER FIFTEEN:

THE LIBRARY

A tired looking Martin Carey sat at his kitchen table. He had searched Saturday evening and most of Sunday for information on Rahaduff but was unable to find anything of any real importance. He had just finished off a bowl of microwaved porridge and was now about to put on the toaster and kettle. Nothing like finishing off your breakfast with toast and strong coffee when you're on holidays.

Walking out to the back kitchen he heard the small meow of Cat outside the backdoor no doubt it was seeking its early feed. The water bowl was almost empty. Martin retrieved a can of premium cat food from the press under the sink and forked out half of it into the cat's bowl and refilled the water bowl. All was done as the kettle clicked off, steam billowing upwards from its spout. The hot crispy bread would soon be popping out of the white toaster and as if there was a connection between them, it did. He needed to close the door to keep out the nippy March air slipping in to the kitchen. Looking down as he began pushing the door he saw Cat staring up at him with a look, a strange look. The expression on the cat's face was a knowing one. Martin stared at his friend, possibly his only real friend, and seemed a little baffled. Cat's white marking, that gave him the tuxedo look seemed to have shrunk in size. It was like the cat could have

The Blackthorn Legacy

pulled his black dinner jacket a little tighter to keep out the cold, the March cold. Was he just imagining this? And his fur, he looked bushier, more fur on his body giving the cat a stronger look although the 'smile' or whatever it was on its face right then gave a different impression.

He knows too.

Why was that stupid voice persisting in his head? He closed the door and went about preparing the remainder of his breakfast.

The plan for the day was first of all to make a visit to the library in Fellowmore to find out what he could about Rahaduff. Surely there was something in that public building. Of course there is, he convinced himself. His own book collection, fantastic though it was, was not of any real assistance in his hunt for pertinent information. Following that, he planned to call into Legal, Wrights. The name of the firm still made him smile. He would see if he could get an appointment with Deirdre King, bitch.

Almo Stace.

That bloody voice in his head again. He couldn't even understand what it was saying. Was it a thing or a person is repeatedly referred to? It was driving him a little mad, maybe even a little crazy. No, crazy was jumping out of a plane without a parachute. Maybe just a little mad then. He tried to remember back if he'd always had that deep annoying voice in his head. He ran through his memory bank as best he could but nothing, until recently that was. Why had it just begun then? Did those dreams have anything to do with it? He dismissed that though out of hand almost as soon as it came into his head. The last thing he wanted was to bring back that terrible feeling of near reality in an unreal world where he was suffering as he sat beside a babbling brook. What had become of the much more enjoyable dreams where he was the hero?

After finishing his meal, he tidied up and readied himself for his day away. Would it all be going according to plan? He

The Blackthorn Legacy

would learn a lot about himself and what problems faced him, and how he would deal with them.

The Gardaí, two detectives in particular had marked his card and they had clocked him in. Who knew how long that card would remain in use? Hopefully a solicitor would fill him in.

Was he ready to go now?

Martin liked to sip water during the day. So he thought it a good idea to bring some of his own fine tasting naturally flowing water with him. He found an empty plastic bottle under the sink. It looked clean but he couldn't be sure how long it was in the press. The tap began its gurgling sound again. The chrome spout shook prior to the water spilling out in fits and starts before the clear sparkling constant stream flowed out. He washed and filled the plastic bottle and was then ready to begin his day's work.

*****

He parked his car in one of the town's public car parks and paid the full day rate. He expected would be a couple of hours anyway.

The library was in the old square off the main street. The old square, recently transformed by the council into a pedestrian only area, was officially called Memorial Square. It had once been a parking area for the people of Fellowmore, but after much debate and listening to the people of the town – their voters – the Council created an area where cars or lorries were not allowed to enter. The decision to make the alteration had initially upset locals, but after becoming accustomed to it, they embraced the idea and it would take much promising by politicians to revert to the bad old way.

The Square itself was one of the original parts of town. It had never really been affected by modernisation or improvement for that matter. Yes, businesses had opened

The Blackthorn Legacy

there, but the Square itself remained as a square, the communal centre of Fellowmore.

To the front centre there was a tall unpainted or undecorated concrete monument commemorating the life of the first person shot dead in some war or other. The fact was that nobody knew who it commemorated. But it was always a marker, a place to direct visitors to. The mass concrete that formed the monument was two feet square at the base, rising up almost fifteen feet into the air and narrowing slightly as it rose into the Fellowmore sky, almost to a point, but not fully. It wasn't one of world renown but it meant something to the people of the town, or at least the local politicians said it did. Most people living there now never even noticed it as anything but a concrete column in Memorial Square.

As he turned the corner from Main Street to enter the square's open space he was hit with the stiff cold breeze. The breeze blew freely in the open space which was not available elsewhere in the town crowded by two storey and three storey concrete buildings. Martin's eyes watered as the sharp draft hit him straight on, tickling his nose while also feeling like it was freezing his eyeballs. He shut his eyes tight in a futile attempt at drying the tears of cold gathered around his lower eye lashes. Also it was just to give his eyes time to adjust to the swift change in the weather conditions that were facing him in the square. He took a step forward and almost fell as he blindly stumbled over something on the pathway. Almost falling headlong to the ground he managed to get his balance from the wall of the bank building that bordered the pathway most of the way down that side of the square. Like most bank edifices seen in many towns, both big and small, it was a boring yet dominating concrete grey structure.

Gaining his composure, regaining his balance, Martin looked around to see what it was that lay stupidly near the corner of Main Street and Memorial Square. He was both astonished and horrified to see that it was a woman with black scraggy hair; predominantly covered by multi-coloured

The Blackthorn Legacy

headscarf, yet some rat's tails blew down by the side of her wrinkled and weathered face. She was dressed in her beggar's uniform. As with all the other beggars or 'Agents of the State', as Martin secretly called them, she was kneeling on the impossibly clean cardboard sheeting and holding out a brown paper coffee cup. He quickly figured out that it was her, The Agent who had caused the obstruction. Martin glanced around and saw the hole in the wall bank machine just up from him. Damn, he said to himself, they would have caught all that on camera.

Then it hit him.

A strange, sickening feeling.

Was it Vertigo? The whole Memorial Square seemed to be revolving around him. There went the concrete monument whirring by in a clockwise direction. Martin watched it whizz by as everything else went out of focus, a mish mash of colour behind it.

He closed his eyes tightly and counted to ten in his head. On reopening his eyes it took a moment for him to readjust to the daylight and then everything was as it should have been and where it should have been. All circular clockwise motion had ceased and his stomach had settled down. It was time to move away from this cursed position.

He looked back and noticed that the beggar had almost immediately lost interest in Martin when she realised that he wouldn't be handing over some of his money. He believed that this was definitely one of those Governmental spies when she completely ignored him even though he had made an ass of himself on the street. He looked around the square and saw people carry on their daily business or whatever it may have been on a Monday morning. Another reason for him to believe that it was more than this 'beggar' that had been working for the Government. He was feeling more alone in the world now than before. Everybody was watching him, trying to catch him out – but he wasn't falling for it. Or at least he was going to make it difficult for them, all of them. It made it more difficult for him to concentrate on his work because he knew there were eyes everywhere. In every street, on every wall and they were seeking out people like him. The ones that knew the truth. He could feel it in his waters. He knew he was right.

Martin shook himself and tried to delete that memory from his mind and remove the shakes from his hands and arms. He shook them both out. He was feeling better already.

At least he would be safe in the library – no CCTV cameras in there.

The Blackthorn Legacy

CHAPTER SIXTEEN:

WHAT WAS RAHADUFF?

THE Fellowmore Town Library had been reconstructed and re-opened two years previously. Prior to that it had shared the building it occupied with the area Education Committee, which was to the front of the old structure. This meant it was difficult for the library to attract new members when people didn't know where it actually was. Newcomers to the town wouldn't have known of its existence. Following an amalgamation of area Education Committees; the library became the sole operator within the building. With some capital funding and voluntary contributions a new building was designed and eventually built.

The new development was a futuristic style construction, containing large glass walls to the front. The architects had obviously decided to use the natural light as much as possible and considering it faced south; why not indeed make use of it.

Martin approached the automatic door which opened when the sensors realised he was there.

Once in, he approached the middle aged lady standing behind the pine fronted and black granite counter. Fellowmore Library was always sparklingly clean, always shining and always tidy. The librarian was not the type-cast black haired pony tail, red faced woman, balancing thick black framed spectacles at the end of her nose. No, she was balancing frameless spectacles on her narrow nose but that was where the similarities ended. She has short wavy hair edging a thin intelligent pleasant looking face which sat comfortable above a slender body. She looked up helpfully as Martin advanced to her counter.

"Hi, can I be of any help to you sir?" She spoke clearly but softly. It must have taken some amount of training to get enough strength in her voice to sound loud enough to Martin while simultaneously managing not to affect any of the other users in there, and there were a few.

He leaned up against the granite counter top and looked at the librarian expectantly.

"I'm searching for information on Shayleigh. Especially old archived stuff and Ordnance Survey maps. Do you think you might have that here?"

"Let me just check for you." The librarian turned to her computer. Martin heard her as she click-clacked on the keyboard. His face changed colour as a spreadsheet of some sort flashed up on screen and reflected its colours onto the librarian's pale skin. Her face showed a level of concentration he hadn't seen in some time. This woman was without doubt working in the correct place. Anybody who went in there looking for information would have been treated the same way, and experienced the same gusto to please. She pulled her eyes away from the screen to face Martin. "As it happens, sir, we have all Ordnance Survey maps etc. uploaded on micro fiche rolls. If you make your way down there to the far left corner you will see a reader. All the micro fiche rolls are labelled and the particular one you are seeking is V22/17. I will drop down other related information to you in a couple of minutes, ok?"

"That's fine." Martin was a little unsure. He had never used a micro fiche reader before. The librarian looked at him and if she had read his thoughts she smiled and walked out from behind the counter. "I'll show you how to set it up. It's simple really." She glanced at a note on the desk. "V22/17", she

The Blackthorn Legacy

repeated to herself. "It works quite like a video player. Instead of sound, it produces pictures and you the user can look at them as slow or as quickly as you please."

Martin felt somewhat uncomfortable walking behind the librarian through the building. There were five study desks, of which three of them were occupied. The first two had older men sitting back by themselves reading the daily newspaper. The third table had two young women writing and reading. They were either studying or preparing a project of some sort. They seemed to be working together. It was the two solo readers that made him uneasy. Were they planted in there by the Government? Was he being watched everywhere he went now?

They reached the corner where he had been directed and within seconds the librarian had located the roll V22/17. It resembled a spool and within another short period of time Martin was set-up and ready to investigate the old Shayleigh files. He was left alone and he felt an electric current of excitement run through his body. His blood coursed through his veins with the same excitement. What was he going to find on these stills? Would it answer his questions or would it raise more? He couldn't wait. He was like the boy at the country fair who had pulled out the winning ticket for the mystery prize. He was nervous but excited. It was now time to unveil that prize.

He scrolled through the film and watched it pass him on the large micro fiche's screen.

Nothing much.

Martin was just about to give up when he saw a small newspaper by-line dating back to 1894.

'Three hoodlums suffer unexplained death at Rahaduff.'

He fell back in the plastic charcoal seat, almost losing his balance and falling off. He looked entirely out of place in building that normally hosted silent and almost motionless people. His flailing arms and legs made him look like the goalkeeper in Handball, coming out to put off the on-coming attacker. It was his good luck that the chair did not have any squeaky joints.

He sat back, embarrassed and afraid to look around to see if he had been noticed by anyone within the naturally well-lit room. Nobody had seen a thing, not even the ones he had picked out as possible Government spies. With the embarrassment seeping away slowly, he resumed his search on the bright screen. His breathing was not what it should have been and he felt as if he had been punched in the stomach by some heavy weight boxing champion. His lungs were however beginning to find the oxygen they needed for him to breathe again with some semblance of normality was returning. He leaned back up to the screen and read the article under the horrifying by-line.

He sat back again after going through the piece. What was so frightening was its resemblance to what had occurred as his house three days previously. What he did find most horrifying was that the piece mentioned the incident had happened at Rahaduff. What was Rahaduff? Was it not a place? He made a few notes for himself on a piece of paper he had found in his pocket. He searched again and located his notepad. He knew he would not have left his house without it. Not a chance. He mentally told himself off for a moment and returned back to the real world. His real world.

With that the librarian came over and laid down three books, a large dusty chestnut brown hardback book. It was called Local History – The Ages, according to the books spine. The gold calligraphy on the spine was the first thing he noticed. It was masterfully engraved on the cover. He could see the depression on the cover's material, caused by the original calligrapher. The detail was fantastic.

Two smaller books were resting on top, both reference books of some sort. Martin looked up appreciatively at the librarian who returned her 'I hope that helps you smile' and left immediately. He watched as she walked away, liking what he saw but not completely sure what had made him feel that way.

The Blackthorn Legacy

Returning to the micro fiche reader, he continued his search for information. Finding nothing more than an old Ordnance Survey map so old in fact, that the place names were almost completely worn off. However somewhere in the region of where he though his house was situated was the letters FF in jet black print. The letters were easily made out on the copy of the original purple paper map he was staring at. There was also an underground stream coming from the right of the FF or the North in geographical terms. He noted all of these items on his pad but he unable to figure out what FF could mean. For several moments he stared blankly at the letters, trying to force their meaning out of them. Nothing. He decided not to spend any more time on it and chose to continue fact finding. After another glancing look at the map, he believed that he had found all that seemed to of interest to him on the micro fiche and so he turned his attention to the old large brown book decorated brilliantly in the golden calligraphy.

He prised open the front cover of the old book and could smell the decades wafting up from the discoloured pages. It felt as though the cover was meant to be left closed in the library. Too late for that now. He had already crossed that line. The smell though, that old smell was like the expected aroma of new history on old pages.

Looking at the early pages first, he noticed that the book had been updated four times, the last being 38 years previously. The first edition was printed in 1892. Was it a coincidence? Just two years prior to the frightening newspaper article that had taken the wind from him just earlier. That embarrassing episode just moments earlier, when he would have entertained the others in the library had they chosen to look in his direction as he almost fell off the chair?

He looked at the back of the thick book. It appeared and no doubt looked the shape of a concrete block and was almost as thick. He flittered through the book until the last page. Almost 1,500 pages on Fellowmore and the surrounding

The Blackthorn Legacy

area? Unbelievable. He licked his thumb and rolled the corners of the pages from the rear of hardback until he came upon an index. There at his fingers was the list of all the information included within, in alphabetical order. Martin slid his finger over the words and turned pages until he found what he was looking for – Rahaduff pages 118-127. The book slipped from his grip and the pages turned of their own accord and finally stopped at page 118.

Another coincidence?

Martin stared at the book, feeling the hairs on his neck stiffen and a cold shiver flow down his back in a wave-like motion. He closed the book and stared at it closed for a moment. Nothing happened. Had he imagined the book opening by itself?

Looking nervously around the hushed chamber he noticed that the loudest noise in there was in fact its silence.

Nobody was paying any attention to him. He wondered if that was more to be worried about? There was the odd glance in his direction now and then, but that was just human nature. People most likely wondering what the guy down in the corner was doing, his brain suggested and he accepted.

Martin once again had to prise open the book. It was like trying to remove a plunger that had been pressed onto a smooth floor surface. Did it not want to be opened? The cover eventually released and just as before, the pages flittered and turned as if an unfelt breeze had caught the sheets of paper. Just as before is finally came to rest at pages 118 and 119.

Don't be afraid Marty, you know who's doing this, don't you?

The voice, the untouchable, meddling voice that just would not go away. It was like someone up there in his head directing the traffic in his brain. He hadn't asked for any help, so why the hell was he or it still up there? The problem was that he recognised the tone, the expression and the accent even if it wasn't his normal talking to himself voice. He had to forget about it for now and proceed with this job,

The Blackthorn Legacy

unusual as it had turned out to be up to that time. He wiped his brain clear of any thoughts. Just like a clean slate and began examining the pages of the self-opening book. He smiled a hopeful smile just for himself. A warm stink of breath came from over his left shoulder. Martin froze and slowly looked over his shoulder.

Nothing.

No one.

He was still alone. A cold breeze surrounded him, taking hold and then melted away as soon as it had been there. He shook his head, his imagination; he told himself, was messing with his head.

Martin returned his attention to the book. The first lines of page 118 provided information to him that he hadn't even considered. Rahaduff according to this was in fact a combination of two old Irish or Gaelic words. Raha meaning Fort and Duff an anglicised version of dubh meaning black. In other words Rahaduff was a BlackFort.

He scanned down the rest of the page but nothing else seemed to catch his attention. He turned the page and almost fell off the chair again. The old grainy black and white photo was of a circle of trees on a mound. The ground looked very familiar but what really shocked him was on the right side of the picture. Just making it inside the border was without doubt Slieve Lea, the mountain Martin could see from Ard Lane. In the photo the base of the mountain was covered in a thick mist resembling the Tutus worn by those ballet dancers in Swan Lake – thick and fluffy. The mist seemed to be hugging only the mountain's base.

It was a Fairy Fort (*Black Fort*) – and that, he decided, must be what the circled FF stood for on that Ordnance Survey map. He noted his new find on the notepad and re-examined the photo. The ring of trees was tall gangly types. Most likely of the Blackthorn variety and that seemed to make perfect sense to him given the name of the fort. The trunks seemed to be set in a perfect circle, but a couple of them appeared to have been growing outwards above the

The Blackthorn Legacy

trunk with branches like arms from a fanatical crowd, each trying to catch whoever or whatever came within reach. There was a demonic look about them and the expectation was that they could possibly move at any time and snatch up any passing, living item.

It was definitely an eerie photograph. The over-dark foliage being held up by what could only be likened to misshapen but strong timber arms. It was that particular segment of the uncanny photo that seemed to be the first item that came into the viewer's focus, so unusual and unnerving was the shape and sight of life-like branches. The dark overcast sky in the grainy photo didn't help. Martin stared at it in disbelief for, he didn't know how long. The monochrome photo development added to the creepiness of the scene.

Turning the page he didn't expect to see anything as disturbing as that photo on page 118.

How wrong he was.

The page described the Fairy Fort following the felling of the trees that formed the perfect circle on the mound. Four men had apparently instigated the cutting down of the Blackthorn trees. The decision was made solely for financial reasons. Houses were to be built on the site where the landowner and the local Council would profit from their construction and ultimately their sale. A cosy agreement if you were either of these parties. They had forecast a huge monetary return.

Below this description of what had prevailed was another black and white photograph although not as grainy as the previous but it looked a little distorted. It contained four men standing behind the treeless Fairy Fort site. They were smiling for the camera, or at least two of them were, in any case. Those photographed were identified as Tom Dunphy, Mick Kennedy Johnny Devery and Donagh Winters. The four obviously stood perfectly still as the cameraman shot the scene but what had eventually been developed must have caused him to examine and re-examine his camera.

The Blackthorn Legacy

The landowner and Council official – Tom Dunphy and Donagh Winters were beaming. They were definitely holding practiced smiles, they had to have been. A circus clown's smile would only have been a slight over exaggeration of both these men's stupid facial expressions. However it was the two men in the centre of the camera shot that caught Martin's attention in the first instance. The two men in the centre were the lumber jacks who had been employed by Dunphy and Winters to topple the Blackthorn.

Kennedy and Devery had turned up as usual to do a days or several day's work and ended up as part of a publicity stunt. Nonetheless they could never have expected what became of them. In this picture they were not recognisable. It looked like the flesh on their faces had been pulled away from the bone and it hung there from their skulls like fresh dough on a stick. It was sickening to look at.

He read the paragraph below the large snapshot and discovered that all four men died shortly after the proposed publicity stunt had taken place.

Both the lumber jacks were killed in a freak work accident exactly seven days after the photo. One was struck in the forehead by the head of a pick axe that inexplicably flew off its handle and other man was crushed by the tree they were in the process of felling. The two organisers – Dunphy and Winters lost their minds, it appeared and within two months of first becoming uncontrollable, they both died by their own hands.

Martin sat back after reading it all. The book or something wanted him to see what made the place what it was. The blood in Martin's face appeared as though it had flowed elsewhere and he had a sudden cold feeling all over his body. Shivers spread from the top of his head all the way to his feet like ripples on a placid lake surface.

He was in shock.

Almo Stace

That was the last thing he wanted to hear right now. That voice, that bloody voice. Almo Stace wasn't even English, was

The Blackthorn Legacy

it? His mouth went dry and his throat felt like sandpaper. He reached down to his bag and pulled out his bottle of water. His own water and he gulped down two large mouthfuls. How refreshing that was. Pure water, from his own well. His dry throat was drenched by the sparkling fluid and he felt a surge of electricity through his body.

Martin saw movement in the corner of his eye up the library. A shadow was it? He glanced up – nothing. Was it them? Had they discovered where he was and what he had been looking at? What had he been looking at anyway? Then from nowhere a hand rested on his shoulder.

"Are you ok sir?" The smooth and controlled voice of the librarian. She was dressed in a dark A-Line skirt. Was it her that had been in his peripheral vision?

"I'm fine thanks." The reply sounded feeble in Martin's head but it seemed to work alright.

"It's just you've been here for a few hours now and I was getting a little worried."

"What?" That can't be right, he thought. He pulled up his sleeve and glimpsed at his watch. "Jesus, I didn't realise it was that time." Martin had been caught off guard – it was almost four in the afternoon. He had spent the best part of five hours looking for information. Where had the time gone to? He shook his head. That was something his father would have said and he didn't want to turn into the man who had died from essentially being a coward.

Martin recapped his water bottle, folded over his notebook and closed the *haunted* brown book. He stood up and was about to lift the book but the librarian fired a patronising smile at him followed by her words that came from the height she believed she was looking down at Martin.

"I'll look after the books; you can go about your business, sir."

Looking at her momentarily with a *how dare you talk to me like that* expression Martin decided it was better to leave it and just to say nothing. She had after all provided him with the information he was looking for.

The Blackthorn Legacy

Bitch.

Now he was going to see another menace, a solicitor. As he walked out into the nippy air he considered his options. It was almost four in the afternoon and he was feeling peckish. Actually he was extremely hungry now that he thought about it.

Food it was then.

The Blackthorn Legacy

CHAPTER SEVENTEEN:

CCTV CAMERAS

WALKING out of the eatery where the food had been rather tasty, Martin took another slug of his water, just to properly wash it all down. The surge of power through his body tingled all his nerve endings and it was an experience to behold. He felt like a new man. He was ready to take on the world.

The sky above him was covered in an uneven quilt of ominous looking grey rain clouds. The overhead greyness also ensured that the length of daylight would be coming to an early end that particular day. A cloak of darkness would once again cover the entire sky, as far as one could see, within the next hour or two.

The air was still quite chilly. It seemed somewhat different from earlier and he wondered if in fact, it was the same cool breeze that was still whizzing around the streets of Fellowmore? More than likely it was the wind just seeking a way out of this old concrete forest. The area was more enclosed where he now was with two storey buildings on either side of the street. Narrow gateways were interspersed along the way, but the wind seemed unable to find its way out of the concrete net. Let nature take care of itself, he thought and decided to continue with his plans.

The Blackthorn Legacy

He removed the business card from his pocket and looked for the address of Legal, Wrights. He had an idea where the office was located. Further up the town and typically, as far as he was concerned, it was situated down a dark laneway off one of the side streets.

Why did that not surprise him?

He stepped down off the path to cross the street ignorant of what was happening around him, and was brought back to the real world by the sharp toot of a car horn. He had completely forgotten where he was and looked around in shame at the relatively small numbers of walkers along the street only to see nobody else was paying any attention to him or his predicament. One or two nosey parkers looked but they lost interest pretty quickly when then he realised that nothing had become of the occurrence. Quickly scanning the house and shop fronts he didn't see any CCTV cameras. Maybe he was in a black spot. Something to remember for the future, he noted mentally.

The driver of the car was waving a clenched fist in annoyance in Martin's direction. Just stick it where the monkey stuck the nut was the first thought that came into Martin's mind. Looking up and down the street he realised that the horn blower was the only road user at that time.

He crossed the street and began his journey to Legal, Wrights.

The Blackthorn Legacy

CHAPTER EIGHTEEN:

THE SUPERINTENDENT

JOEY had felt differently that afternoon. Although he was due to be off work that certain Monday, he sensed the need to be in the Garda Station. He had been called in but it was re-iterated to him in the phone call that he was to only wear his civvies. Was this the first day of the rest of his life? Was he about to be promoted to detective?

Waiting in the room often referred to as the Triage Holding Area, because it was where complainants waited before giving their stories and in some cases their statements. The voice on the other end of the phone earlier in the afternoon had been that of the Super's private secretary – Joan Barry. It was an instruction rather than a request. She had more or less demanded his appearance in the Station. But that was her way. Joan always demanded, never asked.

Sitting on his own in the poorly lit room gave him an idea of what it was like for the 'normal' people who waited to face the system. The dark green carpet was not as clean as it once was. Dark oval forms of discarded chewing gum, trampled into the flooring surrounded by discolouring which he didn't want to even hazard a guess at the cause.

It was unnerving; looking at the posters pinned up on the boring grey coloured wall. Posters provided by criminal

The Blackthorn Legacy

lawyers, doctors, the Samaritans, help line numbers etc. All depressing paraphernalia it had to be said. It was a gloomy space, probably even more so than the holding cells further down the many corridors of the station.

Was it any wonder some people backed out at the last minute before providing intelligence to what were supposed to be the guardians of peace? That was why he was here, wasn't it? He was here today to be told that he was going to provide the much lacking intelligence. He could feel it; he was going to be the reason for the rebirth of Justice in Fellowmore. The Super and some of the others would laud him with praise. Yes, he was going to be the man, as and from the ending of this impromptu meeting with his superior.

Joey was lost in his own heroic dreams when the door of the triage room opened and the stern faced Joan appeared in the opening.

"Joseph Thornsberry?"

Joey gulped and almost wet his trousers in terror and near ecstasy all at once.

"Yes", he replied in a small boyish voice.

"This way." This was a demand. Her sharp voice was not one you could or would dismiss. It went through his head, slicing through the second thoughts he may have had about going home. He was here and Joan Barry made sure he was not escaping. Her shrill severe tone.

He rose slowly and everything seemed to happen in slow motion even though Joey didn't remember the walk to the Super's office. The first thing he remembered was sitting opposite his superior, drinking a glass of water, in the hope it would lubricate his tight voice box. The Super sat behind his desk, clear, except for the personnel file open before him. Continuing to look down at the buff coloured file he began the interview.

"Joey, that's what your colleagues call you."

Unsure if it was a statement or a question, Joey treated it as the latter.

The Blackthorn Legacy

"Yessir."

The room contained a nervous energy, thick, almost tangible. Joey could feel it. Closing in around him.

"I see you've been with us for almost six years Joey; do you enjoy your work here?"

Nothing. Joey was unable to speak. He was happy, well sort of. It was a job, sure, but he could do it better if he was allowed to, but how would he say that to his boss when the man questioning him actually thought he was running a good shop?

"Yes." He mumbled unconvincingly.

"Good", came the quick reply. A high-pitched response that didn't seem to convey the word coming from his mouth, "But you do know that you are working as part of a team here, right?"

Joey was stumped. Where the hell was this coming from, or more importantly, where was it going?

"Yessir."

"Good man. It's just that it had been brought to my attention that you have recorded something, an occurrence or possible occurrence in Interview Room 2 in the last few days. Would that be a fair comment?" This was beginning to feel like an interrogation. But Joey felt that he had to put his case forward. No point in lying down, now that he had come this far.

"Yessir. What I fou...

The Super cut right across him snappily

"If you intend to go down the Whistleblower track Garda, I recommend you talk to your union representative beforehand. If you decide to do some further investigation of your own I think you'll find that you are going down a lonesome road that has no turns and nowhere to hide. You will be a labelled Garda, working where ever it is you go to. I think you understand what I'm saying. I recommend you drop this now. I have it on good authority that what you found is nothing to get yourself tangled up in. Do you

The Blackthorn Legacy

understand Garda Thornsberry?" It was not a question but the Super's words stuffed into Joey's mouth

"Yessir."

"Good man. Come back to me when you are back on duty and we will have a talk about this again. I'll see you are looked after. Is that all then?"

"Just one question for you Super. How would anyone know if I was a Whistleblower if I do it anonymously?"

"Think about it Garda. I advise you as your superior to not go down this road. In fact I am ordering you to leave it right now. Thank you, you can leave now."

Joey sat there for a moment just staring at the Super. The feeling of tension that had been closing in around him at the beginning of the meeting had totally covered him. Almost choking him. Maybe it had obscured the Super's view and therefore he had come to the wrong conclusion. It was obvious, it had to be. It's just a mistake, thought Joey; maybe the man is having a bad day.

"Are you still here Garda Thornsberry?" The Super's agitated voice brought Joey back to reality. He slowly rose from the seat and sluggishly left the office. Maybe he was wrong after all. The man didn't want to know. Why?

As he left the station Joey felt a fire of retaliation lighting for a slow burn deep in his stomach. He made a to-do list in his head which consisted of two items. The first was that he would seek retribution for the way Detective Walsh had treated him on the previous Friday night. The second was also going to be a case of retribution seeking. This one featured the Superintendent.

The Blackthorn Legacy

CHAPTER NINETEEN:

THE ROOFLESS TUNNEL

MARTIN turned down Molesworth Lane where the office of Legal, Wrights was located. It was a narrow laneway only capable of catering for pedestrian traffic. Daylight was fading and it became considerably darker as he entered Molesworth Lane.

It was a throughway or a short-cut to a printing shop at the very end of the lane and like many local printing offices; it was on its last legs. There were other cheaper ways of getting documents published now. Every town had its own printing shop of some size or other. It was a business that did relatively well but was now generally in decline. The passing of time and the introduction of the internet had seen to that.

On either side of it were high dull walls. The only break in the boring aged wall plaster was two small dark windows, one with a cracked window pane. The fissures in the glass itself seemed to rise from the top left corner and reach out to the remainder of the window like searching tentacles, finding nothing to grab onto but managing to stay in place all the same.

Rising damp was also a feature of the walls as was the moss growing in dark green clumps. Some of these clumps were bigger than others. Maybe they were in competition

The Blackthorn Legacy

with each other to see which would be crowned the chief moss clump.

On the left hand side of the laneway, about one hundred meters down the roofless tunnel was a bright white building. It stood out in the dreary, darkness of the walkway surroundings.

It was, as expected, the Legal, Wrights office. The shop front was painted in bright white paint with cobalt blue window frames and door. The name above the door and the large single window was also of the same blue. The types of law Legal, Wrights specialised in was professionally printed on the front window along with their contact details – phone, fax, e-mail and Facebook. None of these methods of contact suited him, but he knew how they worked, more or less.

He looked back up the lane towards the thoroughfare he had left to walk down this mostly grim walkway and saw the orange sodium lights blinking as they came to life. A similar type of light mounted high up on the dark wall just up from the solicitor's office began buzzing and flickering simultaneously. At least he would be able to see his way out of here when he re-emerged.

The Blackthorn Legacy

CHAPTER TWENTY:

THE WAITING ROOM

AS Martin Carey pushed in the office door he was met with a rush of brightness and a gush of nicely warmed air. He could hear the low continuous hum of the electric fan heater that was creating the welcome warmth. The office itself was a sea of fresh light compared with the dark lane he had just left outside.

The floor covering was a light beige marmoleum surface, shining, reflecting the light from the bulbs recessed in the light grey ceiling. The walls were a pure white. All the furniture was natural pine, or at least it looked like natural pine. In the far corner on the right was a quadrant shaped desk, also of pine colour, where a professional looking lady sat behind the curved desk, tapping away rapidly on her keyboard, full attention was being given to her work.

Martin approached the quadrant reception styled area, to talk to the woman playing the computer keyboard like a concert pianist might delicately but elegantly touch the ebony and ivory keys. The desk looked more like a quarter moon as he stood at it. He noticed the secretary's long fair hair that was tied back in a tight ponytail allowing a thin but noticeable face the full attention of the office light. Though it was just an artificial source of brightness, it made her perfect skin radiate, something. He wasn't sure what exactly. As he

The Blackthorn Legacy

reached there he noticed an alcove opposite the desk which seemed to have been turned into a waiting room. A waiting room in a solicitor's office? The guy inside sat alone, looking rather solemn. He felt it was safe to surmise that anybody in a waiting room in a solicitor's office had reason to be solemn. At the quadrant he waited a moment as the typing continued. Finishing a sentence maybe. Better than facing a sentence, like that guy waiting in the waiting room.

He slipped into a daze and there he was in the big meadow again, walking through the long golden grass. He was approaching the stream again. Something was interfering with his dream. A noise. His attention was being drawn, was it him the voice was calling. Then he felt a light tap on his hand.

The shock. It was the sting of static electricity.

He automatically returned to the there and then.

"Sir, sir, are you alright?"

It was the typist, she had broken his dream. He shook his head and rubbed his eyes and focussed on the lady behind the counter.

"Sorry" he put on a fake laugh, "I was day dreaming". The stony faced secretary remained so. "I'm looking to meet with Ms Deirdre King", he continued a little shakily.

"Do you have a pre-arranged meeting, sir?"

"Eh...no. Do I need one?" The confusion in Martin's voice was more obvious that he had thought. The look he received from the typist told him so.

"I'm afraid you do. I'll look in the diary and see what's available." The frosty reply confirmed it for him.

"Thanks."

She leafed through the diary, finally reaching the pages she sought. It was apparent from this small task how thorough she was in her work. Turning over and back, making perfectly sure she was right. Precision, that was good. He liked that.

"Sir, the next readily available slot for Ms King is 12 noon on Wednesday. However Ms Wright should be available in

The Blackthorn Legacy

the next half hour if you would like to remain in the waiting room."

Martin thought about it for a moment and then decided it was probably a good idea to get a foot in the door first and then if he felt he needed to change his legal representation within the company, he would do so.

"I'll take it. Half an hour or there abouts?"

"Yes sir. Can I have your name please?" There was still a little frost in that voice.

"Martin Carey."

"That's fine Mr Carey. Please take a seat in the room opposite. You'll be called". More directions. No such thing as please or thank you, he noticed.

Martin nodded and feigned a smile in the typist's direction. One like all the others she had probably seen since opening for business that morning. He slowly stepped into the waiting room and sat on one of the comfortable looking cushioned benches. There were three of those benches which could possibly cater for three people each at a time. The man already in the waiting room sat on the bench nearest the door, facing outwards. He barely noticed Martin as he ambled in past the man already seated. His full attention was on his Smart phone. Probably messaging someone.

"Hi", Martin whispered.

The man looked up for a second and acknowledged Martin with just a nod of his head and returned back to his phone. He was a butty man wearing a navy hoody under a black leather jacket. Of course the hood was out over the back collar. That was the way now. His shaved head gave him a dangerous look, but sitting there in the waiting room as he was, the man seemed to be pretty normal.

There was a literature holder on the wall near where the butty man was seated. Martin stared at it first as there was nothing else to look at except his co-waiter.

"You in any type of trouble", the man asked out of the blue. The question caught Martin off guard. Without thinking he answered the man. What was he supposed to do in a

The Blackthorn Legacy

solicitor's office waiting room? Ignore the only other person waiting there with him?

"I'm not sure, to be honest. The Gardaí are asking me questions about something I had nothing to do with and have asked me to stick around. To be perfectly honest I am feeling uncomfortable about the whole thing and I thought maybe a little legal advice wouldn't go astray. How about you?"

"It's the cops, they don't like me much either. I'll have the last laugh, 'cos I'm going to bring them to court the way they been treating me. Not them all, just one prick. Yeah"

Almo Stace

Almo Stace

Jesus Christ, leave me alone, he thought. Then a new voice, or another version of the same voice, but deeper and like a voice coming through a cardboard roll – echoey, whilst also resembling the voice of someone dependent on tobacco for countless years.

JJ needs to be gone

A new cryptic message. Great. How much more of this shit was going to be thrown his way? In fact it was flung at him from inside his own head. He had slipped out of his brain for a moment only to be dragged back again by his new waiting friend.

"That copper needs to be put in his place. Nobody can just throw their weight around and hope everyone just takes it as the way he says it is. Nah, I seen him last Friday night outside a house where these three were done. You probably heard about it. What am I saying, everybody heard about it. Some fucking psycho killed three...three young men. Sure they may have been in some trouble but.... You heard about it, everybody did. Anyway the cop started givin' me grief. Fu... Sorry."

Martin sat back in horror. This man had been at his house on the Friday night and a copper, a Garda gave him abuse. Shit, how coincidental was this meeting? He was completely stunned.

The Blackthorn Legacy

"You ok, man?" There was audible concern in the butty man's voice. More so because he wanted to tell anyone who would listen to his story and how he was going to bring the system to its knees. Single handed.

By the look of him though, Martin thought it better to just play along.

"Eh...I...yeah."

JJ needs to be gone.

It was a much stronger rasp in his head this time. This wasn't just the usual voice talking to him; it was raised, in excitement, anticipation. For what though?

"I hope they get that psycho. I wouldn't care even..."

The door outside opened. Butty man looked up to see who it was, craning his neck and ducked back like a man on a set spring. Like a Jack in the Box. The colour had visibly drained from his face. He moved over close to Martin and put his finger up to his lips indicating that he thought silence was the best course of action or in-action. The horror in his face was almost contagious.

"What?" Martin mouthed.

Again the signal to be quiet from the other man. The heavy footsteps outside in the main office were clear as Detective Walsh walked up to the counter with an air of superiority about him.

"Is she in?"

The voice, he recognised something in it. It took his attention for a moment as he racked his memory bank.

"She's a little tied up at the moment Ed. Can you call back in forty minutes or so?"

"She must be practising her knots. I'll show her a thing or two. She loves that kind of thing. Maybe I could teach you a thing or two as well." The sneering look in his face was audible even in the waiting room. Butty man's face began to redden as rage was building up inside him. Martin could see it and was bracing himself for when his waiting room friend would boil over and things got a little more...colourful.

The Blackthorn Legacy

"Ok then, I'll be back in a while. Do not forget to tell her, you understand?" Talk about looking down at someone, which was exactly how it sounded to Martin. He definitely needed to be taken down a peg or two.

The sound of the footsteps resumed as their owner made his way towards the door. "Tell her to call me if she's going to be held up. Can you do that?" Martin, sitting in the waiting area, sat listening to the voice as he began to hate the speaker more and more for his tone. Just then he recognised the voice's owner. He knew who it was and he wasn't very comfortable. The footsteps could be heard until the sound of the door closing behind them broke the sound.

"Shit." The respite in the man's voice and the returning colour in his cheeks were a relief to Martin. Butty man blew out his cheeks and moved back to where he had been sitting.

"What was that all about?" Martin's inquisitive nature was getting the better of him. Normally he wouldn't have asked someone he barely knew a question like that.

"That was him, the copper. The one I'm going to take down. Motherfucker better get used being on his own, except when he's in the shower. He'll get it then alright." The loathing was obvious from the man's tone and it seemed he couldn't wait to seek the revenge he believed was due him.

"That wasn't Detective Walsh by any chance, was it?" Martin asked the question not really hoping for an answer or at least not the one he got.

"You had a run-in with Steady Eddie too. Yeah, it was him." It was like the man was forming a revenge attack in his head there and then. The look of determination on his face as he balled up his hands and stared blankly at the bare wall opposite him was like a scene from a Robert De Nero film. He was full of determination.

"You know why he hates me?" Now he was talking through his closed teeth. Revenge was probably not that far away. The sinews in his neck stuck out like bridge cables.

From the butty man's appearance right at that time, Martin thought there was the distinct possibility that the man's sought after day in court might not be the appearance he dreamed of. Instead of putting a case before a court for damages he could very possibly be sitting before a Judge in the High Court for something far more serious, defending his actions.

A door around the corner to the left opened and a troubled looking man passed by the waiting room, his chin almost on his chest and the weight of the world on his hunched up shoulders. The gloomy look on his face told a story – he was in some sort of pickle. Female voices could be heard, one of which belonged to the frosty typist. Quick short sharp footsteps approached the waiting room. The footstep came to a halt as she; Deirdre King came to the entrance. She had the same clothes, or at least the same looking clothes as the day she and Martin had met on the street.

The stern look was exactly as Martin had remembered from their previous encounter. The tough looking solicitor camouflaged as a woman.

A very neat trick indeed.

Her blonde hair however was styled differently to how he remembered it. This time it was tied up in a neat bun, resting on the crown of her head. "Jimmy Jones", she announced very matter of factly. She demanded that her next client came forward. That's how it sounded in any case. The butty man rose from his seat and looked back at Martin. Jimmy Jones smiled a smile of relief and happiness rolled into one. A strange type of look on his face, but he definitely got some satisfaction from it. His plan to rid the Garda force of Detective Walsh was well on its way, in Jimmy Jones' head anyway, as of that moment.

"I'll tell you that story another day, man. Good luck." There was a certain sense of certainty in the man's voice and demeanour as he walked out of the room, following Ms King. Martin was astonished to think that the man he had befriended in a backstreet solicitor's waiting room was interested in telling his story, his whole story. So it wasn't just a show of power, he said to himself. He sat back and

The Blackthorn Legacy

waited his turn to be called. He still hadn't forgiven that bitch Deirdre King yet though. Bitch.

JJ needs to be gone. You know what you have to do, Marty. For you to have some space you have to take things into your own hands. It needs to be done, Marty. You know it does.

Martin closed his eyes tight, trying with all his might to squeeze the voice out of his head. It was driving him mad, the voice that seemed to have laid its dark hat somewhere in the back of his very own head. It was a voice he recognised but he wasn't sure from where. It was gnawing at him, eating at him. His eyes shut so that he might calm himself. He held his nose and tried to force the voice, or its owner out through his ears. His ears popped under the pressure. After what seemed like an eternity of pushing from within and looking into the blackness and dark grey shading of his eyelids he re-opened them. He had also run out of breath and so removed the fingers that had been holding his nose. The adjustment to the brightness of his surroundings took only a moment. He stared at the blank white wall before him, almost expecting to see a black splashed out dirty shapeless splurge from his brain on the bright paint.

Nothing there.

He felt he had to try something. The voice had quietened and he thought, no he hoped, that maybe he had pushed it out totally, somewhere into the ether. His own thoughts began flowing through his head and filling the space vacated by the speech machine located in some obscure part of his head.

The new thoughts moved across his mind's eye quickly and seemed to be glued together as each virtual story board ran into the next and his mind began to clutter up. The intermingled stories ran in fast forward motion, whizzing past his internal eye. Unexpectedly he jumped; an involuntary action. It felt like the shock he had sometimes felt in his sleep when falling in a dream. The jump was quickly followed up by a shiver. A bright light flashed before

The Blackthorn Legacy

his eyes. It must have just been for his eyes only because there wasn't an exclamation from anybody else in the building. A moment of clarity maybe? Then it formed, the thought, the result of the gush of power he had just experienced.

He had been wondering, in fact searching his brain as to whom or what *JJ* was, and now he knew because the answer had landed on his lap, almost. *JJ* had been sitting beside him. He had been with him, in the very same waiting room. *JJ* had almost sat on top of him when Detective Walsh had made his cameo appearance into the office. What had Jimmy Jones to do with anything? Why did he or it, the voice, want him gone anyway? The voice seemed to be very sure about the need to rid the world of Jimmy Jones.

Martin was considering this and trying to discover any possible reasons that Jones needed to put away – for good and then he stopped. Why was he even thinking like a killer? He didn't need to know why Jimmy Jones needed to be gone, because he wanted no hand, act or part in it.

None.

He stole a glimpse at his watch and realised it had been over thirty minutes since he had been at the quadrant talking to the typist about the appointment he was now awaiting. Well, he had spoken to her and she talked at him. She would need to be considered for payment, a final payment, really final. That bitch should be ahead of JJ on the waiting list. He considered this for a moment and realised he was talking like a hit-man again.

Stop it Martin, that's not you. The more regular concerned voice in his head. The one that operated at the front of his brain, the one who saw everything he did. It was good to hear it again. Comforting, in a strange sort of way.

He heard an office door open and he felt as though something had awoken in his stomach. The butterflies had awoken from their hibernation and it felt like there could have been a flying insect riot going on down there. He put his hands together; intertwining his fingers as he awaited a call

The Blackthorn Legacy

from Ms Wright, the solicitor. Nerves were beginning to consume him and he was forced to take a deep breath just to get his regular breathing pattern back. It was a terribly overwhelming sensation. The last time he had suffered from an attack of nervous tension like this was sitting in the driving test centre, waiting to be told the result of his exam. Of course he had passed, but the waiting that time seemed endless, much like this waiting episode.

Voices. A woman's and then a man's. Then JJ came to the waiting area and glanced in at the uneasy Martin Carey who was now rocking forward and backwards, hands clasped together on his stomach. The tension had reached his hands and his knuckles were pure white.

"You not in yet?" JJ stood there smiling in at Martin, more in astonishment than any sort of entertainment he could have gleaned from having been called in, been seen, and out before Martin moved at all. Martin shook his head but without looking in JJ's direction. He couldn't. He didn't want those feelings of the butty man's destruction to return. The agent of destruction in his head must have fallen asleep – there was not a peep from it.

"Right then, good luck. I'm off." JJ turned and quickly strode towards the door. Then it came. It wasn't a voice this time but a shriek.

NOW, GET HIM, MARTY, JJ NEEDS TO BE GONE. NOW!

He had experienced outrageous screeching when he was much younger once when he had unknowingly stood beside a large box at a country fair which had in fact turned out to be a speaker, carrying the sound of a poor attempt at rock music. But it was nothing compared this pain. The voice was pushing him, almost controlling him into carrying out a feat he knew not how to even go about completing. The voice wanted and expected him to remotely kill JJ. Then it came again and now it was even louder.

NOW, GET HIM, MARTY, JJ NEEDS TO BE GONE. NOW!

The Blackthorn Legacy

The pain, the agony. It was almost too much. Then he felt the discomfort subsiding and words were coming from his mouth. Not his own words. His own voice had dropped an octave.

"Do you feel the way you hate, or do you hate the way...." No, he thought. A flicker of a memory. He had said this recently. He saw faceless people falling before him. His memory was over riding the screaming voice within. Three bodies collapsed before him in the memory or vision. Whichever it was, a memory or a vision, he seemed to realise that those words he had mysteriously uttered in another voice would lead to destruction – even death. He pushed it back, hoping it would smother the lunatic screeching tone in the black unreachable alcove at the back of his head. He fought hard, pushed hard. He could hear the voice or whatever it was up there in his head moving around, pushing down on him. Claustrophobia was taking hold. His breathing became difficult and he was beginning to panic. Where had this happened to him? Was he in a field?

No, he wasn't going to do whatever it was that he – the voice – wanted him to do to JJ.

No.

Not yet anyway.

The pressure from inside his head was becoming intolerable. His skull felt like it was going to burst like an over-inflated balloon. He detangled his fingers and placed his hands over his ears, pushing in at them. Maybe that compressed sound, a sound similar to a far off storm would rid him of the voice. He moved the palms of his hands a little, amplifying the sound over his earholes in an attempt to drown out the unwanted sound from within.

"Do you feel the way you hate, or do you hate the way you...." That deep tone again.

He was struggling.

The pressure.

He wasn't going to be able to withstand it for much longer. The ceiling tiles above him began vibrating and he could just

The Blackthorn Legacy

about hear a scream coming from the general office outside. The scream was immediately followed by something glassy having fallen and smashed on the floor outside in the main office. The lights began flashing, blinking. A warm gloopy fluid trickled from his left nostril, like a big tear, to his upper lip. He removed his right hand from his right ear to wipe the wetness away only to see a crimson streak on the back of his hand. He could smell it, that smell, a smell he had experienced lately. Where was it? The whiff of thick blood was almost overpowering.

Something popped inside the bridge of his nose and red drops began cascading down and hitting the floor between his feet. The first, creating a crown like image on the beige marmoleum floor covering.

The screaming in his head had stopped and the building had settled back to its lifeless state once more. Martin's head was pounding. It felt like a stainless steel belt had been wrapped around his head and it was being tightened with each passing minute. He had experienced serious headaches before but this was excruciating. It went through his skull from every possible angle and the pain waves seemed to meet in the centre and caused this unbearable pumping ache.

Martin's eyes were still closed, sitting forward he had his hand cupped under his nose in an attempt to make sure no more droplets fell from his bleeding nose and onto the shiny clean floor.

Outside in the main office he heard the commotion beginning again. He could make out the vocal sounds of three females but he was unable to comprehend what they were saying. All three were spoke hurriedly and at the same time and at each other. Then they all fell silent at once and heavy panting could be heard as if all three were breathing at once. Then Martin's presence came to one of them. He presumed it was the typist.

"Jesus, oh Jesus."

The Blackthorn Legacy

"What?" This was a voice he hadn't heard before, a softer tone than that of Deirdre King, most likely Ms Wright, he thought.

"Oh God, there's a man in the waiting room. Oh Christ. I'm sorry Jean, I forgot. He's here to see you. Oh my God. I hope...Is he alright?"

Martin's headache was beginning to subside a little. It seemed that the invisible stainless steel belt had been let out a couple of notches. He was sitting, but almost doubled over, his eyes closed shut as he recovered from the attack. His head aching, his nose bleeding and his lungs recovering from their unexpected call into action.

That was exactly how he felt. He had been attacked by the voice. How was that even possible? Could something as insubstantial as a voice actually cause such destruction? The answer seemed to be a resounding YES.

His eyes were still closed and this seemed to soothe him somewhat. Looking into the darkness disturbed only by the dark grey shapeless silhouette forms that passed irregularly in slow motion. The player within his head had slowed down considerably. As he became accustomed to this sight and was able to shut out the unease evident in the three female voices the far side of the wall, he began to calm himself. This must be how those monks do it, he supposed. It was then however, just as tranquillity was finally setting in that it happened. The grey silhouettes were still floating around on the black background. Then another colour seemed to appear. Was it a message? It was like looking at a banner that was being pulled behind a plane over a town or some public meeting place. From left to right the multi-coloured letters moved across the inside of his eyelids. They moved together at equal speed as the invisible banner bringing the message floated over the silhouettes.

URME UNO UR. What the hell did that even mean? Then he heard the quick short footsteps approaching. He remained in the same position to ensure he didn't miss anymore of the show he was actually putting on all by himself. Was it a

The Blackthorn Legacy

memo, a communication or subtitles for the grey silhouette show? He opened his eyes and quickly searched his pockets for a pen and paper and wrote down the letters in the order he had seen them.

"Mr Carey?"

Martin looked up quickly. A woman he hadn't seen before was standing at the doorway. She was ashen faced. He wasn't sure if it was because of what she had just witnessed or because of his condition. He looked down at the floor.

"Oh, I'm sorry about this. I'll clean up the blood."

"No don't move Mr Carey, I'll do it. Are you sure you're ok?" There was real concern about her, her body language and her voice.

"I'm...Yes I'm grand." He considered telling her about his headache but thought better of it.

"Sorry, how rude of me." She stepped forward to introduce herself and stuck out her hand. "I'm Jean Wright."

"I won't shake your hand." Jean Wright frowned a little and then looked a little hurt. "My hand's got some blood on it. When I get cleaned up a little I'll complete the salutation."

Her face warmed up immediately. "Of course, Mr Carey. The Washroom is just across the way."

"Martin, my name's Martin." He smiled as he said this endearing the solicitor to him. Rising to his feet he struggled, slightly unbalanced. However not enough to cause him to fall or even stumble. Just a split second minor version of vertigo.

Jean took two steps back from the opening of the waiting area and looked at the two other women who appeared to be waiting in baited breath. They seemed to have been expecting the worst. What's the worst thing that could have happened? Well, it was a solicitor's office of course. It was always possible that a serious injury could lead to a much unwanted court case. That would have been disastrous. As Martin walked out of the room slowly, smiling at the two waiting women; he could see from the bitch's face that the small wheels turning in Deirdre King's brain. Her face said it all really. She was going to try to avoid as much bad publicity

The Blackthorn Legacy

as possible, as easily as she could possible manage to do so. It didn't matter whose head or shoulders she had to step on the get it. Not to her. Bitch. Yep, she needed a little bit of medicine, and not the type she could get in a pharmacy...Martin Carey was going to administer it.

He eventually made it into the Washroom pushing the door, but not closing it out fully. Leaving it slightly ajar. The conversation between the women outside on the office floor became animated. Well, two in particular anyway.

"Deirdre, can you fetch the First Aid Kit in the back room? Sally, can you get me a wet cloth? There's some blood on the floor inside in the waiting room. We just need to clean it up." That was then first time he had heard the typist's name. Sally.

"Are you serious Jean?" Deirdre King's indignation was very apparent, even to Martin in the Washroom.

"Excuse me?" Jean Wright could not believe the question from Deirdre. She knew her employee was hot-headed, albeit normally on the side of caution. But this was a little further than she expected her to overstep any mark.

"Are you serious about getting the First Aid Kit for him?" Deirdre King said with some venom in her voice as she pointed directly at the Washroom. "That's almost as good as admitting liability. I mean we will be more or less telling him that we know we are at fault." She continued. Her face had reddened with anger.

"Deirdre, please get the First Aid Kit. The man is hurt. Would you prefer he would walk out of here injured and report us for not even attempting to assist him in his time of need. Get the bloody kit." Jean's temper was fraying a little too.

The conversation was followed audible noise of distinctly unhappy footsteps following a pause. Martin guessed it was a stand-off between the two women. They were different to the sound of happy or contented ones. That bitch. She needed to be brought down screaming and shouting. Bitch. Martin

The Blackthorn Legacy

began to think that the word was in fact invented because of people like her. Bitch.

Martin was all cleaned up and he left the little room and walked back to the quadrant where he had first met Sally – the typist. Over in the corner of the office he noticed changes in the floor, light in different colours gleaming at him. He stepped on something small and solid and the brittle sound underfoot along with the gleaming rainbow of colours from across the room had informed him that he was after stepping on smithereens of smashed glass. He remembered hearing the shattering sound in the middle of all of the preceding commotion. He glanced around and saw the water and flowers that had been resting in the now fragmented glass vase.

He almost jumped at the sound of the brittle crushing noise under the sole of his shoe, shocked at the unexpected sound.

"Oh my", exclaimed Jean, "I better clean that up too. We don't want any more accidents." On her way to retrieve some cleaning implements she came face to face with Ms King, coming in the opposite direction, carrying a crisp white bag. The Red Cross on the cover over flap was the real giveaway as to what she brought.

Jean Wright and Sally the typist finalised the cleaning of the office. The blood was cleaned from the floor in the waiting area and the glass swept up onto a sweeping pan. Martin steadied himself and looked at the three women, more particularly Jean Wright.

"You don't have to worry guys, I'm not a money grabbing, situation seeking person. I will not be looking for any sort of...whatever for my bloody nose. I'll be on my way and leave you three to it. Thanks for looking after me." He turned back towards the door and could feel three sets of eyes staring at him, one of which was burning a hole in his back, no doubt.

"That's extremely honourable of you Mr...sorry, Martin." He nodded and walked out the door.

The Blackthorn Legacy

CHAPTER TWENTY ONE:

THE ALLEYWAY OPENING

AS Jimmy Jones had left Legal, Wrights he had a good feeling in his waters. He had a great case according to his solicitor and he was going to be able to create a reasonable doubt in a court of law as to whether Detective Ed Walsh should be holding the position he did in the Gardaí. The bonus was the possibility, although slim, of earning some money – State owned money – in the process. That didn't really bother him all that much because that's where his substantial weekly payments came from.

The office door clicked closed behind him and he was out in the dark alley. The orange sodium light was shining some light but darkness was more powerful than any light. It shone down from the bright bulb high above, but the further the illumination spread, the lesser it became. Darkness never seemed to face that trouble. Unlike light, be it natural or created, darkness could fill corners, and was even stronger the further it spread from its source – whatever it was that caused blackness.

Jimmy Jones took his first steps towards the fully lighted street up ahead at the top of Molesworth Lane and he was all of a sudden beginning to feel unwell. His face began to feel as though it was being stretched from behind and seconds later he heard something, was it a recording? Or was it in fact his own head talking to him. The deep throated tone began talking. 'Do you feel the way you hate, or do you hate the way you....' His face, the stretching, the agony, the fear.

"What's happening t..." His gullet began constricting ever so slightly, but enough to feel as though he was suffocating. He stumbled forward, trying to remain on his feet. He realised that if he fell on the ground of the badly lit alley, it could be ages before he would've been found.

The pain was becoming unbearable as his facial skin was being pulled unnaturally; even further that it was capable of stretching.

Would his skin tear?

He could feel the heat in on his nose as the membrane must have been on the verge of splitting. Just as he was about to scream, expecting his epidermis to begin peeling he heard a loud crack. He heard it inside and outside his head like a stereo sound. The ethmoid bone on the bridge of his nose had shattered. Tears of agonising pain filled his eyes as he felt the tear in his nasal septum. Strangely however, it provided some comfort as his skin had some room for extra movement. There was almost a sense of looseness about it.

Everything is relative.

JJ lost his bearings for a moment and fell against the wall, leaning on it with his left shoulder. He wobbled forward, dislodging a large clump of moist moss from the damp wall as he headed towards the street lights ahead of him like a drunkard.

A ninety second walk took a good ten minutes and JJ looked up and down the street as he reached the alleyway opening. The air was fresher, it seemed. His mind was racing and both his hands were over his nose trying to catch the blood that had begun pumping profusely down his lower face. He looked and felt as though he had stood in a ring and was pummelled by a pissed off world champion of some physical sport. A sport where the referee had decided not to intervene. He was weak and the blood loss was making him weaker.

After a couple of minutes standing there in a state of confusion, disorientation and a world of pain, he saw a taxi coming up the street towards him. He stuck out his hand, catching the driver's attention and got a lift to the hospital.

The Blackthorn Legacy

CHAPTER TWENTY TWO:

HIS OWN REFLECTION

MARTIN left Legal, Wrights in the dark. He was badly shaken and the sense of what he had endured was only beginning to manifest itself now. It was only for the benefit of those women in the office that he had acted so strong and in his devil may care fashion. The fresh air affected him the same way it would have affected a mere mortal leaving a public house after much alcohol consumption.

He stared up at the orange sodium light. It pressed out its illumination as best it could but it was no match for the murkiness that surrounded otherwise surrounded him and lurked in the alleyway away from the light's touch. Standing there outside the office, shivering almost uncontrollably he decided to close up his jacket even though he knew it wasn't the air temperature that caused his drop in temperature. It was most definitely the shock he had suffered, the headache and the power that was inside his head, of which he had absolutely no influence over. That was the frightening part. He had inadvertently tried to kill a man he knew nothing about. However when he tried – and finally succeeded – in putting a stop the force, he suffered horrendously. The question is though; would he have felt any worse or better if he had in fact allowed JJ to die – at his hands.

The Blackthorn Legacy

That was not a question he was in a position to answer there and then because of the way his body and soul were feeling. His head was reeling, his body was cold and he felt nauseous. The only thing he knew for certain was that he needed to get home. Martin put his hands in his pockets in the hope that he could trick his brain into thinking that he was getting warmer. A bit of luck at last. His bottle of water, with some still remaining was in his jacket's right hand pocket. Time for a slug, even if the liquid was now tepid. Maybe this could be another way of convincing his tired brain that he was heating up, he hoped.

Looking up at the orange light again and then up ahead at the street, Martin felt an improvement in his general being. Maybe it was the slug of water that had done it. No matter what had brought it on, he was going home now. Remember, he said to himself, one foot in front of the other. Each step forward was going to be one less to his car which was parked a good half mile away the far side of town. One step at a time, that's how he would do it. He was going to aim for individual markers. First was going to be the overhead orange sodium light just up ahead.

As he moved forward, slow as it was to begin with, he could see the concrete pathway become clearer as he came closer to the source of the light. He noticed his clear dark shadow catching up with him, attached to his shoes. Directly under the strong orange beam, he was walking on himself, crushing his own dark reflection on which he strode.

He had reached his first marker and was beginning to feel a sense of accomplishment. However he knew that this was not the time to stop and pat himself on the back. Yes, progress was being made. But that's all it was, progress. A lot done but more to do. That was put forward at one time as a political slogan by an election winning machine. Nothing much more than election winning had been accomplished, but that's the reality of politics – all talk and little or no memorable action.

The Blackthorn Legacy

Passing the light, leaving it behind him he saw his shadow pass him and quickly lengthen on his right hand side. It was an exact black mirror image of himself until it seemed to stop replicating his movements and somehow it waved at him. He stopped and looked at his own hands. They were swinging by his own sides, not over his head like his shadow – his own bloody shadow.

Why had his own reflection done something he hadn't? It didn't seem to properly register with him that what had happened was unbelievably abnormal, no outlandish.

Next what had been his shadow seemed to rise from the ground, head first, until its waist was perpendicular to the remainder of his own reflection. It was only then he realised what had actually happened. Martin's knees buckled and he nearly fell to the ground. He covered his face with his hands. The heat from his sweaty palms made it difficult to breath. He removed them and stared unbelievably at the distorted reflection. His mind had almost reached the point of meltdown. A shadow, not as clear as that of himself passed over the alleyway. It had to have been something up high because of its gloomy shapeless shadow. Whatever it was cast a narrow amorphous light grey form across the ground, the width of the entire walkway; travelling at speed. It seemed to have come from somewhere further down in the darker regions of the alley. It caused him to tremble in terrible fear.

The surrounding cold air grasped him, encircled him. A cold shiver slithered down his back. His neck and arm hairs stiffened, standing to attention, almost. He knew then that he shouldn't have stopped moving forward. (The part of the brain that produced hindsight should be removed from the brain).

Maybe his mind was playing tricks on him, but he knew better. It had actually happened and he was frozen in position three quarters way up the alley. The main street ahead was almost in touching distance, but still so far away. Fear was taken over his body once more and the shivering he

The Blackthorn Legacy

had experienced on walking into the evening air seemed to have totally vanished. This time he wasn't at all cold, but petrified. He looked down at his long shadow again. The shaded reflection lying on the ground which was connected to him at his feet was motionless, but it didn't look like his dark image anymore. It definitely belonged to someone else.

He closed his eyes shut and held his breath. The blackness with grey shading was there just like before. Just like it always was. He decided to count to ten quietly. By the time he was finished counting, all would be fine.

He hoped.

He had reached just two on his count when the darkness of his lids lightened a little and the message he had witness earlier appeared once more. URME UNO UR. Kaleidoscopic colours filled in behind the passing image on the interior of his eyelids. The dancing colours were continuously changing shape and design. It was mesmeric, but he knew deep down that it had not been created by his own brain. And the writing, it was in the same style again, he noticed.

He jolted open his eyes and found it difficult to re-adjust to the darkness this time. White specks fluttered before his eyes momentarily until they eventually cleared from his field of vision. He had blinked quickly a number of times and the specks disappeared from view.

He looked at the black reflection, stretched out, connected to him, ahead of him, where it should have been – on the ground – he felt a little better. It was his own again. Still somewhat shaken, without much energy left in his muscles, in his body in general, but relatively better.

Everything is relative.

The return of that nonsense message had really flustered him. It wasn't even English as far as he could make out. What did the voice want from him or of him? Had he done something in a previous life to earn this punishment, because he certainly hadn't done anything he could think of that should see him earning this persecution he was suffering at the hands (or brain) of some unseen source. He inhaled large gulps of air and tried to clear his head. It worked – to a degree. He felt somewhat fresher and looked ahead, setting a marker for himself to reach, and he set off once more. He looked ahead, picking a point near the top of the door on a building up ahead, across the street.

One step in front of the other. Slowly he reached his second position. The breeze was much colder now that daylight had been pushed away westwards by the predictable onslaught of darkness. He had seen it before, the sun being forced down below the horizon by an unseen force. Another pointer to the strength of darkness and how it always seemed to overcome light.

Martin continued his trek home in stages, very slowly.

The Blackthorn Legacy

CHAPTER TWENTY THREE:

RULERS OF THE UNDERWORLD

MARTIN drove his car up close to his back door. He had already closed and locked the damaged gate behind him. The sight of the destroyed timber gate was something he was beginning to become accustomed to. He was certainly a changing man.

As he approached his back door he heard the unmistakeable sound of Cat. It sounded rather different but recognisable all the same. He waited at the door, his keys in hand. The cat padded over to him lightly, although it did appear to Martin to be somewhat larger than the last time he had laid eyes on it. It was standing at his dark backdoor, with only the pale pastel-like light from the three quarters moon high up in the clear sky available to him. It was only light was around as far as he could see; that allowed him to see in the gloom that seemed to be totally entombing him and his house and maybe even the whole of Shayleigh for all he knew.

A three quarter moon.

Was that where the man on the moon decided he didn't need to see so much of the shit that happened down on Earth, or was it really just a case of light and shadow? Maybe the man up there created the illusion of shadow when in fact he had just turned his face a little, away from full view?

The Blackthorn Legacy

The cat stopped about three feet from Martin and sat back, never taking its eyes from its master. However it probably didn't see the human as its master because cats are the rulers of the underworld – everybody knew that, even if they didn't know it, they knew. Unlike dogs, cats are not playful animals. They expect to be approached.

They always walked along the tops of high walls. They could be seen sitting high on shed roofs, or in trees. Some people believed it to be for reasons of self-preservation. That was partly true, but why did they care if they were attacked or singled out by an aggressor? Didn't they have nine lives? What other animal or living creature for that matter, could survive like that. There was definitely something sinister about cats. It was Martin's belief that the felines were not of this world.

They spend hours quietly planning where the next meal would come from and how they were going to get it as easily and as efficiently as possible. They knew that most animals living in Western Europe were stupid and that their own superiority in everything is what would ensure that they would prevail as leaders – everywhere. Cats leave their regular habitat during daylight hours and then nocturnally they attack, killing, terrorising, and displacing others.

Cats could always be seen skulked around everywhere, if proper attention was paid. During the hours of darkness they always seemed to stroll in a carefree manner, close in to walls, ditches, or whatever they walked beside. This seemed to be in order that they could retain their anonymity in the shadows hidden or at least remaining as small as possible. Yes, cats had to be the rulers of the Underworld. Why else would they move through darkness unperturbed? They understood much more than we humans have ever given them credit for and they also recognise this fact.

Martin looked at his cat and realised that the white triangle – the tuxedo effect – was almost completely gone. His feline friend – hanger on – was changing. The fatigue he

The Blackthorn Legacy

was very obviously experiencing ensured he did not query the changes in the animal.

"Do you want some food Cat?" he asked in a voice normally reserved for talking to small children – high pitched, squeaky. The response terrified him. The cat pulled back its lips to reveal thick gums holding in place long sharp and bloody red teeth. It hissed a frightening threat at Martin. The cat stood up on all fours and even in the gloomy surrounds, Martin was able to make out the huge tiger like shoulders on the enlarged cat. It took a menacing step towards the tired and frightened man. Martin was like death propped up on shaky legs, barely able to move but as soon as his adrenalin kicked in – from somewhere – he moved more quickly, and more steadily, towards the back door. He injected the key into the keyhole and in a single motion unlocked the door, opening it into his dark back kitchen. He stumbled over the threshold. Luck was on his side for the first time that day and he managed to stay on his feet, staggered in past the door and banged it closed behind him with his foot. He stood there, leaning against the closed door in the safe darkness of his back kitchen for several moments, trying to build up a little oomph, or just any bit at all. He was shattered. The day's actions had taken their toll on him and all he was ready to do right then and there was sleep. The short adrenalin boost had completely disappeared and all that was left was a withering, tiring man. He felt as though he might have even slept standing with his back to the door.

Martin must have stayed there for five minutes, alone in the dark silence. Complete silence. Too quiet. He could hear the sound of silence, a quivering low pitched wave of sound. There was another sound though. A repetitive sharp but low sound. A double sound. *Tick Tock, Tick Tock.* His wall clock over the fire place. The normally irritating sound in times of complete silence was rather comforting on this occasion. It brought a sense of reality back to the evening.

The stillness outside was also broken. It was a strange sound. It seemed like some sort of metal object was being

The Blackthorn Legacy

dragged across his driveway. What did he have out there that was metallic? Think Martin, he shouted to himself, in his head. It was almost impossible for him to put proper thoughts together or in any real order. His brain was like marshmallow now. Soft and gooey from tiredness. Weariness had affected his ability to be afraid. He hung in there however and a memory slipped into his head – the cat's water dish. It was a baking tray, thingy. Shit, the cat was moving it, but why now? What did it want? Then the screeching began. A sound combining what sounded like a long howl and a high pitched very out of tune musical note. A noise that grated on him, reverberating around his head. A scrowl he decided it was called. A new word but it defined the sound he was hearing outside.

Even Martin's tired mind knew that he wouldn't get any sleep where he stood – even if he could sleep standing up. He managed to push himself away from the back door and wander into his kitchen in the dark. He hadn't noticed the cold in his house until that moment. The fire hadn't been lit all day. It could wait until tomorrow, he decided. He was too exhausted to be affected by the lower temperature. He would sleep on shards of broken glass right at that moment.

There was that noise from the cat again. "I don't even want to know what it wants", he said under his breath to himself and walked into his bedroom. He collapsed onto the bed, slipping off his shoes and pulled the quilt up over him. Within seconds he was fast asleep. The cat let out another one of those loud burst, a scrowl he had called it, but Martin was dead to the world.

CHAPTER TWENTY FOUR:

THICK GREY FOG

AMBLING once again was Martin, through the golden meadow once more. His right hand was extended out catching some of the seeds of the long sunshine coloured grass. The sun was shining from a cloudless blue sky although there wasn't much heat in it. It was however, perfect for strolling through fields alone.

On this occasion as he walked through the luscious meadow he could feel his heart beating, no it was pounding.

The fear.

His heart felt like it was going to burst through his ribcage. Would the air quality fall as before and cause him to fight for breath. Even he decided he wanted to turn back he had nowhere to go. How did he get into the field? Where had he come from? All these questions ran through his mind at a hundred miles an hour. No matter how he thought about getting out of the place, he knew he just had to proceed. Something he had no control over was making sure he just walked on.

He was looking around the meadow. His head swivelled like an owl as he scoped the entire area. His neck comfortably allowed his head to move the way it did as if it was a natural movement. His ears were cocked and as he climbed over the mound he had seen on, on his last visit and

The Blackthorn Legacy

this time he managed to reach the bottom on the other side. He could feel himself straining his ears even more. The only sound he could hear at first was the noise he was making as the long golden grass swished this way and that around him, under his feet.

The air was completely still as was the complete scene. Only the grass falling beneath his steps was the only movement other than his own. Another few steps and there it was, the weirdly shaped stone holding up the wooden handle over to his left. Maybe thirty or forty yards away. The handle of some large or important tool, most likely. That metallic smell.

It was a strong smell of something he should know. What was it? He knew he should have known the origin or the cause of the odour.

Forget that though, he decided; and he pushed it to the back of his mind because he was hearing the calming resonance of the babbling stream. The crystal liquid that flowed through this bizarre location that probably only existed in his dreams. Martin shook his head.

How did he even know he was in his dream?

That wasn't normal was it?

It had just become stranger and stranger. His mind completely changed thoughts when he came close to the flowing stream, hidden from sight. He decided to kneel down beside the coursing water, dipping his fingers in to test the flow. The cold liquid flowed easily around his fingers. A memory from his day at the library came into his mind. It was a strange feeling. He imagined that he was a pawn in a game and whoever was playing had slipped him a clue based on the information available to them. Except it wasn't exactly handed to him, it was slipped into his head. It felt as though it had been done the way a child slipped a coin into a piggy bank – just slipped in. Follow the course of the stream, said the new thought. There was no voice, just something like a speech bubble very much akin to a comic book, available only to his mind's eye.

The Blackthorn Legacy

It felt like a good idea and so the dreaming Martin decided to do as was suggested. As he moved, the tall trees on the right began to thin out and eventually cleared away making it possible to see in every direction for as far as was possible, only he wished the clearing hadn't appeared or that the trees had disappeared. What he saw to the right was in some way disturbing. He was closer, much closer to Slieve Lea. Much closer than he was when looked at it from his own house. He looked back to where he thought his house might be. Nothing, but long golden grass and rolling mounds covered in the same gilded deep carpet he was currently standing in. It was the same in every direction except behind him where all he could see was the golden mound he had descended to reach the point to where he now stood, perplexed and confused in this chaotic dream land.

He was feeling a little flustered now but something told him he had been here before, right here. Behind him to his left and now about fifty yards away was the misshapen stone holding the wooden tool handle in position. A flash of screaming and dark red came into his head and immediately he looked away and it stopped. But the strong metallic smell lingered a second longer and then it too blew away on the non-existent breeze. Something bad had happened there and he sensed it.

He felt it in his waters.

Speaking of which he decided he needed some and bent down to the sparkling stream. He knelt down and cupped his hands to collect some of the cool clear liquid to splash on his face. His mind needed to be clear.

Splashing the cold water on his face did indeed awaken him, but only in his dream.

A moment of clarity?

Not exactly, but he felt so much better. It was like an injection of energy. Was this how those sports stars who had been found guilty of taking performance enhancing products had felt after a hit? If it was the sensation they had felt it was no wonder they did take the products. He tried to imagine

The Blackthorn Legacy

the combination of this feeling he now felt and being presented with a gold medal. What could be better? No, stop thinking like this, he chastised himself, silently.

However just as it had occurred the last time he had used the stream's water, that deep guttural tone, the disquieting voice came loud and clear in his head. *Well done, now let's clear it up.* It echoed inside the walls of his skull, just like a sound in an enclosed cave might do. Then it was gone, just switched off and all was silent again or at least back to the original silence that existed there.

What did that even mean?

Why was he being praised, and what did he even do?

He didn't like it but at least it was gone. Some sort of normality had returned to this unearthly world.

It was time to follow the suggestion already given to him. He stood up and moved slowly along the non-existent path of the flowing water. As he did so, the flash of screaming and dark red entered his head again and then a moment later by the disturbing voice telling him how good he was. This was becoming disorienting and he was beginning to lose his balance as he walked through the long grass along the stream's bank. Then he saw something he hoped that he would never see, after the last sighting. Before his eyes in black powder of some sort and just hovering in the air was the message. That message. **URME UNO UR**. It just hung there before him although it seemed far off. He balled his hands and rubbed his eyes with his knuckles until it should have hurt. He couldn't feel anything, but that may have been the choice of the Martin Carey back in his bed in Shayleigh. In dreams some things happen because the dreamer allows them or wants them to. In Martin's case, he seemed to be in charge of very little except rubbing his eyes.

He re-opened his eyes and the hovering powdered message had vaporised. No doubt, he was shaken by it but he had to proceed. He had no idea how to get out of this place. He was in his own dream, a world of his own making, but emergency

The Blackthorn Legacy

exits didn't exist. The only way he had of escape was waking up. That seemed a little bit away at this particular time.

As he walked on it felt as though he was on a treadmill and he wasn't actually moving forward but the terrain was coming to him. In fact it seemed to be moving faster than he was. It was as if he was walking into a fast forwarded scene. Within moments that sound of the gurgling stream became somewhat louder. With that he stopped walking. The moving landscape also came to a sudden stop.

Was he in charge of all around him or was he being told by the universe that his future was in his own hands now?

He felt that maybe he was thinking too much into it; after all, he was dreaming this, wasn't he?

The increased sound of rolling water had caused him to stop where he had, and he folded his legs down to a kneeling position. Martin pulled back the lengthy golden grass and peered down at the gushing stream of liquid crystal, bubbling as it flowed past him but then just seemed to disappear. He followed the line of the stream and after some looking he realised that the water was falling into a hole in the ground.

How was that even possible?

Where was it going?

Did the water gush into an Artisian Well like in London City?

The questions were endless.

Martin pulled up his grey jumper sleeve on his right arm and rolled up his shirt sleeve to his elbow. He reached his hand down to feel the hole that accepted the quick flowing water. He could feel the blackness with his hand. An all-encompassing blackness. He only put his hand into the hole and the powerful flow of the water drew his hand in. It was a curious sensation. There was no light down there, the long grass on all sides helped with that as did the little opening allowing the water through. It was cold and the chilliness of the stream's water did nothing to help. The increased sound of water was because of the lowness of the natural stone archway through which the stream flowed. Some of the water

The Blackthorn Legacy

was bashed back by the old dark grey stones, forcing it to try again to get into the darkness. Up to his elbow was now feeling the cold and he wasn't getting any more used to it. What was really strange was the dryness of the underground stone. Although he could sense the total gloominess that existed inside the hole he was unable to fathom the depth. It was deep, that he was certain of.

He withdrew his hand and could feel the cold more so, now that it was out in the air. His hand and arm as far as his elbow was red raw from the cold. The pain would begin soon as the blood began flowing to his fingertips once more. But he wasn't going to remember if he felt that throbbing pain, that aching discomfort because his attention was now drawn elsewhere, in fact it would be his own head that had his full attention. He sensed a weak version of the flash of screaming and dark red that had come into his head earlier. He closed his eyes. Even though it was much weaker than before, it was hard to take. The comfort of the black and greyness of his eyelids only lasted a few seconds before the URME UNO UR message appeared and then the disturbing voice - *well done, now let's clear it up* entered his head. He kept his eyes closed and pressed the palms of his hands on his ears. His eyes were shut tight in the hope that maybe, just maybe that would keep the silly message from appearing on the inside of his eyelids on the kaleidoscopic colouring that now danced across the blackness there.

Nothing for a moment. Maybe it had all gone, but he wasn't really expecting that. He lowered himself carefully down onto the long grass on his back with his legs bent and knees pointing up to the perfectly cloudless blue sky. His ears were still covered by his hands. Then came the flash of screaming and dark red – much stronger this time. The flash also included something else he was unable to quite make out, but that didn't exactly worry him right then. Just as that vision subsided the message across his eyelids followed and then the chilling voice. This alarming attack continued over and over again. Each time there was less and less of an

The Blackthorn Legacy

interval between the bouts and then it became just a singular noise.

Martin wasn't able to take much more of this, he could feel it. He began convulsing on the grass breaking out in a cold sweat. His head was becoming tender and raw inside, and he believed that he might not last much longer. The ringing, shouting and re-mix sounds in his head were becoming intolerable. This attack on him which could not be heard outside the walls of his own head and the hollow echoes reverberating off the interior of his skull were really taking it out of him.

He began shaking his head from side to side. Suddenly it all felt differently. The noise was gone, his head was still vibrating but lying as he was on his back, there was something more comforting, he felt more at home. But inside his head still wasn't so relaxed. In fact there was a residual heat in there. It felt as though hot steam had built up, with nowhere to go and he needed a pressure valve to relieve it. However it was better, if only slightly better, than what he had gone through over the past...how long had it lasted. Time was immeasurable. Everything was relative.

He opened his eyes. It became clear why he felt more at home because that's just where he was – at home, on his own bed lying just as he had last seen or imagined himself in his dream, legs bent and feet flat on the bed's mattress. Grey light poked in his bedroom window. He always closed his curtains.

Always. Why were they opened? He pondered this.

Then he came back to him, he had fallen into bed on the verge of exhaustion just hours ago.

The light coming in seemed dimmer than he would have expected at this time...whatever time of the day it was. Time didn't particularly matter to him just then. On his back, knees bent and pointing to the ceiling. El Che's portrait was still staring at his from the poster on the wall. Was he telling him something as well or was that just some form of

The Blackthorn Legacy

paranoia setting in? No El Che was remaining still. At least Martin seemed to have someone on his side.

He slowly removed his hands from his ears, unsure of what to expect. The feeling, this fantastic feeling. It was as though his ears were in fact that pressure valve he thought he needed. The heat and steam he believed had built up inside his skull seemed to just drain silently from his head and it deflated to its original size – that's how it felt in any case.

His senses slowly returned to him and normality began clinging to him. He looked at his wrist watch. It was just after half nine. Why was the daylight so dim?

His eyes felt sore. He looked at his arms, as his right arm felt differently to his left. His left arm was fully covered but the sleeves of his shirt and jumper were rolled up on the right. That arm looked rather raw. His lower jaw fell open and he stared at the ceiling in astonishment and fear. He had been in his own dream, really in it.

Was there any way out of this world he had unknowingly gotten himself into?

It was becoming much too much for him to take. What did he have to do to stay out? He decided there and then that he would do just about anything to open the door, a door that would remain open at all times. A door to return from the dream world back to reality. But how could he even do that? All of a sudden he realised how much he enjoyed the boring place he actually resided in – his real life. He also realised now that the saying he had heard occasionally from older people did or could in fact apply to anybody, even him. Desperate times called for desperate measures. Never did it mean so much to Martin.

The poor light quality coming through the window was nagging him. He swung his legs down off the bed and walked towards the window. Leaning on the window board and staring out, he couldn't believe what he was seeing. Maybe his eyes were just hazy with sleep. He balled up his hands to rub his eyes, but as soon as he began rubbing them he pulled away automatically. A reflex action. The soreness in and around his eyes was...well eye watering. Martin opened his sore eyes wide to ensure they were clear and he was seeing what he was actually seeing. How much worse could it get. A thick grey fog had risen over night and hung there malevolently. He leaned up to the glass pane and glanced left and right. The mist obliterated his view of anything past twenty feet. The trees across the road were invisible as was the view on either side of his house. If paranoia had in fact set in, he might have thought that an opaque dome had descended around him, ensuring he could not move from his house. Of course the up side to this was that nobody could bother him.

The thought of the dome fleetingly crossed his mind but disappeared into the fog of his forgotten memories much like the trees across the lane had done so in the hanging mist outside. He had to figure a way out of this mess. There and then he decided that that would be only goal for the day.

The Blackthorn Legacy

CHAPTER TWENTY FIVE:

A LITTLE CRUMB OF EVIDENCE

GARDA Joseph Thornsberry parked his car in the relatively empty car park. He sat there taking deep breaths readying himself for the job ahead. It was just after nine but he wasn't due to clock in until half past. He wanted some time on his own to search through the computerised records to find out all he could about the connection or lack of it between Jimmy Jones and Detective Ed Walsh. There was also the matter of what he perceived to be a cover-up by the Super. He was going to sort this out once and for all. Joey felt it was about time for him to come to the fore, and he believed it had come and that he was going to prove all the higher ups wrong, and also demonstrate that he was ready to be a detective.

He got out of the car once he had finished his breathing exercises and was ready for the work of his life to begin. The fog was extremely heavy that particular morning and he could smell the pong of spent carbon fuels and industrial smoke captured like scent fossils in the heavy mist. He never remembered any haze as thick as this one ever before.

The roads had been quiet on his way in thus not slowing his down journey too much. The mist just hung there motionlessly, clinging to everything and surrounding the scene completely. There was no getting away from it. No

The Blackthorn Legacy

matter how fast or slowly he moved the fog remained the same distance away. Always the same distance away. As he began moving he could see some of the water droplets swirling as his large mass disturbed them.

Joey flashed his card against the reader outside and proceeded in through the back door and the long walk up to his kiosk as per usual. Only today he was a little more enthusiastic about being in work. The walk didn't seem as long. All the same he couldn't get there quick enough.

It was he who had introduced the saying 'same shit different bucket' to the station in Fellowmore. He was proud of this as it was now a widely used phrase on dark mornings after long breaks away from the office or weekends. Before this it had been just the simple 'another day, another dollar'. What did that even mean if you didn't live in a country or territory that used currency other than the dollar? Was it just something to say; just to be saying something? Joey always believed that if you had nothing interesting to say, just keep your trap shut. Simple as.

He opened the door to the kiosk and entered quietly. Denny Spollen was there and boy was he glad to see Joey enter the room. Denny was a younger, thinner, taller and quieter version of Joey. In fact, the men were nothing alike.

The younger surprised man glanced at the clock high up on the wall and then looked back at the smiling face of Joey.

"It's only just after nine. What are you doin' here already?"

"Do you wanna go home or do you wanna go to jail?" Joey often quoted the line from a film he had seen some time before but couldn't remember which one it was. A cop flick of some sort. He had enjoyed it as far as he could remember. The delight in his voice was quite unusual, especially for a morning. Joey was not usually a morning person. Anyone who knew him normally stayed out of way before eleven. He was liable to do or say anything before that time.

"What has you all happy and shit, Joey?"

The Blackthorn Legacy

"Go on, get outta here Denny. I'm here now. It was as easy for me to be here now as it would be in half an hour. I was up anyway. Go on, get outta here."

Denny didn't really need to be coaxed that much and almost had his coat on over his uniform before Joey had stopped talking. He was afraid that if he asked any more questions, the real Joey might break out of the shell that looked surprisingly akin to the older version.

"You sure about this?" He didn't really care. He was just saying it for something to say.

"Go!" Demanded Joey.

The door banged out behind Denny and Joey was alone at last. The smile on his face quickly changed. It was time to concentrate and there mightn't be much time to carry out the searches before members came looking for information and whatever else it was that they were just too lazy to find or do for themselves. Anyone on duty now would be ready for the changeover soon enough and wouldn't bother him. That's how it always was. Fellowmore was not a busy town as far as crime was concerned.

He logged into two separate computers and began searching different databases simultaneously. He typed in queries relating to both Jimmy Jones and Detective Walsh individually on the PC's. Nothing had turned up until he accidentally pushed the *LE* keys. Information he hadn't expected to find flashed on the screen before his eyes.

"You beauty." The excitement within him burst out in his voice. He felt like jumping around but his body mass wouldn't have allowed him do so without causing himself, or his clothes for that matter, a serious injury. He almost knew there and then the feeling Archimedes must have experienced in the bath, after making that scientific discovery. Joey's discovery wasn't scientific but it was as a result of perseverance and investigative intuition, he felt. He would enjoy the rest of the day planning how he would use this new information. Now he just had to find out why the Super was involved. No doubt this would be a more difficult

The Blackthorn Legacy

task. But he knew that if he wanted to be considered for detective grade, he would have to have all bases covered. It was well known in public service circles that job number one is CYOA (cover your own ass). The one single disadvantage he felt he had in gaining promotion was that *they* always seemed to promote the wrong ones, the least entitled but most favoured and not always favoured for work reasons. He would buck that trend. Joey anticipated that today's work would see to that.

His search for items associating Walsh and the Super was not as productive although a little crumb of evidence had appeared but it was going to require more work. The searches were going to have to wait because he could hear the sound of multiple footsteps up and down the corridor outside. The day had awoken and he would be on call for the next couple of hours, no doubt. With that the door opened and the first of many lazy queries was made.

The Blackthorn Legacy

CHAPTER TWENTY SIX:

YOU KNOW ME TOO WELL

Molesworth Lane was under the same curtain, and in the enclosed narrow alley it appeared to be darker than the main street, but that was to be expected. Sally made her walk to work before half past nine to open the office for the day's business. The spots of water floating in the fog were being swirled around as she cut straight through the thick mist.

It was no secret among her colleagues in the office that Sally hoped one day to be a singer; and not just a cabaret type performer. No, not Sally, because rightly or wrongly, she had eyes on being a world star. As she walked through the fog, she imagined she was backstage just before making her grand entrance in the MGM in Las Vegas through the billowing dried ice. In her imagination she could hear the crowd calling for her after her opening act, Beyoncé, who seemed to have done a good job in warming up the crowd for her. Sally flicked back her hair and set herself in that thought, in that magical place for a moment longer. That was her dream.

The secretary at Legal, Wrights regularly entered singing competitions and also sang in the local bars and clubs in the hope that someday and agent or someone involved in the music industry might just notice her. As of yet it hadn't

The Blackthorn Legacy

happened but Sally was still full of optimism and that recurring dream in her head could still be a possibility.

There were two Sally's. The day Sally, who dressed looked the part of the professional office secretary, and the evening Sally, who had some star quality about her. She was by no means a striking looking woman but she definitely was someone who might be noticed in a crowd. She was fairly tall standing five foot seven inches, carrying no excess weight. She had however a strikingly pale complexion, that required little make-up for either Day Sally or Night Sally.

She reached the office door and entered. After opening the outer door, she pressed the correct four digits on the alarm pad to turn it off and to put an end to that annoyingly repetitive beeping sound. The cold air inside the office just hung there. She often imagined it sneering at her as she shivered first thing on the cold mornings. Sally pressed the switch near her desk. The drone of the electric fan heater was also a sound that should have annoyed her, but because of the heat that produced by the electrical installation, cutting through the stagnant cold air, she oddly enjoyed it.

Sally left her coat on for a few minutes still as she prepared the office for the day ahead. It certainly was no fun being cold first thing in the morning.

She recognised that it was the pay she accumulated from her work as a secretary that would eventually allow her to follow her dream of singing to millions in the biggest cities. She didn't dare even contemplating losing that wage and that was the reason she put so much into her day's work in Legal, Wrights. Jean Wright had almost come to the point of calling Sally inexpungible because of what she put into and gave to the business day-in, day-out; the lack of sick-leave taken and her willingness to help the business progress any way she possibly could. No matter how many late nights out performing in clubs there were, mixing with her fans and possible fans-to-be, she was first there every morning to open up, without fail. Jean also liked how she dealt with clients. Those who needed to be told where the door was,

The Blackthorn Legacy

found out promptly from Sally. She was generally a good judge of character. Not always right, but more often than not.

The main door of the office opened in and Jean Wright entered with her usual friendly face. It was difficult to believe that the pleasant and welcoming façade belonged to one of Fellowmore's best Criminal Lawyers. It was probably true to say that Jean Wright had a mean streak somewhere in her body, but she maintained it out of sight for the most part. It was happy face and the flirtatious smile that was one if the endearing qualities that helped her to entice clients to seek her assistance and on occasion to entice the justice system to rule in her favour. It could also be, when she wanted it to be, a mesmerising smile.

Jean Wright was a woman of average height. Her dark brown tightly curled hair flowed from her head and rested on her shoulders. Her slightly tanned face had just the faintest traces of any make-up. Her grey fitted business suit gave her an air of superiority with even a hint of over-bearing. Her dress sense always seemed quite simple, yet effective. She turned and closed the office door behind her and stood just there as she unbuttoned the large whire coloured toggle-fasteners on her dark brown duffel coat. She left down her leatherette handbag and the blue plastic bag she had carried in with her, freeing up both hands.

"Morning Sally."

"Hi Jean."

"Where did that fog come from? Unbelievable isn't it?"

"It certainly is." Sally was opening the diaries and setting up for the day. It was obvious that neither of the women wanted to bring up *the thing* that had happened the previous evening. It would be just left aside and completely ignored. They would just forget about it. In reality both of them had secretly felt very foolish at how they had reacted to whatever it was that had caused the occurrence.

"What have we got today then, Sally? Anything pressing?"

"You've got a court appearance with Mr Daisy at 2pm. You know, the speeding fine guy." Sally rolled her eyes.

The Blackthorn Legacy

"Oh yeah, that...client." She smiled at Sally.

"I know that's not what you wanted to say, Jean." Sally reciprocated the smile.

"You know me too well. Anything else I need to worry about today?"

"Well, there is that Mr Carey. You know, the man that was here yesterday during the incident." She paused for a moment – just long enough for an unpleasant silence to develop, but continued before it could take a hold. "Do you want me to set up another appointment with him?"

Jean stared past Sally, at the white wall behind her as she unconsciously moved the tip of her index finger across her lightly glossed lips. Just think about the man, no, the client, she silently corrected herself, returning her eyes to Sally's

"Yes, I think we should. Can you get in contact and find out, as only you can, when would suit. I think we should also work out a special rate with him, given what seems to have happened here in his presence here yesterday? Putting on an act of normality while under pressure was a prerequisite for a lawyer, and Jean had that trait in abundance.

"I don't have a contact number for him, Jean. I just took his name when he arrived in here, and then I requested he wait."

"Where is Vera; we could do with her particular skills on this one. I don't want to lose Martin Carey's business just because *we* didn't try hard enough."

Sally flicked through another appointment diary and after reaching a particular page, she slowly looked down the lines studiously, as she was wont to do, noting all the entries. "She's due back here at around midday." She remarked, lifting her head from the book.

"Send her a message instantly, Sally. Tell her you need all the information she can her her sticky fingers on, pertaining to Martin Carey, and in particular to him being contacted, ok? Right now. It's her new priority."

Jean finished removing her duffel-coat and brought it in and hung it on the coat-hanger in her office. She re-emerged

The Blackthorn Legacy

and retrieved the two bags she had left sitting on the floor inside the main door. From the blue plastic carrier she removed a shapely small glass vase and some elegant dried flowers. She placed the prepared plants in the vase and put it in the place where the other had fallen from and had smashed on the floor the previous day.

"What do you think? Honestly?" She asked Sally. Her opinion was important to Jean. She trusted the woman like no other when it came to the public appearance of the office. Mostly because she understood Sally's need to have her public personae perfectly presented each night, no matter if it was in a big club or some dark corner some pub. To be fair, anytime Jean had seen her, she was always stylishly turned out.

"They're fabulous Jean; they really brighten up that corner.

The door opened loudly this time as Deirdre King almost came through it on her way in. The dour expression on her face said it all. It told her two colleagues that they would have been safer to remain quiet and to just keep their powder dry, for the time being at least. Deirdre trudged straight through the front office and into her own office, and she slammed the door shut behind her.

"At least the flowers will brighten up this place even if Deirdre is a little under the weather."

"A little green under the gills, is my guess", replied Sally.

"I can hear you talking about me." The muffled shout came from Deirdre's office. Jean and Sally glanced fearful looks at each other. Sally threw a shape at Jean indicating that it was most likely man trouble. Agreement was shared between the two. There a moments complete silence.

"Maybe I should bring her with me to court later on. What do you think, Sally?"

"I think that might not be the best idea that you've ever come up with. She is not one for that sort of thing. You've seen her in action. She likes her space in situations such as this. Just let her be for an hour or so, you'll get the best out

The Blackthorn Legacy

of her then. You know as well as I do that Deirdre is a single-minded as they come."

Jean just stared at Sally pensively for a moment. The cogs in her head were grinding. The thinking process was on-going.

"Hmmm", she mumbled. "maybe she should be the one to meet Martin Carey when we convince him to return. I think *that* would be a good move. Neither particularly likes each other but I think it will bring out the necessary, whatever that happens to be."

Sally nodded slowly and then her warm smile spread slowly across her pale face. "That might work. Sure, go with it. Ill text Vera and tell her to prioritise Martin Carey right away."

The Blackthorn Legacy

CHAPTER TWENTY SEVEN:

DESPERATE MEASURES

MARTIN was up, fed and ready to clean the house before starting into what he had planned for the day. In the back kitchen he was standing at the sink, washing up after his breakfast and staring out at the thickening fog. The longer he stared out at the grey mist the denser it seemed to become. It felt like he was being held prisoner in his own house by some greater power. They were going to keep him there for as long as it took to....to what, he asked himself. And who was it that didn't want him leaving his house today? Not that it mattered because he had some checking to do and notes to recap on before he could make his next move. Ultimately he just wanted to find out who or what was working against him. They always seemed to be where he was, putting voices in his head and making or trying to make him execute particular tasks he wasn't completely comfortable in carrying out.

The fog wasn't the only thing keeping him under house arrest. A certain black feline creature that had been 'scrowling' the previous night also had Martin on edge. He firmly believed that entities other than he himself, or anyone else for that matter who knew and understood, were watching, viewing, and observing him. Through the fog, through the darkness at night and at times through his own eyes from within his own head. He would have to learn how to control these voices or at least try to understand them. They had been talking in riddles and were seemingly harmless for the most part except, except the one that had been calling for JJ to be gotten rid of. That was uncomfortable. But if that was what it took to straighten the curve, he would do it. Desperate measures, that's where he was and he needed everything he could muster or understand to free himself of the shackles of fear and dread.

It was like playing Monopoly. Instead of picking the Community Chest card, Martin had chosen the Desperate Measures version in the Shayleigh version of the game. He wasn't exactly sure yet what it entailed, but he would roll the dice again and try to beat the odds.

After finishing the washing up, he set the fire and put a match to it. The fog outside was keeping any heat available from the sun away from him.

"Oh you won't beat me that easily", he mumbled to himself under his breath. "I'm self-sufficient and I can survive here, on my own, for another week or so."

He completed all his chores and collected his notebook and pen from his jacket and placed them neatly on his kitchen table. Martin wasn't relaxed enough. He wasn't as relaxed as he should or wanted to be. Something was missing. He got up and left the kitchen for a couple of moments and returned with his record player. It was a heavy piece of machinery and when it was closed up the way it was in its encased blue box, it could have passed for an old style sowing machine. Setting down the music box on his settee beside the little table that was holding the Banker's Lamp. He searched and found the electrical connection required to work the player. He disappeared once more and returned with a number of records.

Carefully, Martin removed one of the vinyl discs from its sleeve and placed it equally carefully on the perfectly maintained black turntable. The plug had been connected to the wall socket and he could hear the electric current

The Blackthorn Legacy

running through the music playing machine. The black metal tone arm moved robotically and Martin placed it in the first groove. He was starting on Track One. Then it began, first the crackle, and through the built-in speaker it sounded so good. Music was always meant to be recorded and played in this manner. Every other method was a pretence he believed. The music began and his mind began to float. His brain felt like it was being recharged. His head moved on his neck of its own accord in time with the 1960's Pop/Rock song being played out through the old speaker.

Everything suddenly seemed so much better. It was however, time to get to work. Martin had notes to read and probably to re-read to make sense of them.

He sat at the table with his pad and pen before him and he looked up at the ceiling, taking in the music and casting his mind back. Where should he begin this project from? Was it really that important where he started? That was an important question. All of these questions were fighting for attention at the front of his head. Closing his eyes, letting the music calm and settle him, he decided that he needed to start with his memory of the death at the top of Ard Lane, or at least the body found there. Start at the beginning.

He divided the notepad page in two, drawing a freehand line down the centre of the page. The left column he had called Memories and the right side he labelled that column Actions.

Two hours later he had sat back and stared at the pad. He had written non-stop for that time, chronicling everything that had happened up to and including the previous night. The sense of empowerment it brought was intoxicating. It was only after a few moments of looking at his work that he realised that the music was no longer playing. Martin was so caught up in the moment that he had withdrawn himself into some other world. It was a safe and voiceless place with no fog, no scrowling cat or interfering busy bodies. This is where he liked to be – a world of his own creation. He sat back and he admired his accomplishment on the pad before him on the kitchen table. It was time to complete the Actions column for each of the many Memories he had logged.

He knew that this was probably going to be a laborious task, but probably the most important job he would do for some time. It was inevitable that some of the Memories would not have accompanying actions or at least actions that he could produce as yet. This is exactly how it panned out for the first few entries. Then he came to Almo Stace. There was something nagging about this phrase. It wasn't English but nor did it feel like it belonged to any other known or widely used language. He played around with the letters on a stray page. After creating several combinations of the letters he sat back wide-eyed, staring at the scribbles on the sheet of paper. There on the page were two words Almost Ace. To most people they would seem unimportant, but not to Martin. Especially in the context of when he had heard the voice spouting the message Almo Stace. How had he not figured this out before, he wondered. But then he had to admit that he wasn't listening to the voice, just hearing it, that annoying tone coming from an unreachable part of his head. A dark corner. Almost Ace, Anyone who played cards would know that in most games the ace is the strongest card and next in line is the King. Given that he had heard this voice at times associated with JJ and was being directed to him, it stood to reason that King was in fact Deirdre King.

What was he going to place in the Actions column opposite Almo Stace. Maybe he should leave it momentarily and return at a later date. It was possible and probable that some of his Memories were connected. He decided to write the Bitch's name in the Actions column. Just in case he would forget what it actually meant.

As he sat there considering his next move, a wave came across him, a feeling, a longing he hadn't had in years. Twelve years since the previous January to be exact. The need for the sickly taste of tobacco in his mouth was strong. In fact it was stronger than he remembered it ever being even when he was addicted to the chemically altered stuff.

The Blackthorn Legacy

Twelve years. It was a long time. He began to get fidgety and the need to smoke was becoming more and more necessary. It felt like he wouldn't last without at least one drag.

A cold sweat broke out on his face and palms of his hands had become tacky with the false heat created by the craving. He had to do something. He needed to find a cigarette.

The shakes were becoming insufferable. His shoulders were moving of their own accord and his knees were jigging at a rate of knots under the table. He stood up from the chair. He had to stand up. How was he going to make it through this debacle now? He wracked his brains and then remembered something. It brought a sly smile to his lips, only his lips. A knowing leer. Martin Carey had hidden the last box of cigarettes he had bought all those years ago. Yes, he had put them away so that if cold turkey became unbearable, he could have a puff. Now, where did he put them? He remembered putting them somewhere near but hidden when he moved into his current dwelling.

After ten minutes of hunting and rummaging through presses in his kitchen, the room went from being the neatest known. It could have been mistaken for a tenement house in the East End of London in 1940 after the fifty seven days of Luftwaffe bombings. But that didn't seem to bother Martin now, because he had found what he was looking for. A cool bright blue coloured box of cigarettes with six smokes still remaining. He knelt on the floor where he was, glee on his face, and warmth in his skin. A palpable calmness had descended on Martin. Now all he needed was a light. He knew where he had one of those.

Getting up and looking around the cluttered floor and worktop of the normally pristine kitchen, he unusually just ignored it all. This was the man who always had everything in its own place. He did not care about the state of his kitchen at that particular moment, he just wanted his hit. He needed his hit.

The glass full of nick-knacks was where he was headed. The shelf on the wall just inside the door into the kitchen

The Blackthorn Legacy

from the back kitchen. That was where he had kept his lighter. It was also a plan B in case he had run out of matches for the fire. Martin believed that there was only one proper taste when smoking and that was created by the gas fire. The taste and smell created by burning phosphorus at the end of small wooden stick was pungent and it never really appealed to him. Reaching the shelf, he picked up the glass and heeled out the contents onto the wooden ledge. There it was, his plastic red lighter. He picked it up, the cold, rounded plastic container with metallic fittings and wheel on top. His cigarette lighter. It felt so good holding it in his right hand. Rolling the wheel back, igniting a spark which was then fuelled by the pressurised gasoline. He lit the end of the cigarette and sucked in the navy velvet smoke and blew out a cloud of grey tension into his kitchen. That was worth searching for, he thought. A second drag quickly followed as did the dizziness often experienced by first timers or those like Martin who hadn't inhaled tobacco smoke for some time.

He was able to block everything completely from his mind as he smoked the cigarette. The mess on the ledge was going to be easy to clear up and would only take several seconds but he decided that it could have to wait until he was finished his well-earned time-out. The dead grey ash that had extended at the end of the ciggy was like a shrivelled up decaying lifeless object. He walked to the fireplace and cast the deadness into the burning embers. One more big drag and to hell with the woozy sensation he was feeling in his head, he thought to himself. Just finish it off at the fireplace and then start the tidying up job.

Back at the shelf, Martin gathered up a group of pens, nail-clippers, a nail file, a screw and such like to deposit them back in the glass. Two attempts would be enough to gather all the items and replace them in the rightful place. Martin began scooping up the remaining items and noticed something that shouldn't have been there. A pen, a Parker Pen. He lifted it up and examined the navy and silver writing implement. There was an inscription on it. He had to squint

The Blackthorn Legacy

his eyes to read the small writing. After much staring in the diminished light he made it out *Det E W - V.*

What the hell?

Why was that in his house?

What did even mean?

JJ knows, Marty. JJ still needs to be gone. Now you have something. What the f..? The bloody voice. After so long alone with his own thoughts. He stared around the kitchen and almost expected to find someone standing there. He almost hoped there was someone standing there. Had the walls got eyes and ears? Was everybody watching him now? The feeling of claustrophobia was folding in around him again. The kitchen was becoming smaller, or so it appeared. The fog outside the window was becoming thicker. He was beginning to think that he might be in one of those decorative globes, but instead of snow he was surrounded by fog. Did they want him to remain here? Sure, he could last for a couple of days. Then what? His supplies would run out by the weekend. *JJ still needs to be gone. You need to deal with him, Marty. Remember what you said yesterday, desperate times call for desperate measures. Deal with it, sooner rather than later.*

The blood left Martin's face and it felt like the tide was going out, leaving him marooned on this island.

Rahaduff Island.

Weakness was engulfing him, taking the space left in what seemed to be a kitchen which was ever decreasing in dimension. It was closing in, whatever *it* was. He stared around the room; eyes wide open in fear and panic, as the walls moved in time with his palpitating heartbeat. This must be how it felt to suffocate.

The air seemed to becoming heavier in the kitchen. He felt as though it was trying to press him down. Rolling waves of mist and fog and heavy haze were now moving around him in slow motion. Circling as if waiting for him to lose his remaining strength and then no doubt it would swallow him whole and take his remaining breaths. His mind was running

The Blackthorn Legacy

amok and he was close to delirium. He fought, he clawed at the shapeless enemy.

How could the mist have gotten inside his walls?

The windows were all closed, weren't they?

He was seeing something that did not exist, only in his imagination, his wild imagination. But it was draining him.

If there was a thermometer to illustrate energy levels, and it was there in the kitchen, the mercury in Martin's contraption would be moving steadily down the glass, contracting quickly. He mustered up enough strength to move a little to look at his windows in the kitchen. Indeed they were closed, as was the back door and back kitchen window. How had the mist, now darker in colour, gotten inside? Was it really even in here with him? He didn't care much anymore. Standing there trying to figure out this new problem, for which he had no answer was going to wear him out even more. Preserve your energy Martin, he told himself in a weak voice. Looking around his room for some solace, for some help, for which there was none visible. And then everything became a whole lot worse. On each of the four walls he could see the letters **URME UNO UR**. It was only getting worse. *JJ needs to be gone, Marty. You know what you have to do.* The problem was he hadn't a clue. No matter how much the insistent voice told him he had, he didn't know what to do.

The heat, the difficulty in breathing, the pulsating kitchen walls and now the messages on those very walls. It was all becoming too much to take. As much as tried to fight it, he was becoming weaker. His legs gave way initially, falling to his knees first and then he collapsed and fells forward heavily onto his floor. Martin Carey was out cold.

The Blackthorn Legacy

CHAPTER TWENTY EIGHT:

A PREPARED STATEMENT

OUTSIDE the Garda Station, Garda Superintendent Philip Morahan was overseeing the setting up his podium. In the following minutes he would prepare to give a press conference concerning the investigation into the death of three youths in Shayleigh on the previous Friday night. The podium itself was a lightweight timber structure with a microphone attached to the slanted notes holding plate. Further microphone holders were also attached for the media organisations. Only the media groups he considered to be to his taste had been cordially invited. All was being set up on a portable stand to give the man who considered himself to be of great importance, a height advantage. Talking down to people was his way of maintaining a sense of superiority. That was always how he liked to do it.

The Superintendent, a man who measured five feet nine and a half inches, (the half inch was extremely important), walked out the main door of the station in a dry run. He stepped up onto the wooden platform and addressed the empty space before him. Yes, they will love me, he said under his breath. The slick smile and patronising wink of his eye to no one, demonstrating the air of superiority he carried with him. Not that he needed to show the world his self-professed pre-eminence, most of those who would attend the press

The Blackthorn Legacy

conference later knew already how superior the man believed he was. He carried bagfuls of his own dominance with him, on his person.

One of the young Gardaí came out and adjusted the wiring to the microphone and set up a light behind the platform, just how the Super liked it. Show me in a good light, he always joked in his dry sense of humour. Only those who wanted something from him ever laughed (which was generally most people working in his proximity).

A large white van with the name of a TV station plastered on its side pulled up with twenty meters to the right of the barracks.

"Another twenty minutes Super", Said the willing to please Garda. The Super just nodded, a fake smile broke across his lips. "Do you need anything else, sir?" Asked the over-eager Garda. The Super just raised his hand and waved it in a regal fashion as he passed the young man. Almost demeaning him. *Thanks but no thanks, you little person.* It was time for him to prepare himself to give the world the news they sought. The truth was he had nothing, no ideas, and no plans, nothing worthwhile. But that was not how he was going to give it from the stand. He would talk to the media; get his picture on the papers and all the top TV stations. Morahan was more a politician than a proper policeman. He craved attention and he was able to decide when he got what he wanted. Power, power with no responsibility. He was the cox on this big boat. He had all the power but if he appeared in a bad light, it would be someone else's fault. Yes, all the power.

*****

At a minute after four in the afternoon, a minute late, the Superintendent walked out to the podium flanked by two young Gardaí, one on each side. Cameras began flashing and the mumbling crowd quietened down to a mere hum. The only discernible sound was that of the clicking cameras.

The Blackthorn Legacy

Morahan raised his hand to the crowd as if looking for silence, the silence that already existed. He coughed into his hand and moved in closer to his microphone which was now surrounded by wireless media versions covered in coloured foam with media station logos.

"Thank you all for coming today", he began, reading from a prepared statement. "The prevention and investigation of crime and disorder is the primary function of every police organisation countrywide and this Garda Station and its workers are no different. Over the years, you will recognise that there has been modernisation with enhancements to the processes and technology used to investigate crime in Fellowmore, but a holistic view has not yet been the driver; but rather the crisis of the day. This approach may have been sufficient to address serious issues in this great town in the past; but today's policing environment needs and is getting a much more comprehensive solution to overcome the challenges, thanks to changes, I as Superintendent have introduced in recent times. With this sliver of information in mind, I wish to inform you that, in relation to the recent serious incidents that occurred in Shayleigh, are indeed being treated with the utmost importance. We are working with all relevant parties to bring the investigation to a successful conclusion. With regard to the suspicious deaths recorded just last Friday, we are following a definite line of enquiry and I have my best people working on it. We have already had one person in for questioning and they are helping us with our enquiry." At this stage he raised his head and looked down at the intently listening and scribbling crowd. TV cameramen had fought for the best vantage point and he beamed a sincere looking smile back at them. Anybody who knew Morahan would have known that this was all part of the choreography he had practiced for up to twenty minutes earlier in the day. "I'm afraid I am not in a position to divulge any further information. All our collated information is considered pertinent at present and I do not want to spoil any of the hard work my investigators have

The Blackthorn Legacy

carried out to date", he continued without missing a beat. It was a truly professional lie, but well presented. He had the attention of all of those in attendance. "I will answer any questions you may have as best I can. However I will not answer anything directly related to the on-going investigation that I feel may jeopardise a positive result being achieved by the Fellowmore Gardaí." The circus ringmaster was definitely calling the shots.

The crowd leaned forward all at once and raised hands attached to screaming bodies, as they sought attention to and to be chosen to ask the first question. It seemed to him to be no different a scene than would be seen at a concert or a football match where the adoring fans sought a piece of the star. He believed he was Fellowmore's very own idol.

Morahan loved the attention, no he craved it, and he looked out at the crowd, all of whom were staring at him, wanting to know what he knew. This was how it felt for those rock stars on stage in front of a devoted crowd, he thought. He was lapping it up, what he considered to be adoration. Waiting a moment before choosing the first question just to drag it out his enjoyment of the little people wanting of him, as much as possible. Then he pointed down at one of the journalists he recognised. "Please identify yourself and the media outlet you represent", he requested.

"Steve James, Fellowmore Tribune", announced the bearded fifty something year old reporter. Morahan nodded in his direction as if to give the man the signal to go ahead. "This is the second major crime in your jurisdiction in eighteen months, Superintendent. Is it because of recent budget cuts that you are finding difficulty in preventing such crime or is there still a disconnect between your organisation and the general public? Because prior to this the crime level in Shayleigh alone was almost non-existent." The question caught Morahan by surprise. He needed to answer this in such a way nobody would be offended. A politician's answer. A position he aimed for down the line.

The Blackthorn Legacy

"Crime prevention is a science. It requires preparedness and for all our members to be ready at all times. Like all sciences, it is not possible to get it right all of the time. We are developing and improving here in Fellowmore every day and I feel that in general we are building a better rapport with local people and businesses. If I was in a position to predict where crime would occur, I think I would probably be able to predict the Lotto numbers and retire gracefully". His answer flowed from him and a few giggles broke out on the right of the crowd. Exactly what he was looking for. "Unfortunately, this particular crime happened in an unusual place in an unusual time, made it virtually impossible to prevent it."

"But Superintendent..."

Morahan ignored the bearded reporter and sought out another question. He found a delicate looking young woman. A good looking blonde with bright sparkling eyes. She had just cut off a phone call, putting her device into her jacket pocket and smiling up at the podium, with a wide smile on her face. Like that of a Cheshire Cat.

"Miss", he said pointing to her, in anticipation of a nice question.

"Thank you. Sophie LaFare, The Times. Superintendent Morahan is it true that you are covering for one of your Detectives. Is it not true that a member of the public is attempting to bring a case of verbal and physical abuse against the said Detective, for a second time?" Morahan was totally flummoxed by the question. How could she, the one he had chosen for her looks do that to him? Who the hell had told her anyway? Was there a rat in his building? A picture of Joey Thornsberry crossed his mind. What was the name of that nobody uniform he called up to his office the other day?

The Superintendent hoped that the discomfort he was feeling was not showing on his face or in his general demeanour. He knew he had to play this correctly. Like a politician

He just had to.

The Blackthorn Legacy

All his good work, or the work he believed to be so, would go up in smoke because of that stupid… That's it, he thought. He quickly refocused and lost the rabbit in headlights look instantly. He realised he had been staring into oblivion for the last few seconds, creating, manufacturing a reply to this leftfield question. The look of authority with a touch of arrogance was again on full view on the sly expression that was almost always omnipresent on that face of his. He had formed an answer that he was ready to share with his public.

"I'm afraid the incident you refer to Miss; is a matter for the individuals involved and will in no way interfere with this extremely important on-going operation. I can assure you that it will continue to be an all hands on deck investigation. That will include my own input when it is required." He spoke with vigour and stared intently at Miss LaFare as he had provided the half-truth. The look of reproach was very evident to Sophie. The reporter however, never batted an eyelid, because she knew that this attack was his way of trying to cover up the real story. When he had finished, she smiled timidly, tongue in cheek. She knew there was a story worth digging for. This she would have to thank her friend, Deirdre King, for the phone call just moments earlier where she had provided the information.

Morahan pulled up his sleeve and glanced at his watch, and turned to his left and whispered a word to the young Garda standing slightly behind him. Both men nodded and the Superintendent returned to the microphone and announced the end of the press conference.

"I'm sorry ladies and gentlemen, but I have been informed of a more insistent matter needing my attention at this moment. I will keep you up to date on this investigation regularly. Thank you for your time."

The discontentment was clearly audible as he turned from the podium. It felt like a needle through his soul. His reputation as a fine orator and organiser had taken a hit. Philip Morahan will return stronger, he told himself. He had to find the rat first. The rat that had spread the word about

The Blackthorn Legacy

Detective Walsh and that troublemaker Jones. That needed to be sorted *tout suite* he told himself. In truth he would have little or no input into detecting a person he believed had made a mockery of him, the Superintendent, before an audience of invited guests. Philip Morahan would just point his well looked after index finger at individuals until he found out what he needed to know. There was no panache in that, just a creation of fear among the staff working under him. He wasn't leader just because of his ability as a Garda. (It was nothing to do his ability as a Garda – he had none – he was a politician through and through).

When the three men disappeared from the crowds view behind the closed doors of the Garda Station, the Superintendent stopped walking and grabbed both the younger men flanking men. He glared at them and they watched as the rage visibly grew in his already reddened face. An even redder wave seemed to wash up to his forehead like a red tide. The older man took a deep breath, considerably calming him but not quietening him.

"Get me the overweight prick who works in the kiosk. I want him in my office first thing tomorrow morning. If he's not on duty, drag him in. I want him there. You got that? Don't fuck it up." The ire that seemed to have disappeared from his face must have only just departed from view and reappeared in Morahan's voice where it was pushed out into the open. He was not to be messed with when he was like that. Both of the young Gardaí knew that much.

The Superintendent left the two Gardaí behind in a state of dread as he stormed off towards his office. The ruthless Super would have their guts for garters if they didn't do as he had bid.

The Blackthorn Legacy

CHAPTER TWENTY NINE:

VERA BABALU

"...ter ..rey"
BANG BANG BANG
Martin could hear the noise, the banging sound. It seemed to be coming from far away, through the haze in his head, far away.

"..ister Carey."
BANG BANG BANG BANG BANG
It was a little clearer. It seemed to be a little closer. What was it? Martin wasn't really sure where he was. He was uncomfortable wherever he was. He tried to open his eyes but the Sandman's glue was of good quality. His mind began to work, but very slowly. He managed to move his legs a little. Martin reached down along his body to pull the covers over him to keep the cold out.

No bed covers. Why was he wearing day clothes in bed instead of his night clothes? Daylight was endeavouring to push through his closed eyelids. Something seemed amiss. The unusually cold air was draped around him, causing him to shiver.

"Mister Carey", a ladies voice, now closer than it had seemed however long it had been since the last call. Had somebody been trying to contact him?
BANG BANG BANG BANG

The Blackthorn Legacy

"Are you alright in there Mr Carey?" Much clearer this time. It caused Martin to shake himself. He felt a dribble of warm sticky saliva slowly oozed down his lower cheek. He lifted his head, eyes still stuck closed. He wiped the wetness from the side of his face with his sleeve. Why did his mattress seems so hard and cold? He knew he would have to move at some time and so he felt it was time to investigate what was happened and with great trouble Martin unsealed his eyes and jumped in shock at the sight that met him. Saucepans, plastic bowls, plastic washing-up liquid bottles and clothes pegs were strewn on the floor around him. He jumped to his feet and winced immediately.

The pain.

It was all on the right side of his head and it was excruciating. A throbbing pain and a constant ache at the same time in the same particular spot on the side of his skull. In fact it felt like the throbbing pain had been coming from deep within his head and as it escaped through the bone structure of his cranium, it caused the terrible ache.

"Mister Carey". An echoey voice. A female voice coming from the hallway.

"I know you're in there. Can I talk to you please? Mr Carey." The woman's voice sounded strange. He couldn't figure out what was making it sound peculiar. His mind drifted again.

Martin stared at the mess on his floor. There were at least four saucepans strewn on the floor like they had been just thrown there without any thought put into it. They had. What had happened? He still could not remember. Why had he been lying on his kitchen floor? He cast his mind back trying to recall what had happened. Then he remembered the fog outside. The thick grey mist that had been hovering around his house on all sides almost like a dense haze, somehow ensuring Martin would not leave his home. *They* must have wanted him inside. Creating a sense of claustrophobia, pressing him in, condensing the very air he was breathing. Glancing outside he realised that the very fog

The Blackthorn Legacy

he had been afraid of some hours back, had dissipated completely, if in fact, it had been there at all. A clear blue unblemished sky covered the entire area like a happy looking ceiling. It curved down to meet the line of the horizon, lightening in colour as it did so. The view up the fields from the rear window in his kitchen lifted his spirits although starting from a low base; it wouldn't have taken much to manage this improved sentiment. Looking out from the side window, the perfectly blue canvas was only interrupted by the tall bare trees along the line of the laneway. Trees with bare branches resembling malfunctioning fingers pointing up to the sky.

He heard a quiet squeak as springs were being extended against their will. Then the rumble in his stomach told him that he needed food, but he also needed to know who was calling him.

What did they want?

He took an unsure step towards the door and as he moved a bright light appeared in his peripheral vision to his left. He looked over and immediately spotted the origin of the vivid beam – the shaving mirror on the window sill over the sink. Maybe I should just see how I look before I open that door, he decided.

Martin moved directly to the window and raised his hand to examine his reflection in the glass only to realise he already had something in his right hand – a Parker Pen. Memories and thoughts flooded into his mind in a jumble, like a bale of compressed recycled goods ready to be dispersed. His reflection was not as he would have imagined and it startled him slightly. After a couple of long blinks, in the hope of correcting what he had seen, he stared into the mirror again. He noticed his face's pale almost see-through complexion which was more pronounced by his raisin like dark eyes which looked like they had been set into his doughy face by an amateur baker while he was unconscious. His pupils were fully dilated. So much so, the pupils and irises were almost one. His black eyes, black terrifying eyes.

The Blackthorn Legacy

He couldn't do anything about them right then. It was time to see the voice and so he turned to the hallway and in doing so set off another screaming pain in his head, reducing immediately to a dull painful throb alternating with the existing throb. Maybe a sub-Saharan percussion styled band had set up residence in his skull and they had begun to beat out a tune. Not one Martin was getting enjoyment from, it has to be said.

He was a mess of pain and hunger, but who did the female voice belong to?

Martin struggled but forced himself to walk out in the direction of his hall and saw the metal flap of the letterbox being pushed in causing squeaking noise he had heard.

"Who's there?" He stood in the middle of his own hallway. Even speaking was a chore in his current state. "Who are you, I asked?"

"My name is Vera Babula and I am working with Jean Wright of Legal, Wrights. Can I come in, please?"

The pen in Martin's hand seemed to have increased in mass just at that moment. He lifted his right hand and looked at the pen, in his strong safe grip. It would be safe.

Let her in Marty. You can sort out your problems with her help. You need to sort out the JJ situation.

"Go away." Martin hadn't meant to speak it aloud, but it happened. The voice in the darkness of his head was somehow surviving in amongst the aches and pains that were flittering around up there.

"Excuse me." Vera was not expecting to be told to go away. "I need to speak to you Mr Carey, please let me in", She continued with hopefulness in that strange voice of hers. Martin reached the front door and opened it slowly, the creak was still there. The opened door revealed a pale faced slip of a woman without even a touch of make-up – or even the need for it. She was a tall, extremely good looking woman, with a slight body frame. Her long shiny jet black hair fell down around her ceramic looking facial features and over the front and back of the navy fishtailed military style

The Blackthorn Legacy

coat. Her skinny jeans looked like they may have been painted on to her exceptionally lean legs. The Burberry handbag hanging from her wrist gave her the look of a serious shopper. This way she could hide in plain sight. It was impossible to even hazard a guess at her age. But if he had been forced to, he would have said somewhere in the region of thirty five.

"Hello", said Martin, almost too embarrassed to look at the very attractive woman standing on his doorstep. The woman put her hand into her left pocket and fished out a business card, much like Deirdre King's, except the name and profession were distinctly different. Ms Vera Babula was an investigator, according to the card in his hand.

"How did you find me, Vera?"

"That's what I do, I find people." Now he knew what made her voice seem strange. It was her accent. It was quite probable that Vera Babula was originally from Eastern Europe, although she had picked up some of the pronunciations used locally.

"Come in", he said, a little uncomfortably, given the woman's good looks and his inability to deal with it. "Please beware that I have made a mess in the kitchen, the second door on the left", he continued.

After he entered the kitchen, he pointed to a chair at the table, inviting Vera to take a seat. The fuzzy feeling in his head was being whisked around in there by the throbbing and aching pains, like lumpy cream in a baking bowl. He was however becoming more comfortable with his visitor with each passing minute. All tension fully evaporated when Vera carefully placed her expensive looking handbag on the floor beside her feet.

"Would you like something to drink? Tea, coffee, water? I don't have much else."

"I'm fine, I will not be here very long, Mr Carey." Martin sat at the table, realising that Vera was here on business and business alone. Unknown to himself he was playing with the Parker Pen under the table, out of the woman's sight. It

The Blackthorn Legacy

wasn't really a secret, was it? He was being advised, or at least his sub-conscious was being advised by an *other* that it was safer to keep it out of Vera's sight. "Jean Wright, I believe you met her yesterday". Martin nodded. "She would like to set up another appointment with you. She is very sorry about what happened in her office and will cut her consultation fee to make it up to you. That is why I'm here." Vera looked around the kitchen and out the windows, taking it all in. "You are difficult to find Mr Carey." He ignored this last comment as he thought about it for a moment and remembered the voice's latest ramblings. Martin stared at Vera for a moment, looking through her as he thought.

"I have to get in contact with a client of Ms Wright's. I met him in the waiting room yesterday. His name is James Jones. He gave me a number to contact him on, but alas, I lost it in the disturbance and so on. Would that be possible? We both have a common interest." He could see her thinking and endeavouring to work through the question and possible answers. She needed to balance correct with keeping his interest. It was imperative that she did not lose the interest of the man sitting opposite her, especially after all the work she had put into finding him and the expenses she would be claiming from her employer for this work. Of course she would be unable to claim the full amount if Martin Carey declined to take the bait.

"Maybe I could get your message to him", she said with an air of plain hope in her voice. Martin recognised something in her speech. Was it despair? No, not despair exactly, but it was close to it, to some degree in any case.

"Well, I'd like to see him again. We had a connection and as I said, I've no way of contacting him." The poor me in Martin's voice was having an effect on Vera Babula. He could see it in her eyes, her beautiful, dark green eyes.

"Can I check with my...?"

Martin did not let her complete her question. He knew what she was about to say and it didn't cut the cheese as far

The Blackthorn Legacy

as he was concerned. He decided to proceed with his own form of attack.

Ask more questions.

He had one in particular that would stop her in her thinking tracks, completely derail her thought process.

"Do you know Detective Walsh? You do don't you?"

The woman's reaction was unbelievable.

Her naturally pale complexion became paler, insipid. Her lower jaw became unhinged as her mouth just fell open, and remained so until she blinked her eyes in what seemed like slow motion and only her attempt at a dry swallow, forced her mouth closed. She was visibly shocked at the question. In the ten seconds it took for Vera to lose control of her facial functions, Martin's head aches and internal sub-Saharan percussions ceased, completely. A warm sensation filled his head in his place. There it was, osmosis at work – cool warmth filling the void left by the burning agony.

"Yes."

"Sorry", enquired Martin.

"Yes, I do know Detective Walsh." The sheepishly presented reply was all he needed to know. He had already thought it to be true, but he was going to dig farther. He had to, to be sure.

"Did you meet him last night?"

"You don't need to know this Mr Carey, nor do I need to tell you my personal movements." The indignant reply further nailed it on for him. She pulled her military style coat in around her and was edging to stand up. After a moment's consideration she did rise to her feet and she rashly grabbed her bag, "I must leave now. I do not need to stay here any longer to talk to you Mr Carey." The accent of her motherland was more defined now. Still she stood motionless as if waiting for direction from Martin.

"What will you tell Ms Wright? Will I be making an appointment with her or not? Is that not what you came to find out? You came for a specific answer, but I have not yet

The Blackthorn Legacy

answered your question. I believe you need to know in order that you can earn your earned pay. Am I right?"

She stood there still, not moving, just looking at the wall. She was definitely torn between answering his questions and getting paid fully for her work. The question in her own mind was; which was more important to her? She stared down at Martin resentfully. It was clear that she was thinking clearly again. She had made her decision. She sat down on the chair once more, although she remained on the edge of it, while she rested her Burberry bag on her knees. Martin knew by looking at her as she sat primed for out that he had to be careful. This woman would only take so much, before she would up and leave, payment or no payment for work done.

Yes Marty, yes. This is brilliant. Do it. Just do it.

This time it didn't feel so irritated hearing that voice from the darkness, from the shady corner of his mind.

"Here's the thing Ms Babula. Your friend Detective Walsh, your reaction tells me that you are close friends". Martin created inverted commas with his fingers when he said *friends*, illustrating the fact that he knew that they were more than just acquaintances, they knew each other better than that. "Anyway", he continued, "I know that the Detective is after Mr Jones, but has been unable to find him. So, if I can be put in contact with Jimmy Jones, I can then make him 'available' for Detective Walsh. What do you think? Oh, and you will be kept out of it. It will be choreographed for the Detective's part and it will appear wholly coincidental." He waited a moment, watching her facial expression change several times as she thought it over. Vera was obviously giving it some serious consideration. "Are you in?" That was the question, the contractual question. She was still mulling over it, sitting back at little further in the chair. More comfortable, it seemed. She brought her right hand up to her face and slowly and delicately stroked her bottom lip with a manicured finger nail.

"I will not be implicated in any of this, right?"

The Blackthorn Legacy

"Not by me."

"Yes, I will do." Her Eastern European accent was fully out now, for all and sundry to hear. She was at ease, at least more at ease than she had been minutes earlier. Her face opened and a thought crossed Vera's mind. "But why should I not tell him? I am ze investigator, I cut find Mr Jones and set up meeting." She spoke as though she had just arrived off the boat or plane from where she originally took flight. Was it possible that this woman may just actually have been falling back into her old ways? It was becoming clear to Martin from Vera's mannerisms that she could have been an investigator of some sort in her home country. Martin hadn't expected this and he was thrown by her retort.

It's too risky Marty, too risky. Think of the implications.

"Thanks Vera, but if you want to remain clear of this, I think it's in your own best interest to have as little involvement as possible. It would be too risky to be involved any more than I'm asking of you, ok." She nodded and thought some more about it. It was obvious the investigator was deep in thought. Her right hand came down to rest on her bag and she then brought her left hand up to her face and then moved it to stroke strands of hair.

"How do I get in contact with you?"

"You don't. Leave a message for me in Duigan's Camp Shop. Address the envelope to me, name only and have it there by ten tomorrow morning. It should contain details of Jimmy Jones and confirmation that Detective Walsh will be at the Library tomorrow afternoon at one o'clock. Is that ok?"

The single nod of Vera Babula's head meant that she was serious about this and would have the information he sought. She leaned forward, opened her bag and rummaged through its contents until she found what she needed – a notebook. Opening the little book, she flicked through pages and located what she sought. Vera extended the notebook towards Martin.

"That is the information I have on Jones. Take it down and use eet as you please, but I do not want to know what you do with eet. Is that clear Mr Carey?" Her real accent was much clearer.

He took it and looked up at her, breaking into a smile.

"Perfect. Tell Ms Wright that I would love to rearrange another appointment."

He recorded the information in shorthand on his wrist. He then returned the pen to below the table top where he recommenced stroking the pen, feeling an increased strength.

The Blackthorn Legacy

CHAPTER THIRTY:

THE STREAM

FELLOWMORE Library was unexpectedly busy at half twelve in the afternoon. Martin had brought in some of his notes to examine. He was seated on a soft sofa style seat near one of the large window panes. Memorial Square was also a hive of activity and inactivity simultaneously. It was full of people of all shapes and sizes, of all ages and ethnicity. An older man sat outside the window on the concrete bench, calmly and serenely watching all those moved around him, taking in the fresh air that freely whisked passed him, while occasionally glancing down at the redtop newspaper he had brought with him.

Some others in the square conducted business on Smart phones and laptops, tapping continuously on the screens or on keyboards. Some had earbuds in their ears talking while holding the phones in their hands. This was something that Martin couldn't quite understand. Why would they carry out conversations on mobile devices which were initially designed to be held to their ears? Was it just so they could be seen by others? If that was the case, it worked because Martin had noticed them. It didn't have any real effect on him only to ponder on the stupidity of it.

The Blackthorn Legacy

It worried him to use such items as mobile phones and laptop computers. It was fine and dandy seeing all these people talking and working on the move but where did the information they produced and generated actually go? If it was breezy, was there the possibility that the waves that carried the data could be pushed in another direction, somewhere it wasn't supposed to go to? All information was collated somewhere or in some places where, as he knew or at least surmised, it could be and probably was assessed and surveyed by the secret Government agencies. He was having none of that. He had it tough enough getting to the library without stepping on a manhole cover or falling over one of those beggar spies. Life was tough enough without having someone spying on your every conversation or on-line creation.

A queue of younger suited and booted people had formed outside the newly opened funky sandwich shop on his left as he watched out through the large window. Lunchtime was a busy time in Fellowmore. It would be interesting to see how many of all those people outside in the square would have actually been out there, had it been raining. There would have been many less than occupied it now, he reasoned.

Martin returned back to his notes. The diagram of the stream caught his attention. He noted where it rose – Slieve Lea, or close to it, and ran to...Jesus.

That couldn't be right, he thought to himself. He had only just commenced his study and already he was sick of it. Sick of what he thought he might have found. He cast his mind back to his last dream. That was the strange thing about his vivid dreams. They stayed with him as memories of incidents that could have actually occurred, even though he had never been there in that meadow, wherever *it* was.

Thinking back, he remembered walking up to the stream and following its course and there, after some trekking was Slieve Lea on his right hand side. If he was reading his notes properly, and if he had recorded them accurately, the stream

The Blackthorn Legacy

flowed right up to the point marked as Rahaduff. That meant...no it couldn't. It had better not be.

The Blackthorn Legacy

CHAPTER THIRTY ONE:

MEMORIAL SQUARE

THE cool March breeze was blowing this way and that in Memorial Square, swirling as it deflected off all of the tall but seriously dull and drab looking surrounding buildings. Detective Ed Walsh was leaning against the grey concrete monument attempting to look as inconspicuous as possible. He was looking in the direction of the library, while his right shoulder held his weight. He had a tightly rolled up newspaper in his left hand. He was uneasy and this could be determined by anyone by the way he tapped the paper off his knee in an irregular beat.

Walsh must have missed the classes in Detective school concerning tailing or camouflaging while in street settings. He stood out like a sore thumb amongst all the individuals and groups passing through or walking round the square. He hadn't really even attempted to hide himself from view. He had only one thing on his mind – Jimmy Jones. The thought of meeting him one on one was the one thing that was making him jittery, excitedly jittery. He badly wanted to see him face to face especially as that man was not expecting this confrontation.

He peered at his watched – 12:53. Another seven minutes and some. Jones was probably going to be late. He was a layabout anyway. Walsh was sure of this even though he

The Blackthorn Legacy

knew very little of what Jones with his days if he had a job, or if even he had a family of any sort. He did know that the man was a parasite on Fellowmore.

The more he thought about that man the tighter he gripped the rolled up newspaper. He wanted this so much. He wasn't entirely sure what he would do or how he would handle the situation, but he wanted to face him – really badly. He could feel his temper rising, his neck sinews tightening and teeth tightly gritted. Jones had caused him, Detective Walsh, personal trouble. He had been called before a committee to explain his actions following a complaint lodged by the lout. Oh yes, he was going to ensure the Jones would pay for his previous deeds.

Walsh had worked himself almost into a frenzy while he was waiting by the concrete monument. The grimace on his face was becoming more pronounced with each passing minute and his tight grip on the newspaper was such that his knuckles were white. Anger came easily to Ed Walsh and this slow build up would need to be dealt with soon before somebody else got hurt. What he required was a stopcock on the side of his head, allowing steam to escape, reducing the pressure that had been building up inside.

He looked at his watch again.

12:57.

No sign yet of the man he so wanted to pay for...everything that had happened to him over the last few months. His marriage break-up, the appearance before that committee and his own working partner's growing distrust of his ability to do the job.

Time was passing more slowly that he would have expected.

12:59.

Walsh's mind was beginning to wander and without his notice, Jones had entered the square. He regained his concentration and his focus. He looked up and there he was right at the window, the library window. Jimmy Jones. He knew that this was his time to get this done, for once and for

The Blackthorn Legacy

all I'll sort him out now, mumbled Walsh to himself. He lifted himself away from the monument, threw the crumpled and shredded newspaper into a nearby rubbish basket and marched towards Jones, no longer caring if he was seen or not. His anger was just about at bursting point.

The Blackthorn Legacy

CHAPTER THIRTY TWO:

THE TANNERY

JIMMY Jones looked at his Smart phone as he closed the door of his well-kept Council house. A metal clip had been placed over his nose at the hospital following his terrifying ordeal down Molesworth Lane. It was still tender. The thick set bandages covering the metal clip over the bridge of his nose made him look like he had lost a street battle. However because he did not have either a black eye or redness on his face which would normally be the result of such a scrap. It would usually have led to questions, but not of Jimmy Jones.

12:49.

I should be there in good time, he thought, smiling to himself. He was unsure as to why Martin Carey would want to meet him outside the library. Something about that dirty detective, but it was unclear in the message that had been left under his house door. He could have rung his doorbell. Why had that man been so secretive about it all? He had been there all last evening and the lights were on, weren't they?

Yes the light had been lit.

What a strange time to organise a meet – one o'clock. It must have been something important, he mused, smiling with nervous anticipation.

The cool breeze was blowing into his face and over his aerodynamically shaved head, causing his eyes to water more

The Blackthorn Legacy

than his paining nose did, but he had dressed for the weather. Jimmy Jones' warm coat acted like a weather shield, but that said, he enjoyed the fresh air. It cleared his mind. He was going to need a clear head this afternoon and the expectation of what lay ahead was growing inside him. Butterflies were flying around freely inside his stomach.

The back streets of Fellowmore were quiet at this time of day. The only business done here was carried out by those who had none or little regard for the rule of law. Most days the only rules that applied were created by street gangs and such like. It was just a case of knowing who not to talk to and who to avoid if one wished to stay clear of unrest.

Jimmy passed two well-known street corner look-outs on his way to the Tannery. The look-outs just nodded in his direction and then re-took their places at the corner, scanning the area for the business and the unwelcome types.

The Tannery was a one-way street that led up to Memorial Square. A route less travelled by many of the inhabitants of Fellowmore. The street held its name from over a hundred years. Back in the day it had been where dead beasts had been brought by farmers for their leather, or the price of it. The Tanners would skin the dead animals and the hide would then be manipulated for the creation of leather. It had been quite a successful business in its time.

The old stone buildings that had been used by the tanners were well built back then but hadn't been properly maintained and had deteriorated over the years. Some of the upper stones of the old walls had become lose and dangerous and grass grew between some of the cracks.

He entered the street and he felt the calm as the tall buildings seemed to hide the Tannery from the cold breeze. On his right was an area that had been marked as a site for a prospective car park, but was now overgrown with weeds and long grass and would most likely never become anything but the den of iniquity it had already become.

Occasionally it was cleaned by the council, and the cleaners often reported finding used needles, used condoms

The Blackthorn Legacy

and empty bottle and cans once holding cheap alcoholic beverages.

Jimmy slowly walked up the sloped street towards the square. He would normally be sitting down to eat a meal at this time, but the nervousness in his stomach was keeping the hunger at bay, at least for the time being. After his meeting with Martin Carey, he would eat something. A celebratory meal no doubt.

As Jimmy continued his walk up the Tannery through the grey and overgrown decrepit areas, he was approached by two roughly dressed characters that seemed to have just materialised from thin air, although more probably they were lying in wait – for someone, for anyone to sell some of their product to. Generally their primary task was to sell but on occasion they had been known to take payment while providing nothing in return except unwanted injuries.

Both of the men were dressed almost alike, as if they were wearing the street uniform – navy shell suit bottoms and crew neck long sleeve light grey jumpers with varying dark grey rope designs across the front, over white t-shirts. Their footwear was made up of white runners with well-known logos in both cases. Their hairstyles both consisted of tightly shaved sides with short back and sides. It looked like there was an overuse of hair gel or possibly just greasy hair, keeping the hair flat to their heads. Except for the silly tassel style fringes.

Both of them approached Jones, walking in that cocky way those who have control, or at least believe they have, are wont to do. The scene could have been from any of those Hollywood films where the underdog, a small man, comes up against two larger unsuspecting types. Not in this case however. The men stopped before Jones who greeted them amiably and began pointing in the direction he had come from and producing a list of some sort for his attentive listeners. He was a leader of men, men who followed every word he uttered.

The Blackthorn Legacy

The only other movement in the Tannery at that particular time was a light plain blue plastic convenience store shopping bag that was dancing to an inaudible tune, being conducted by the light breeze over in the wasteland once proposed as a possible parking lot.

After concluding their meeting, the two ruffians, for want of a better description, left in the direction Jimmy Jones had come from, with orders. Jones pulled up his sleeve to check the time. He rubbed his clean shaven head and brought his hand down his face as if replacing the existing visage with a new one for a new meeting. He winced at the pain as he rubbed the bridge of his tender nose; bring tears to his eyes once more. Peering up at the sky, he saw the mostly grey carpet broken in places by ever changing sky blue blotches. Could the universe have changed without his knowing and the clouds had become blue and the sky's natural colour changed to varying degrees of grey. He refocused his eyes. Everything was as it had been. The thin grey clouds were being blown by the wind across the heavens; forming alternating shapes as it did, forming shapes and letters for some unknown as yet undiscovered code.

12:57.

He would be there at the meeting place on time or even before it. Jimmy Jones was very rarely late for a meeting and believed that tardiness was something that could only be corrected by punishment. By carrying out business in this manner, created a need to concentrate and maintain a sense of time and place. He had seen how it was in the Public Service. Those who made mistakes were promoted just to remove them from a position where problems were being made, and therefore this policy, unwritten though it was, only compounded the problems. On the streets mistakes are punished and this led to those making errors learned from their slip-ups and thus improving one's self and business. There was no room for errors in his line of business. Preserving a level of interest in his product and its distribution was important to him, of the utmost importance.

The Blackthorn Legacy

He had lost three of his runners out in Shayleigh several nights previously. They had been punished, terminally, which was unfortunate and would be costly for a while but someone was going to pay for it. Detective Walsh was someone high up on Jones' list of those who would be making restitution of one kind or another. He smiled to himself as he continued to walk up the slight incline towards Memorial Square which was now coming into sight.

He could feel the cool, sharp breeze again as he approached the entrance to the square and the tingling in his stomach began to become more chaotic as the butterflies must have anticipated the exhilarating feeling that occupied his head at the same time. He believed that nervousness was good; it kept him on his toes.

12:59

Jones met the swirling breeze of the square head on but he continued walking to a position in front of the large window of the library, just beside the now empty bench.

The activity all around him was in keeping with the emotions inside his body.

Manic.

He stood there with his back to Martin who was studying papers on the desk but neither man realised either was there.

The Blackthorn Legacy

CHAPTER THIRTY THREE:

LET IT GO, MARTY, THIS IS FOR THE GOOD OF ALL

ENDEAVOURING to comprehend what he had just discovered in his notes, Martin was oblivious to everything that was happening in or around him. If what he had was in fact recorded, then he had to come to terms with the fact that his dreams seemed to have had some element of reality attached to them. If that was true then the stream really existed and did in fact flow from Slieve Lea. What he knew was that it flowed from the dormant volcano to Rahaduff and to be more exact, it actually flowed to the site his house was built on. How lucky had he been to have bored his well just in the spot where the stream ended? But why did the stream end there? Was it not a law of Mother Nature's that water would always find its own level and eventually make its own way out to the vast seas and oceans?

So many unanswered and unanswerable questions. He leaned back on his chair and glanced out the window to where the groups of seemingly unorganised humans went about their business indifferently. What he did see caused him to freeze for a moment. There, outside the window, with his back to Martin and moving from one foot to another in an excited yet somehow uneasy fashion, was Jimmy Jones. Glancing at his watch, Martin saw that it was 12:59. He

The Blackthorn Legacy

looked around the square and there he was, Detective Walsh, marching towards Martin Carey and Jimmy Jones but he only had eyes for one. The detective was swinging his arms and his intention was almost clearly etched across his livid facial expression. The face of thunder.

Let it go, Marty. This is going to be for the good of all.

Another outrageous communication from the dark passenger in his head. But these were desperate times for Martin and desperate measures were called for. The desperation involved was not something he entirely understood, but some part of him, his darker side, was willing to let it play out this time. He tried to predict what the outcome of the upcoming meeting between Jones and Walsh might be. After a couple of seconds of wrangling with himself he decided to let it go and to watch with an open mind. The next few moments would provide the solution to his nagging questions.

The Blackthorn Legacy

CHAPTER THIRTY FOUR:

THE BENCH

THERE was a first time for everything, though Jimmy Jones as he saw the detective trudging towards him, and immediately recognised the body language of the raging man and smiled at the stupidity of the openly aggressive detective. A raging pig in the town square, he quipped to himself. I though those days were long gone, his mind's voice said as he coolly waited for the expected confrontation.

Jones casually leaned his hand against the back of the bench as the detective neared him. Walsh came around to his left and Jones turned to face him, removing his hand from the bench and taking a step away from it.

"Detective", he said with a little tinge of sarcasm in his voice.

"Do not Detective me, you little shit. I'm going to bring you and yours down. I will build case after case on you and your little house of cards and it will fall all around you." The venom in the detective's voice was unexpected. Spittle flew from his mouth in pure passion, or stupidity. However, Jones being who he was and what he was, just calmly wiped his face dry with his sleeve.

"I don't enjoy being spat on Detective Walsh, but if you feel as strongly as you obviously do, then I recommend you go see someone. Maybe your investigator friend could find the right someone for you. A nice bit of stuff she is too." The wild and crooked smile that crossed his face riled the Detective even more. Jones could feel as well as see the heat rising in the man standing opposite him.

Walsh took a deliberate, threatening step towards Jones and both men were almost standing toe to toe. The smaller, balder man could smell the vile breath of the almost unhinged detective. Anyone who had been watching the incident could see for themselves who the aggressor was. Raising his hand and pointing in the face of Jones, he felt like wringing the little shit's neck. Nobody, but nobody treated *him*, Edward Walsh, the way he was being treated here and now. His blood was beginning to boil, as it done on many a previous occasion, with regrettable results on many of those times. The fast flowing, hot bubbly blood had a mind of its own and it nearly always seemed to direct the detective's unstable emotions.

"Are you going to assault me, again Ed?" That was the last straw. Walsh's was like a wound up spring, ready to jump into action. Somewhere, though in his head he knew that this wasn't the way to deal with the problem he faced, but it would feel particularly good. A coolness of some sort came over and descended upon him and he suddenly realised, through the red mist in his mind, that actions there and then would do nothing. He stopped and stared at Jones. That talk of Vera was tough to hear, but she would never be with, or even talk to a shit like the hoodlum standing before him. He knew her too well. She would have nothing to do with any of this type of thing. Yes, he knew her too well. Just as all these thoughts were flying through his head. Being soft didn't suit him. Standing there, still poised to whack Jones, he felt a paralysing sensation followed immediately by an awareness of something intangible rummaging around inside his head. Something sinister, something that didn't belong in there, inside his head. His eyes rolled aimlessly and he then leaned his head back a little and closed his eyes, followed by the words – "Do you feel the way you hate, or do you hate the

The Blackthorn Legacy

way you feel." There was real venom in his words. A gravelly hateful voice, sounding mostly like that of Edward Walsh, but more chilling. Although he had no idea where the voice had come from. His mouth had moved but it was as though a ventriloquist was in control. Then it was gone and Walsh felt as though he had been awoken from a deep sleep, the daylight shocked his eyes and he blinked deeply and then re-opened his lids. He saw a terrified Jimmy Jones standing before him. Walsh's rage re-ignited inside his mind and chest and he looked as though he was about to grab the bald butty man by the collar of his coat, but instead, he dropped his hands by his side and began shouting.

"I'll f..."

Walsh leaned in closely and stopped mid-sentence as he watched Jones grab his own throat and saw what appeared to be anguish and pain across the man's face. The detective stood there, frozen for a moment and then when he moved in to grab Jones, the man fell backwards, slamming his head off the edge of the bench he had been leaning against only moments earlier.

The sickening hollow sound as his skull cracked off the permanent bench was awful. Everyone in close proximity seemed to turn at once at the revolting thud. Jones' body eventually came to rest with his neck in an unusual and horrible looking angle and blood began seeping from the back of his head, trickling first and then flowing steadily. Forming an expanding crimson blotch on the pathway.

Some of the witnesses, and there were many at the scene, had vomited where they stood, having observed the dreadful incident that had just played out before them. Some had seen the entire skirmish, but most of them had just heard it, even above the din of traffic on the Main Street behind them. Some had taken out their Smart phones and the good Samaritans called the emergency services while others were more interested in taking the momentous photograph to post up on a social media site, as was their 'norm' nowadays. One lady had collapsed in a heap on the ground where she had

The Blackthorn Legacy

been standing, near the busy sandwich bar. The sight of Jones' darkening bloody blotch spreading out across the pathway from under his motionless body right there in front of the library was creating a general queasiness. The red had changed to maroon on the concrete pavement and it looked like it was expanding in slow motion.

Those on-lookers who had managed to maintain their food, just stood transfixed. Hands over open mouths, looking at a scene that was comparable to that of a scene from a high end Hollywood production.

Walsh stood over him in disbelief and stared around at the growing crowd, looking for support. He could see from the gazes and the changing expressions that they believed him guilty of causing the death of the bloody mess lying on the pavement.

Within seconds multiple sirens could be heard coming through the town. Two patrol cars and an ambulance halted on the street at the square, blocking all traffic coming from both directions. Diversions would be put in place as men and women bailed out of the emergency vehicles.

The Blackthorn Legacy

CHAPTER THIRTY FIVE:

EQUAL AND OPPOSITE REACTION

SITTING in the front row for the most anticipated show of the year is not always as good as it sounds at time of the ticket purchase. This front row seat was no different. He spent several seconds, comfortably seated, moving his eyes from left to right like a spectator at a Table Tennis match. He was watching the determined approach of Walsh and Jones' reaction over the seconds as the coming together was about to occur.

Jones' obviously noticed that Walsh was moving in his direction and Martin could see the mocking smile form on the butty man's lips. The determination in Walsh's step was the giveaway. However the butty man seemed unperturbed by it, surprising when he had been expecting to meet the man who was actually sitting inside the window, directly behind him.

The front row seats are sporting occasions give the best view of proceedings but on certain occasions, infrequent as it might be, injury or the unexpected has been known to occur. Martin had a bad feeling about this. There he sat in the best seat in the whole arena, probably the best seat in the entire town of Fellowmore. But he felt particularly uneasy – inexplicably so. He watched intently as Walsh made his final

The Blackthorn Legacy

approach and landed to the left of Jones, who turned to face his nemesis.

Both of these men hated each other, that was patently obvious from how they acted in each other's company, but there was no respect for each other's abilities in their individual fields of expertise.

Walsh stopped and quickly glanced around, in the window and almost directly at Martin who immediately looked down at his notes to hide his face from the rampant detective. He stared at his table, his own notes of everything and the first and only thing he saw written there was the message he had seen numerous times. He was always disturbed by that message **URME UNO UR** whenever he had seen it and this time it was no more unusual that the previous occasions. A shiver went up his arms, holding for a split second in his armpits and then down his sides, causing him to quiver a little. He peeled his eyes away from his notes and cautiously glanced back to the window where Walsh and Jones were still in conversation, agitated conversation.

The exchange between the two men was getting a little heated.

This is it, Marty. Take him out. This has to be done and now you have the chance. Walsh's head will direct you and he will...help. Just do it this time.

That dark voice from wherever it came, the same dark unused place inside his head, sounded more reasonable now. It hadn't changed but Martin was becoming more comfortable around it. The voice would help him. This he seemed to know, somehow.

URME UNO UR

He had to clear his head of all the voices and thoughts so that he could do this, this something new. He seemed to know what he had to do even though he had never done it, nor did he really understand what it was he was about to accomplish.

Martin felt himself floating and passing through the glass. He looked back and saw his own body still sitting in the

The Blackthorn Legacy

comfortable seat at the table inside the library, right at the window. This was an out of body experience. His see-through self that had just passed through the large window pane, wrapped itself around the head of Ed Walsh, pulling his head back at a slight angle. Martin could see the relaxation, but not the cause, as the Detective closed his eyes. Walsh relaxed and his eyes rolled in his head. Martin could feel the mass increase inside his own head. It seemed like the expanding dark mass was going to blow his skull apart at any second if the pressure was not released. It felt like his head was inflating like a balloon and soon it would reach the point where it could no longer swell and the library would be covered by pieces of skull and brain tissue. On the bright side, the dark voice would be gone forever, but then again so would his head. Neither was really a good result. His mind started racing. The murkiness deep in his mind began creating a dark rhythmic beat, slow but even and calming. Within seconds he was looking at Jones face to face – through Walsh's eyes. Even this weirdness was unable to bring Martin out of the calmness created inside his head by the rhythmic beat. Then came the words, the death wish –

"Do you feel the way you hate, or do you hate the way you feel."

The fear on Jones' face was something to behold. Walsh was operating under the control of an *other* – Martin Carey. The man sitting inside the library was the puppeteer although there was someone or something else directing proceedings. Something happened. A fall, a sickening hollow sound and screaming.

The mixture of fear and elation inside Martin's human body combined to create a delirium. Possibly like the delirium his parents had suffered before they had died. The shock, the thought, the repulsive memories rushed through Martin's head as he remembered that night his parents were executed before his very eyes. The sounds of his father screaming in agonising pain, his mother's panicky voice and then the sounds of life being taken from them by a tool handle.

A tool handle, he questioned it. Could it have been like the tool handle he had seen in his dream, or premonition or whatever the hell it was? No, he thought, deciding to reseal that secret envelope up there in that hiding place in his mind.

It was over, Martin's job, because the see-through version of himself just seemed to slip out from the top of Detective Walsh's head, a horrified, a frozen Detective Walsh, and it simply returned to its owner – through the large library window. Martin felt it settling inside him, a warm sickly feeling. Warm gassy acidic liquid rose up his gullet to his throat, but he somehow managed to keep it in. The burning taste at the back of his mouth was powerful and almost took his breath away. It brought him back to where he was, in the real world. Staring out the window at the body on the ground he could see the fluttering closed eyelids of Jones as he lay there otherwise motionlessly. Then the body's last breath was pushed out slowly and evenly. A look of fear engraved on the dead man's grey face. His lifeless colour more pronounced because of the unevenly spread maroon discolouration on the pavement outside. The spilled blood already had that sticky look about it and even though it was a cold March day, a few flies had gathered for a taste.

Every action has an equal and opposite reaction, Marty. It just had to be done.

The dark voice's explanation for what had happened. For what Martin had been a party to.

What are you talking about? What does that even mean?

The voice of a reality in Martin's past life. It had been some time since it had made itself heard in Martin's clustered head. He wasn't sure if he wanted to hear that voice right now. He was at a crossroads as regards his feelings. He had witnessed to death of another human being. A killing he had been a part of, and he wasn't sure if he was satisfied or repulsed by it. The voice of reason and reality had asked

The Blackthorn Legacy

what the dark voice had meant. He wanted, no, scratch that, he needed to know what it meant.

The Gardaí and Emergency Services appeared together at the scene. One of the Gardaí turned and ran to the nearest street side bin he could find and vomited into it. It was too much to take for him, all that blood around an inert human body, lying in a peculiar and unbelievable position. The other three stared for a moment. One went and raised his hands to all those that had been standing around watching the proceedings. It was impossible to hear what was being said through the triple glazed windows. Another got on his walkie-talkie and spoke to someone else.

The crowd members that were being interviewed all seemed to point in Detective Ed Walsh's direction as they spoke. The look of incredibility etched on the Garda's face as he turned in what appeared like slow motion to look at the individual being singled out for the crime. They would all tell how they saw Jones being thrown to the ground by Walsh, even though that wasn't what had happened. It's all about perception. Illusionists use that trick when preforming on stage – they direct the audience to look at something in particular, a dancer, a flashing screen, something other than they want the audience to see.

Deception.

The audience had been deceived, but this time it was in an open air auditorium although applause was not sought by the magician – not in this instance. Nor was it given.

Moments later Detective Mason appeared on the scene, ashen faced, as he approached his work partner. Without speaking a word he cuffed Walsh's wrists behind his back and directed him back to one of the squad cars. The slow walk of shame.

The universe works on balance. Both these individuals were throwing it all out of kilter. They have taken each other out with your help, Marty. You should feel proud. We work well together, Marty you know we do.

The Blackthorn Legacy

That was one feeling Martin was definitely not experiencing – pride. Nor did he like the fact that he was told that he had been involved in JJ's death. He may have known he was a party to it. But hearing it?

Other see-through people were now visible on the library window. Who were they? Why were they here? Had they come to punish him for what he had been a part of? All of these questions and many others raced through his over-worked and tired brain. Distress was beginning to grow and dig into his flesh, possibly aiming for his bones.

Then he heard the voices.

More voices? He wouldn't be able to handle any more than the ones he was listening to. A panic stricken Martin shifted in his seat and out of the corner of his eye he saw something move. He was almost afraid to look further, but curiosity got the better of him.

A number of people who had been in the library had gathered at the window, behind Martin's set-up, talking, whispering, muttering grave and sombre stories. Their reflections in the glass had confused him. However he quickly realised mistake. His over-active imagination had run away with him again, but the realisation at what he had actually seen in the glass was a relief. A reprieve from the terrible and upsetting feelings he had suffered in the previous few minutes. He looked back further to see them all focussed on the deathly scene outside on the path. The people inside never took their eyes from the dead man even while talking to those standing around them. Martin was then sure that it was those on-lookers voices he had heard and not some other dark lurking predator, hiding in the blackness of his mind. The weight of the heavy dark stone of terror that was resting invisibly on his chest had noticeably decreased with that realisation. One of those who had been looking out at goings on leaned down to Martin.

"Terrible situation, isn't it? I mean, nobody liked that man. But I wouldn't have wished that sort of an end to him. Terrible."

The Blackthorn Legacy

Martin just nodded. He had no idea what to say to that sort of comment. Did he agree with the man? Or was the questioner trying to find out where he stood on the issue. The Government had all sorts of people everywhere trying to find out all sorts of things. Maybe the man knew something about what happened and was trying to find out a little more.

"Look", he said pointing out towards the street. "The media are on to the story already. Didn't take them long, did it?" He paused. If he had been waiting for a response from Martin, he had been disappointed because yet again he refused to be engaged in conversation with someone he wasn't sure he could trust. "Maybe if we go outside we might get on the news tonight. Are you coming?" The excitement in the man's voice was that of someone searching for his chance to shine. A thrill seeker, even. Martin could guess from his reaction to the appearance of the media – national and otherwise – that this guy was just an on-looker, hoping to be noticed. The man was of middle age, well dressed and well spoken. If he was a member of the library, the chances were he had taken early retirement, was on leave or was between jobs and was gathering information for the purposes on an interview. A little nobody trying to become a somebody at the expense of somebody else. "Come on", he encouraged, "You might get to see yourself on telly tonight", he continued.

"I don't watch TV and I certainly don't listen to the news, mister,"

The look of dismay in the man's face was almost worth it for Martin to have said it. Within a flash, it was as if the middle aged man had put on the dismayed look mask, replacing the nosey, and fame seeking one.

"Wha...What? You don't watch telly or listen to the new...Are you...? Why the hell not?" The low voice he was using was similar to the voice in his head, but a little squeakier. Martin wasn't sure what had caused the most consternation for the questioner – no TV or no news. He decided to give the man a pointer.

The Blackthorn Legacy

"Look", said Martin, "The news is Governmental sponsored psychological terrorism." He could see that he had frightened his new student. "Everything the Government wants you to buy, the places they want you to go, all that stuff, they put it in the news. You may have noticed back all those years ago when it was reported there was to be a petrol shortage. What happened? People queued at stations. Queues for hundreds of meters at every fuel station. Then what happened? An announcement to say that there had been a mistake. That there enough fuel"

The man went into thought for a moment, hand over his mouth, eyes closing and opening again, slowly. He was taking the information in but analysing it. He opened his eyes and there was light in them.

"That was a mistake though, they admitted to it. Once it happened. That's not a reason to boycott the news."

"It happens all the time. The prediction that an extremely cold weather front is on the way and people panic buy. Then what happens? We get the same weather we always get. You gotta wake up to the way we're being told what to do and when to do it by our fine politicians. No, you carry on outside, mister, I'm staying put. I'll see all I want to from here. In fact, I've probably seen enough already."

The man straightened up slowly, obviously still thinking about what Martin had said, however the approach of television cameras lured him out. Fame was the draw.

The Blackthorn Legacy

CHAPTER THIRTY SIX:

THE KEY

MARTIN got out of his warm car and stepped into the cool evening air, to close the damaged gate behind him. He still did it in the expectation of separating him from the rest of the world. The latch slipped into place and he turned the key in the locking mechanism to ensure he would remain alone for the evening. Alone in the world of quietness and solitude, self-imposed solitude. The stillness was only broken by the engine sound of his car. The sound seemed to have being directed out through the exhaust pipe. Strange how that seemed to be the case when the motor was actually at the front of the car, under a closed bonnet.

No matter.

This was the place where he was at his happiest – in Ard Lane or Rahaduff as he now knew it to be called. He smiled a pleased smile to himself as he got back into his car to bring it around the corner near to the back door.

This time of day – dusk – was the strangest of all segments of daytime. Daylight was slipping away and being replaced by the darkness. The blue screen above the world began changing colour to a dark purple. It happened at an alarming speed, yet it was impossible to see the change in shades of blue as it darkened. First it was blue, then reddish brown and

The Blackthorn Legacy

finally purple before ultimately becoming black, invisibly occurring before the eyes of everyone, yet never noticed.

The dimmed lights of the car cast grey white cone shapes on the gravel before him as he edged the car into his regular parking spot. The cones lessened in strength the further they spread. He pulled the handbrake to ensure the car remained in that position until he required it again. Although Martin may have been the only one who ever parked a car at the rear of his house, he was without doubt a creature of habit when it came to parking his very own car. Four perfect depressions were visible in the gravel where the car wheels rested every day.

When Martin was happy he had parked where he always did, he turned off the engine, but left the music radio channel on for a moment. A fuzzy happy feeling was circling around him within the confines of the car and he wanted to take it in some more before he shut himself inside chez Martin for the night. He looked around his back garden, absent minded, enjoying the tune currently playing. He double looked to his left when something caught his peripheral vision. It was his pump-house. Something odd about how it appeared but it still seemed normal from where he sat behind the steering wheel. Suddenly the fuzzy feeling was replaced by a cool dark slithery uncomfortable sense of foreboding. It may have had something to do with the way the dusk sky replaced the bright day version, but that didn't seem to be it exactly. Whatever it was over at the pump-house, it had a definite draw on Martin. His mind was being dragged over there. It was magnetic. He opened the car door, without removing the key, shut it behind him and very slowly began walking towards the concrete shed.

The grass of the back lawn cracked under his weight like small twigs in a forest floor with each slow step. Was the frost setting in already or was it something else? The cold thin air surrounding him suggested it probably was the workings of Mr Frost. As he reached the pump-house the grass appeared to have changed colour. He remembered

The Blackthorn Legacy

having noticed a slight change in its appearance some days previously. It had looked like an uneven border of dead grass then, but now it had pushed out further. He had observed the burnt orange colour back then and probably intimated to himself that it was the oil or some part of the workings within the pump-house, but now the orange hue had pushed out from the mere edges of the concrete building. The sight of the increased burnt orange made him shudder, the thought of something growing from inside his pump-house out into his lawn. Could something have been incubating below his lawn? He shivered uncontrollably for a split second and the cold in the air seemed to get under his skin and circulate with his blood, like its intention had been to freeze him totally. Again he shivered, shaking this time as though the earth below him shook intensely. He was entranced by the cold but the next strong shiver awoke him from the stupor.

The sky overhead was completely black now. Darkness had taken over without Martin having given any real notice ahead of its colour change. Snap, and there was the daylight, gone. Another eight hours of a deathly black coloured sky. Numbness from the cold was setting in on his fingers and if he didn't soon warm himself, it would begin its crawl up his sleeves and would then take over his whole body like some unwanted terminal disease. He shook his head to rid it of any of those thoughts. He stood still and listened. That sound, what was it? Something was attempting to cut through cold and the darkness. Where was it emanating from? He craned his head as if that would make it easier to figure out the sounds origin. Taking a step to his right, crushing more of the stiff frosty blades of grass, the sound seemed to increase in volume. A small amount, granted, but an increase all the same. He looked up to the sky, at the light peeping through different sized pinholes in the unending blackness, and the origin of the sound came to him. He shot a look to the right and there it was.

His car radio.

The Blackthorn Legacy

Damn, is that all it was? Relief crossed his cold pale face.

It was bloody tiring standing still, he thought. It was the sea of emotions he had been through in such a short period of time that had fatigued him. In fact the whole day's adventure had drained him. He was possibly more susceptible to losing concentration because of his weary condition.

Martin trudged back over the frosty lawn to his car to turn off the car radio and to eventually enter his house. All he wanted was something to eat with a cup of tea and then see how the evening panned out. Notes and findings from earlier today could be added to the information already gathered. Some important pieces of the puzzle to be put in place that he hope would ultimately give him what he was looking for. The problem was he wasn't sure what he was looking for.

The car door was closed once again and the keys had been removed from the ignition. He searched through the assortment of keys and located the one for the back door. As he approached the step up to the house's rear entrance there was a noise in the trees behind him. Something was breaking through, something powerful by the sound of it.

Audible panting.

The only sound was the crashing and breaking of bear leafless branches. Martin lost the key for the door and began searching blindly for the correct one.

Fumbling, shaking hands.

He didn't want to look back over his shoulder; he knew the sight of whatever it might be would only slow him down.

He found it. Yes. The correct key. Raising his shaking hand to the door, groping it for the lock, in the dark. He felt it under the cold fingers of his left hand. Fear was beginning to take hold as he heard padded footsteps from behind. A bit away just yet, but he knew it was still moving, stealthily.

Oh Christ.

The key, just put it in the lock, just put it in the...He screamed silently, probably in his mind only.

"Shit."

The Blackthorn Legacy

The key fell from the grasp of his numbing fingers. He stood perfectly still in the hope that doing so would make him invisible to whatever it was that was moving up behind him. He had to get the keys, had to. He was going to have to move to get the bunch in his hand. Whether he wanted to or not, Martin was going to have to move. Hunching down very slowly, by degrees, he managed to touch the keys and he sneaked a look over the right shoulder straining his eyes to see over his back. He could feel the pull in his sockets; the wrenching feeling was almost too much. He felt as though his eyes would pop out of his head if he tried any harder. He eventually chose to move his head a little more to get a view and then he wished he hadn't.

There, not twenty feet behind him was what used to be Cat. A black...something or other.

Completely black.

An animal halfway between a cat and – a jaguar? It must have been two feet high from paws to muscly front shoulders and then some to the top of its over-sized head. The great shimmering green eyes with a thin downward curved strip of black in the centre of the green eyeball seemed to be staring threateningly at Martin. There was some sort of dead animal between its large intimidating jaws. It was being held in place by the cat's sharp aggressive looking teeth. Thick gloopy saliva was dripping from its mouth. There was also blood falling profusely from the dead animal's carcass, steady heavy drops.

Drip, drip, drip. Splashing on the broken stones beneath the cat's large paws.

He jumped to his feet hurriedly, awkwardly, grabbing the bunch of keys, rummaging through them once more, attempting to locate the correct one to undo the back door lock. He was terrified the cat could hear his thumping heart, so loud was the sound in his own ears. Martin also had a terrible feeling the hunter would hear his blood being pumped quickly through his life veins and it would smell the fear, and then attack him.

The Blackthorn Legacy

He tripped over the step, falling against the door and almost dropping the keys again. Barely clinging on, to both the door and the keys, he fumbled the bunch again.

Find the key, he implored of himself and whatever God would be listening to his silent calls.

He located the one he needed and felt around the door for the lock.

The strong padding sound was coming from behind. The cat was on the move once more.

Martin needed to use the toilet. His nerves were shredded. The key, it reached the lock, but wouldn't go in. He cursed himself; he must have picked the wrong one. More soft, lithe paw steps behinds him. He could hear the breathing. Then a soft growl.

The key.

Put it in the lock.

It still wouldn't go. A drop of cold perspiration had rolled to the end of his nose. The pressure was getting to him.

The key.

Put it in the lock.

Why wouldn't it go?

Shit. It was upside down. Turning it around, teeth side up, it entered the lock.

The door flung open. He fell in with it. He removed the key and looked back and saw his cat – Cat – sitting there looking up at him. It was a dead fox in its fearsome jaws. It dropped the dead animal, about the size of a medium sized house dog, on the ground at its paws and just sat there looking up at Martin and then peered around as if awaiting applause. It turned its head around to look at Martin; its unblinking eyes were almost hypnotic. The green seemed to be circling in a clockwise fashion in the right eye and was moving in the opposite direction in the left one. The curved black downward strip was what gave it the killer look. Sitting there elegantly, yet terrifyingly, showing its kill, reinforced Martin's view – the cat was most definitely the leader of the Underworld. He closed the door never taking his eyes from

The Blackthorn Legacy

the feline animal near his doorway as he did so. He was a long way from being in a trusting mood, especially after the day he had been through. The manual introduction of energy into his system would be needed if he was to solve the codes and notes he had taken over the last few days. No matter what, he was going to solve it (them). That's what Martin Carey did; he solved problems every day in paid employment, and why not do it for himself now.

The Blackthorn Legacy

CHAPTER THIRTY SEVEN:

DO WHAT YOU'RE TOLD

DECREASING light, air temperature reduction and heated discussion were some of the ingredients that were causing a stir in Fellowmore Garda Station. Of course the main ingredient to be added to the mixture was yet to be introduced. Detective Ed Walsh was one person who got tongues wagging in the station under normal circumstances. This however was the farthest from normal imaginable for anyone currently working there.

Groups of officers lined the hallway waiting for a glimpse of the detective on his arrival into the station. Some were agitated while some were smiling within themselves that the dirty apple had been noticed and would be thrown out of the proverbial barrel, at long last. The different levels of anticipation would no doubt create an over-charged atmosphere. In fact the tone in the station was changing minute by minute depending on whose side the new additions to the growing numbers were on.

A perimeter had been set outside the main gateway to prevent the media vultures from interfering with his delivery. Regarding his transport to the station, it had been planned to the nth degree. The Super had personally overseen the entire thing.

The Blackthorn Legacy

At just after five o'clock, two squad cars and an unmarked station wagon pulled into the car park at the rear of the building. A man wearing a beige overcoat over his head alighted from each of the three cars simultaneously. This was done specifically with the press army outside the entrance off the street in mind. Inside the back entrance of the station, all three people retained the coats over their heads and were lead to the stairwell to bring them upstairs to the Super's office. This had been done to retain Walsh's secrecy so that they too would be unsure as to which of the three was the culprit. Detective Mason was leading one of the cuffed men, leading most to believe he was directing his partner through the narrow corridor. This was another part of the deceit. Mason was with a young Garda brought along just for this use. Walsh was the third of the three which was totally unexpected.

Shouts of abuse and some of support were made by the on duty Gardaí waiting further down the hall. The shouts also lead to some jostling by men and women who worked together on a daily basis but were split by the arrest of the detective. Some of those on Walsh's side were only there because of their delight at the death of a hoodlum, a trouble maker. Anytime one of those was taken from the streets either in cuffs or a body-bag, there had been a little short celebration. Unfortunately for Walsh, in this instance, he had been off duty during the altercation. He had broken the law, is how it had been perceived by the majority of those who had witnessed it.

Outside the Super's door, one of the covered men and a young uniformed Garda waited for the call to enter following the knock to the timber door.

"Get in here." A shout, a roar of disapproval from inside. Walsh had not expected this. He had hoped for a hero's welcome from his boss. He had after all rid the streets of Jimmy Jones, even if he hadn't felt he had personally done it. He believed that he was surely due some sort of recognition from the Super. Had he not improved the overall situation

The Blackthorn Legacy

for the Super? Because the boss-man didn't have to look after him, Ed Walsh, against a possible case that may have been brought forward by Jones. It would have been different if he had actually touched him, as much as he would have liked to have done, but he was clean this time, wasn't he? His hands were cuffed, at the front, allowing him some, although restricted movement. He removed the coat from his head and handed it to the officer and then pushed open the door, leaving the young Garda on his own, with the coat. It had obviously been pre-arranged that the young recruit would stand guard out there. Walsh closed the door behind him and walked in, anxiously. He reached the comfortable chair at the desk and pulled it out. The Super was staring down at an open file on his desk, as if he was ignoring his right hand man's entrance to his war room.

There was complete silence for a moment.

"You and me Detective Walsh, we're finished." Morahan continued reading and kept his head down.

"Wha..What sir?"

"We're finished. You'll have your legal support from here or headquarters, but I'll have nothing to do with it." The silence resumed. Walsh's face paled, and he felt alone. If he didn't have the support of the man sitting opposite him, he was in some real trouble. A world of trouble. "We were a good team", he continued, "I was getting the applause for the good work being done, and you were allowed the freedom of these streets, up to a point of course. But now you've gone and fucked it all up Walsh. All of it. My promotion is probably...I don't know. You've ruined me, you stupid shit." Morahan was spitting the words out.

Walsh continued to stare at the top of his superior's head which was still bent, facing the table. "But I...I didn't do it, boss. H...He fell, I never laid a fin..."

Morahan didn't allow him continue.

"Thirty something fucking witnesses say you did. You bloody well murdered a man in broad daylight, in the fucking square." The Super slowly raised his head to reveal his face

The Blackthorn Legacy

covered in rage, hurt and probably a tinge of pay back. He was furious. The whites of his eyes seemed to be almost red as the blood that thrust through his veins at a rate of knots. Such was the fury within him. "Get the hell out of my office." He raised his head further and raised his voice to the man outside. "Come in here officer. This man needs to be put in that cell we talked about, for the time being."

"But sir, I didn't do it." Tears were now beginning to fall from Walsh's eyes and flowed down his pallid complexion. "I swear – I didn't –

"Shut up with your whining. Just do what you're told. This town will want and will get a quick trial, I'll see to it, now get OUT!" He fired his arm out, aiming at the open doorway.

"Oh, and don't worry about your job, I have a replacement readymade for the position."

The Blackthorn Legacy

CHAPTER THIRTY EIGHT:

RECALL

LONELINESS leaned heavily on Walsh in the small holding cell. He sat there with his head in his hands, sitting on the wooden bench that doubled as a seat and a bed. He had put many a person into this place. But never in a million years would he have thought that he would be occupying it himself.

Never.

Shame washed over him in the growing dimness of the evening. He knew the day was passing him by, he could feel the daylight ebbing away through his closed eyes even though his fingers were covering them. The trouble was it wasn't only the light that was ebbing away, his life as he knew it was slipping away from his grasp, tenuous though it may have been. Yes, it was good that he was by himself, but he shouldn't have been by himself. He hadn't done anything, had he? He didn't push Jones? He hadn't hit Jones, had he? He had wanted to, so much, he really wanted to put him out, to kil... He stopped and considered his last. It was possible, maybe he had hit him. The point of eruption had almost come to the surface when that little fat bastard...Maybe I did it, he thought again. Then for the first time since the incident he tried to re-call it. For the first time since he had been sitting alone in the cell he removed his hands from his face

The Blackthorn Legacy

and opened his eyes. It took a moment to accustom himself to a different, greyer type of darkness than that behind his closed eyelids.

He remembered walking right up to the little prick and leaning into him without actually touching off his person. He had been careful not to do something as stupid as that, even though he had come close to hitting Jones. Being pulled up for assault was serious. Not as serious as murder, as it turns out.

"Are you going to assault me, again Ed?" He remembered feeling his blood boil hearing those words. Walsh remembered how he had wanted to make him pay for that. Then what happened? He tried to concentrate. It was difficult to rid his mind of everything given his predicament at that particular moment. Dark shadows were passing through his mind, bad thoughts and some decisions. Concentrate, he told himself. He put his hands over his face again and then a flash. A brilliant white explosion of light. A vision, a memory. He remembered something coming over him at that time, a paralysing sensation.

He shivered as he recovered the memory.

That paralysing feeling was immediately followed by an awareness of something groping around inside his head. Something sinister, something that didn't belong in there, inside his head. Then...a feeling, a sensation. Had he said something, what was it? Come on, he pleaded. There was a buzzing sound in his head. It sounded like a hive of bees in there. He jumped up off the bench.

Do you feel the way you... He couldn't dredge it up, not all of it anyhow, no matter how much he struggled. It began eating away at him. He couldn't recall any more of the incident, just the screaming and the sight of the falling Jones and his expressionless pale face staring up at him when it all finished.

Maybe he was responsible.

Maybe all the other cops were right about him.

The Blackthorn Legacy

It was still nagging him though. Eating away at him. Was this the way it was going to be from now on. His head was full of dark thoughts. Some were memories and some were…well, plans. That paralysing feeling he had gotten outside the library came again, with the same effect as moments earlier – a strong quaking shiver. A momentary convulsion.

He made up his mind. Something had to be done about this. Not having a job was the same as having nothing and so he decided he would be losing nothing. The buzzing returned inside his head. It felt as though the hive was becoming overcrowded. He removed his hands from his face and placed them over his ears, hoping this would dim the sound. His eyes were shut tight. Still it continued – the dark thoughts and the incessant buzzing. Was this what the onset of madness was like? The buzzing, the darkness, the insecurity. On and on it went. He was becoming dizzy with all this stuff going on behind his eyes and between his ears, all fighting for the best place inside the enclosed and limited space of his mind. Insanity was not as good a place to visit as he may have believed. It was horrible. Just do it now, he ordered himself.

Ed Walsh removed his hands from his ears and began unbuckling his waist belt. The indescribable noise and pictures and echoes inside his head were unbearable. Something had to be done. He knew what he had to do.

*****

Detective Mason slipped away from some of the others in the canteen. He wanted to see his partner, alone. He knew Walsh was capable of stupidity. Not only was he capable, but often was the cause of incidents moving from silly to downright senseless. Mason also knew that Walsh was capable of being a good detective though. The streets needed someone like him to keep them honest. He agreed with him

The Blackthorn Legacy

that there should be no free rides for any of those law breaking twats.

Mason strolled down the dimly lit corridor trying to decide what he should say to his colleague. He reached the door of the holding cell and waited a moment. He bowed his head and readied himself for a shock. No matter what anyone says, he knew it would be strange seeing his work partner in that small room ultimately waiting to be moved to wherever it was decided he should be held until all of this was cleared up.

He knew his partner would never kill anyone, not the way they said he did. He wouldn't, no, not Ed.

He knocked on the cell door.

No response.

He knocked again and still nothing. He opened the flap and peered in. Could he be asleep in the cocoon type room?

Mason looked around through the rectangular post box size opening, looking for a shape, a silhouette even.

Shit, what was that? He squinted his eyes, trying to squeeze better sight out of them. Walsh wasn't that tall, was he? What was that tall man doing in his room? Why was his head at that angle?

"Oh Jesus Christ, oh Christ." He jumped away from the door. The sound of incredulity and fear was in his voice. He stared in again, and it was still the same picture.

"Jesus, Ed. Why?" Mason was crying, but no tears were coming. He pushed himself away from the door and then decided maybe his partner was still alive. How many people had been saved, how many had he saved. He took the cell's keys from his pocket and pulled open the door.

Ed Walsh's face was blue. The belt around his neck was attached to two of the bars in the small high up window.

Martin Carey had wondered why the bars were on that window in the first instance. He reasoned that nobody could escape through the tiny opening anyway. Now it turned out that the bars had assisted in Walsh's escape, from his demons.

The Blackthorn Legacy

CHAPTER THIRTY NINE:

THE ANNOYING VOCAL SOUND IN HIS HEAD

STILL in recovery mode from the scare he had suffered outside his back door moments before, Martin eased himself away from it and into his kitchen, moving directly to the Banker's Lamp in the far corner. Throw a bit of light on the subject, as his aunt use to say. It was a silly adage, but it was always nice to chuck it into the conversation every once in a while. Especially when his conversations were mostly with himself. It was quiet except for the incessant tick tock sound from the clock.

He could still feel the fear in his system and why wouldn't he have. Outside his door was what used be his pet cat, now a fox slayer. A fox slayer? If he had been told by one of those idiots in work that their cat had caught and killed a fox, he would have nodded, listened and when the dialogue had completed, he would have laughed to himself at the lunacy of it. Imagine a cat catching and killing a fox.

What the hell was happening, he wanted to know. Why would a cat grow to that size in such a short period of time? Or had he imagined to whole thing? That was a distinct possibility, wasn't it? Especially with what had been happening to him in recent days.

The Blackthorn Legacy

First things first, he decided. It was time for a drink of nice cool water to calm himself down a little. Martin grabbed a mug and returned to the sink. He turned the handle of the cold tap to release the flow of the crystal clear liquid.

Two seconds – no water. A forceful squelching sound came from the base of the arching chrome tap and it began vibrating. It shook at first like a tuning fork might do after the musician or for that matter, the doctor, had tapped its prongs. After a couple of seconds it began gyrating erratically from side to side. At the point where the tap was connected to the sink, the actual point of connection became visible. A dark ring appeared, narrowing and widening according to the tap's movement. The squelching sound was like the noise one would expect to hear if a liquid was splashing around in a half filled but sealed thermos flask. He could hear it coming though. He also felt it coming. The whole kitchen was alive with the shaking at the sink. He could feel its power. Martin stepped back. Several steps. It was about to arrive.

Splushhh.

Water hit the base of the sink with enormous power. So much so, some drops bounced up wetting the ceiling directly overhead. The noise was unbelievable, reverberating off everything that was solid in the kitchen, creating a bizarre echo and an echo of that first sound. It was like a high note hum from a double bass. The tap seemed to have been misshapen with the power of the fast flowing torrent of water. A tsunami of tap water. And just as soon as it began, it stopped and the cool, crystal clear water flowed freely from the slightly out of shape chrome tap.

He moved back to the sink, nervously. One slow step at a time. The water was spilling out in a pure constant flow – like any normal tap. Martin placed his mug in the water flow and gulped down the drink, wiping his wet lips with his sleeve, but the satisfaction was evident on his face. He replenished the mug and swallowed quickly again, before turning off the tap. It was only then that he realised how cold

The Blackthorn Legacy

his house was. Martin's senses were returning to some kind of normal standard.

*****

After eating a tasty easy to prepare meal, Martin fastidiously tidied the kitchen, as he was wont to do. He was feeling so much better. The water, his water, had made him feel electric, and fully charged. No Council water scheme would be able to provide a pure drink to the quality to what had come from his very own well. From his pump-house. Although he had already decided that there was no way in the wide earthly world that he was going to pay for an inadequate, half-assed water system, he was sure of it now. He knew he had been perfectly right to sink his own well.

The fire he had lit in the kitchen fireplace was coming along nicely. It provided the room with odd shaped shadows which danced across the floor and on the walls, surrounded by the orange hue of the fire itself. The heat was rising up and was beginning to push down and overpower the cold air that must have rushed into his kitchen when he had opened the door to get away from the cat.

The fully cleared table was ready to be used as his working desk for the evening. He carefully laid out his notes and left an open notepad with his newly obtained Parker Pen there to make notations, if required.

Deep down, he realised that he had three options available to him to solve the subject of his dream. In truth there were really only two possibilities. The first option was that he would figure out what all the information he had recorded over the last couple of days would lead him to. His second option included going out and finding the field with the long golden grass, the mound and surrounded by high trees up to a point and then opened out the view to Slieve Lea. That was a long shot, but not really as much an outside bet as option three. He knew that his third alternative would probably be more dangerous, but also much less doable. As he saw it, it required him sleeping and getting himself back into that dream. Each time he was in that dream of fields, he saw a little more. Extra information was gathered after each individual visit, scary though that it may have been. He thought it was a good idea to record his three options on a clean sheet of paper and he then tore it from the pad, folded the sheet, and placed it away to his right, away from all the other pages. He looked at what information he had assembled. Martin took a deep breath, held it and blew it out slowly. He considered all the notes he had collected. He would work through all of that first. This was option one of his three and it made the most sense.

Before commencing the tedious job ahead of him, he placed his hands behind his head, laced his fingers and stretched his arms and back. Exercise, no matter how little, was always good before going into lengthy periods of serious concentration. It made the body happier, he believed. He leaned back on the chair reflecting on what had happened today.

Did that only happen today? What a long day it's turned out to be, he thought to himself. He cast his mind back to his front seat view of proceedings outside the library earlier in the day.

He sat up forward abruptly, hands still on the back of his head, although his fingers were slowly loosening, and his hands would eventually come down to the table in what could only be described as live slow motion.

Something...something dark, something mushy in his head, something...The thoughts were all jumbled again. Flashes of recent and not so recent memories. He had to concentrate on the most recent ones. Martin closed his eyes tight, keeping out the dancing shadows, the orange hue from the fiercely burning fire. And the ticking clock.

The voice, the annoying vocal sound in his head, it spoke to him today, again, but...only after JJ was dead. Something else though. What was it? He tried to rewind the event.

The Blackthorn Legacy

A sinister feeling. A dark, murky sensation in his head – or out of his head.

Shit.

He had a foggy memory, like a recollection from years past. Only it happened that very day.

Then he saw it on the dark screens of his eyelids. The day's incidents would be shown on that screen. He felt like he had been given another front seat for what was about to be shown on the screens.

Something happened. He couldn't properly make it out. Then he saw it again and it registered in his brain what he had seen. It was very possible he had been unable to understand what he had seen the first time; his brain was not willing to accept it. He managed to pause and rewind it. On second viewing he saw what had happened. He understood it but could not explain it. His body, it had left him. A ghostie version of himself floated up and through, yes through, the triple glazed library window. Through the bloody triple glazed pane of glass, unbelievably.

Incomprehensible.

It attached itself to Walsh and then the murky, dark mushy brain feeling. JJ fell, bang and his head folded into his chest. His spinal cord had to have snapped and then the sickening smash as his skull cracked off the concrete pavement.

Martin shivered at the thoughts of that sound. Even through the triple glazed window he could hear both head smashing thuds.

He opened his eyes, to relieve himself of the stomach-turning sight of JJ's terrible death. He shook himself and immediately shivered again. The wave of coldness went up through his back and up his front and spread out across his shoulders, evenly. The hairs on his arms and neck were standing to attention following the shuddering chilling sensation. But although he had seen the replay of all that had happened, it was the voice, the message from the voice he wanted to recall. What had he said? Why was he calling it a he? Sure, it was a male sounding voice, but it wasn't human,

The Blackthorn Legacy

it couldn't be. It was in his head. To the best of his knowledge, humans couldn't live within other humans. Even with all the recent advances in sciences. Anyway he surely would have known if a person had been planted in his head.

Surely.

Or should it be surely not. Either way, it couldn't have happened.

No way.

The voice. What did it tell him? He raised his hands and with the index finger on each hand and he began massaging the sides of his head. This will help me concentrate, he tried convincing himself.

All he got were words. *Action. Reaction. Balance, Affecting the Balance.* But then as clear as the water that flowed from his tap came one of the comments. *We work well together, Marty, You know we do.* He stopped everything, even massaging his temples. The shock of what he remembered hearing from the voice numbed him. He had recognised that comment. He had seen it or heard it somewhere recently. Paraphrased even? He also realised that it was also very probable that he had only heard it in his own head, because that's where he had seen and heard most recent matters anyway. What was it though? He looked down at his notes, pushing papers around in a frenzied fashion, searching for something. What exactly he sought, he did not know. He located his main sheet and studied everything. One item stuck out, but he couldn't see how it meant anything. He noted it all the same and then slumped in the chair.

It felt as though someone or something had reached into his body and withdrawn his entire energy levels. Hitting like a punch to the stomach, he felt completely drained. He looked around the kitchen and noticed that the dancing shadows must also have lost their fire. Indeed they had, Martin saw the flames had decreased to just better than glowing embers.

Had he really been entranced for that long? He looked at his watch, realising that it was after eleven o'clock.

The Blackthorn Legacy

Outside he heard a noise. He walked to his back door and put his ear to the timber, hoping it would increase his ability to hear outside. After a moment of listening, he heard padding footsteps or paw steps. There was nothing for a moment and then the shrill noise he had christened the Scrowl. Louder than previously, a long ululating scream.

A blood curdling scream.

At least it was outside, Martin thought. It was a big cat, granted, but clearly there was no need to worry about it breaking through his back door, was there? No, surely not. It was time for him to hit the hay, he was beat. He tidied up the table, sorting out the pages into individual bundles and when finished, he left the kitchen to retire to bed. Sleep was already working its way into his mind, pulling at his eyelids, making them heavy. He wondered if his dream would be alive in his head again. Would he find what he had been looking for?

The Blackthorn Legacy

CHAPTER FORTY:

REACHED THE OTHER SIDE

SLEEP came quickly to Martin. The dark room, the silence of the house all good ingredients to entice sleep with of course a good measure of tiredness. He slept soundly at first, enjoying the silence and the comfort supplied by his own mattress.

After about ninety minutes of heavy uninterrupted slumber his eyelids began creasing and his eyes behind them started moving as though bulging behind their covers.

The dream had commenced.

He had remained in the same position up to that time, but, the onset of the dream saw him begin to move around under his heavy quilt.

The long golden grass was dancing to the tune of the light warm breeze that floated across the dream world. The sky was not as clear as it had been on his previous visits to this particular meadow. Watching the grass move in waves, it reminded him of a time he had been at the seaside, watching the tide come in and wash out. Not so much an ebb and flow as sweeping breakers. Back then times were far simpler.

Martin had reached the stream and the metallic smell was thick in the warm air.

What was it? He thought he recognised the odour but he just couldn't put his finger on where he had smelled it

The Blackthorn Legacy

previously. He racked his brain, trying to figure out the cause or the origin of the odour. It was more difficult because in dreams sensations are generally involuntarily placed in one's subconscious.

He looked back as if he was observing a camera man who was Martin himself in this instance. Even dreaming, Martin got the sense that he was directing the main character, from a distance, even though he himself was that individual.

The water in the stream was gushing at a greater speed that it had been before this. He kneeled down and dipped his hand into the sparkling water and could feel the drive behind the crystal clear liquid. Powerfully gushing forward towards its end. He walked its length, looking up at the mound, from which he had previously descended and most likely had done so, prior to this dream going live.

The tool handle was resting against the misshapen stone, where it had always been, but it was a slightly different angle that he had remembered it from his former visits to this place. Had someone else been here since he had last visited? Hard to see how, because it was his dream, was it not? He stopped to look over at the misshapen stone and for the first time he saw a resemblance to one he had seen before. Just right there – the metallic smell was at its strongest. It had a heavier tinge of something in it just there.

The stone.

It was a strange shape, but it was the same type of stone but not the same shape as the one he thought it had looked like. Definitely strange, he thought.

The din being created by the travelling water returned his attention to the torrent and he continued to follow its line, downstream, taking care not to trip and fall into the gushing water. Reaching the hole, the underground tunnel the stream disappeared into, he was astounded at what he witnessed. The water was not following the normal rules of gravity. Although the water was travelling at enormous speed, it was somehow not wetting the grass on its bank, either one. At the tunnel opening, the water collided off the overhanging stone

The Blackthorn Legacy

and rebounded extremely forcefully. The sound was that which would normally be heard at the base of a large waterfall. The sound was raucous, but invigorating at the same time. Even the water that crashed outwards from the tunnel edges still managed to land back within the edges of the watercourse. The world in which Martin was moving around was very different from that which he moved around in daylight hours. It was a world that he felt he would still be comfortable in, though. He marvelled at the crashing water as it managed to return to the stream and never hitting the grass either side, or in fact over the top of the tunnel, for that matter. Everything had its place and that was just how he liked it to be.

Martin dipped his hand into the stream just where it disappeared into the tunnel. He cupped his hand and brought it up to his mouth, sucking up the water into his mouth.

Well done, now let's clear it up. That strange message again. But it didn't bother him so much this time because the energy given to him by the water was unbelievable. Like a small electric charger had been plugged into him. He was alive and ready to take on the world – the dream world.

Martin looked back over his left shoulder at the misshapen stone. The almost identifiable stone and the worn tool handle leaning against it. It was time to visit this outstanding item and see what he might discover. He felt good about himself and the water had instilled a feeling of greatness within him.

The stone, the misshapen item, unusually placed and out of place in the middle of a meadow comprising millions of long golden grass stalks and a stream. A sparkling rushing stream invisible to the ordinary everyday passer-by. It must have been of some importance in years past because it had been recorded on those old Ordnance Survey maps he had seen at the library. He tried to recall the map, but his dream was dictating what to see and where to go. Still staring, although in an absent minded fashion for the last moment or

The Blackthorn Legacy

so, he decided to make his way over that far. To have a look. The dream director, he himself, wanted him to see what was over there.

The stone and the resting tool handle were at least fifty yards from his current position, at the bottom of the mound. It was to the right of it as he looked in that direction now.

The long golden meadow growth moved around the stone in the breeze like an upside down grass skirt that had no regard for the laws of gravity (much like the stream behind him). As he began his walk in that direction he realised how high the stone must have been. The grass was up to his waste and almost two feet of the stone was visible over the top of the waving golden strands.

The ground underneath his feet was perfectly even which seemed to him to be unusual for such an area of unused land. Then again it may all have been within the imagination, of his own construction, (this he very much doubted however).

As he neared what he called the misshapen stone he realised it was a pillar or the remains of one. It looked to have been masterfully shaped. Without doubt it was a block of limestone. It had all the characteristics of the sedimentary rock with the exception of the sharp edges forming the top to bottom corners. He knew it was Limestone though, he just knew.

Strange memory type slides passed through his mind but not staying within view of his mind's eye as he walked to what he now knew to be a stone pillar. A fuzzy sensation was growing inside his head, nothing to worry about yet, he decided, and continued the last few steps. The metallic odour was very strong and it became thicker, the closer he got to the stone.

It was much bigger than he had first considered it to be. Like an optical illusion, it changed shape as he closed in on it. The top had been hollowed out leaving a V shape – the misshapen look. His limited knowledge of geology told him that the hollowing out process had probably been caused by rough weather conditions over a vast period of time. The

The Blackthorn Legacy

whole rock had evidence of moss and lichens and this told Martin (the amateur Historian/Archaeologist) that it was old, maybe even ancient. The metallic odour was almost overpowering, but he was becoming used to it.

He walked up to the pillar and hugged it, for some reason best known only to himself. Or maybe not even by himself. Rubbing his hands up and down two sides of the huge but damaged pillar, he felt an indentation with his right hand, down low on that face, between moist, soggy moss which clung onto the rock for dear life. Its life. It caused Martin to stop completely and then after a moment's stillness he moved his fingers, his right fingers again, searchingly. He hoped to locate nothing. His hopes were completely and utterly dashed, blown away even. Something had been inscribed into the stone.

Flashes of bright white light.

Memories?

Dreams?

No please not a dream, he demanded. Not a dream in a dream, surely? Images were building in his mind and some he remembered. Some he didn't. The pillar was coming back to him.

He kneeled down and pulled back some of the long golden grass stalks to inspect the indentations in the pillar and after moments of poking around, he leaned back his head, opened his mouth and screamed at the top of his lungs. Or at least he tried to. Silence emerged from his throat. Surrounded by silence in the meadow, what did he expect – normality?

The dream.

The pillar.

The indentations had formed a spelling, a word – RAHADUFF. He had seen it in a previous dream.

He began breathing quickly. His lungs were expelling air quicker than he could take it in. He fell forward onto the ground, on his side, just missing the large stone. His face was reddening as it became almost impossible for him to catch a breath, a proper breath. His chest was heaving, faster and

The Blackthorn Legacy

faster, and he began wheezing. Losing strength. He knew it must be close. Fight, his mind screamed in a small voice. A cool breeze blew through the grass into his face, up his nostrils and down his windpipe. It slowed his racing heart, a little and provided a slight respite for his over-worked lungs. But even he realised that one breeze wasn't going to help he needed more. The old adage *One swallow doesn't create a summer*, crossed his mind, why?

Surely the director would call CUT any second, surely. The odour, the thick, tacky, metallic odour flowed out from behind the pillar. It had a colour, made up of tiny red and white particles. The particles were in equal measure and therefore the actual colour passing through a curved liquid type duct flowed was pink. A steel pink colour. It flowed from behind the pillar Martin had been hugging just moments earlier.

The pillar with the indentation.

The pillar spelling out Rahaduff.

The pillar that supported the tool handle.

The visible odour flowed through the imperceptible duct passed directly towards Martin and fed directly into his open mouth. First he began gagging and then writhing on the ground. However within seconds it brought a strength, like that of the water from his tap. Immediately the influx of the syrupy odour into his system stopped, sensing that it had done what it needed.

His heart beat slowed, his lungs slowed and his face lost the fiery red colour it had held. He began breathing normally; well, like someone who had just sprinted the hundred meter dash in world record time. That kind of normal. His lungs were burning, but he could cope with that kind of problem if he was sure he would be able to catch his regular breathing pattern.

After what seemed like an eternity, the weakness dissipated, completely, and he rose to his feet, slowly, very slowly. He stumbled on the first attempt to stand but he was not about to give up now. Not after what he had been

The Blackthorn Legacy

through. He might never get a chance like this to discover what this and the previous dream had meant. He knew that the secret of the vision was behind this pillar. The Rahaduff Pillar.

Standing weakly, leaning against the out of place stone, in the out of place field, in his strange dream, he took in a few more deep breaths and then attempted to stand without any assistance. Sweat dripped freely from his face. He felt as though he had put in a hard manual labour shift. His chest was tired; he could feel the twinges in the muscles that would no doubt soon become screaming pains. He had soon become warm all over and was soaking in sweat, making it more uncomfortable to move in the cold sticky clothes. You will not give up, he bawled at himself from inside his head or maybe it was from inside his dream. It didn't matter where it came from, he was proceeding with this. He needed answers.

A strong breeze blew again, directly into his face, bringing with it another blast of energy. Blast was probably overstating it, but it had provided a spark of vigour, as if he had been plugged into a small set of jump-leads for a split second.

His face reddened again and his eyes sparkled, but this time with a little oomph. He straightened up and stood to attention almost of his own accord. He felt great, better than great. Now to see what lay behind the pillar, what secrets were hiding there, he had wondered. The easiest thing for him to do would have been to walk around the tall cuboid column of limestone. But that was going to be harder than he had expected.

The long golden unbelievably grass formed an impassable barrier. It had stiffened and was not for moving. He was unable to break through on either side. It, whatever it was, didn't want to make it easy for Martin. The only thing to do was to haul himself up on the stone, using the v-shaped remains of the pillar to hoist himself up.

As he reached the top, and after managing to drag his knees up to the top of the stone, everything just stopped. The

The Blackthorn Legacy

breeze that had been blowing ceased. Everything in the place, this place, became still. Only the odour, the strong thick, syrupy, metallic odour. It had become much more pungent.

Was there a greater being here, he wondered because it felt as though he was being watched from afar and as though *they* had flicked a switch of some sort or maybe a lever had been pulled down, stopping everything. He felt completely alone. How funny was that, he thought. Funny peculiar and not funny ha ha. He had been alone in this dream world all along but now he felt a strong sense of loneliness. It caused him to quiver, a reflex movement. He had to carry on regardless though. He needed to. All the suffering he had endured couldn't be for nought.

His knees were now taking all his weight as he balanced on the pillar's top. Some of the rough edges were digging into him, but his mind was elsewhere. He reached over and grabbed the tool handle that had caught his attention on his previous visits to this place. It was heavy, far heavier than he would have expected. He had seen and felt a handle akin to the one that he was attempting to heave up over the pier. Flashes of red and a sense of unhappiness, no not unhappiness, regret maybe. After a tiresome struggle he finally dragged it up, the exertion, a timeless struggle. The odour was definitely more pungent, potent even.

The tool handle was connected to a pick axe head. A great big pick axe head. A pick axe head covered in blood. He noticed thick syrupy blood drop as it fell heavily to the ground. Each drop looked as though it was being pulled away from the pick axe in slow motion. The slick sound of the drops forming and falling to the ground was sickening to say the least. He almost dropped the tool from his grasp but managed somehow to maintain some control. He put it aside on the pillar, which now seemed to have increased in length. He knew that he was going to have to crawl across its top to get a view of what lay at its base on the far side. He needed to

The Blackthorn Legacy

find out what the blood that was dripping from the large pick axe head belonged to.

Martin shimmied across the ever lengthening pillar until he eventually reached the end. He stopped and gathered his thoughts. It must have taken thirty seconds to move along the pillar, but when he looked back to where he had come from, it was almost within touching distance. This place was messing with his head, although there was no such feeling up there in his head. Either everything had been scrambled or he had unknowingly expected this assault on his senses. He returned his attention to where he wanted to be, and took two deep breaths, blowing them out slowing with puffed cheeks. It was time to lean forward. Seconds after looking down below he fainted after seeing the first, second, third, fourth and then fifth blood drenched items lying lifelessly on the clean grassy ground. Cut flesh with exposed bones protruding through crimson coloured ripped flesh. The shock of it stopped his brain just after it had managed to register what it was he had seen.

CHAPTER FORTY ONE:

HURTLING DOWNWARDS

FALLING.

The awareness of rapid decent was clear in his mind. Martin was falling at breakneck speed through what felt like a black airless vacuum. Hurtling downwards.

His arms and legs were swinging in all direction, in an attempt to reduce the speed of his decent and maybe find something to catch on his fall through the darkness, like film heroes all managed somehow to do.

He heard the sound of that bass drum once again coming from somewhere, but not knowing where. Within seconds he understood that it was his heart which was beating so hard, it was as though the powerful muscle was ready to burst through his ribcage.

He was falling so fast. But there didn't seem to be any ground coming up to meet him. The endless fall, in darkness through a black hole was even scarier than knowing he was most likely going to come to painful end, a bone crushing thump any second now. Even though he was plunging at such speed, the sight of what lay behind the pillar was still with him.

The thoughts going through his mind were abnormal to say the least. He had remembered seeing somewhere that

The Blackthorn Legacy

human beings, who are at the end of their life, heading for the exit door to their demise, would see a bright light approaching them and that their spent life would pass before their very eyes. Martin could dispel that myth there and then. He could neither see a light approaching, nor was the history of his living experiences visible to him. The horror was there, though. The horror of not knowing when to brace himself, of not knowing how much pain he would be in, if he did survive. Also, he feared surviving the fall and being unable to move. Dying where he landed, in darkness, and nobody else knew where he had been. In fact he didn't even know where he had been, himself.

How long had he been hurtling through this dark tunnel?

Eternity? It was incalculable.

He had learnt his secret, or at least the secret of his dreams. Had it been worth it? Well, not if he were to die then, like that, alone.

Suddenly he felt it. His end was on its way up to meet him. At least the ground will break my fall, he said trying to make himself smile. I should be happy dying, no matter how it happens, he said trying to calm himself before the inevitable end.

The Blackthorn Legacy

CHAPTER FORTY TWO:

WELL DONE, NOW LET'S CLEAR IT UP

MARTIN twitched unusually in bed. It was unusual because of the power in the sensation. He actually thought he had bounced up off the mattress – so vigorous was that twitch. The shock of it made him sit up immediately in his bed. The quilt was still over him, barely. He had woken from the terrifying sensation he had experienced of falling to his death. His heart was racing. His lungs were pumping.

Palpitations.

Perspiration was lathered across his brow and neck.

His eyes wide open; he glared at the opposite wall in his bedroom staring blankly until El Che came into focus. Had he been observing him in his hours of sleep and...

"Oh Jesus", he shouted, head upturned and facing the ceiling above him. He dropped his head and buried his face in his hands, falling back onto his pillow. He was drained; every muscle and sinew in his body was weary and was calling out for rest. Unfortunately, that was not going to happen because although his body was utterly fatigued, his mind was acutely alert. He knew it would futile to attempt to stay in bed if his mind wanted to wander, even if he was physically shattered

The Blackthorn Legacy

Wide awake.

He stared up at El Che for advice, none of which was forthcoming. His dream jumped into his mind, screaming for attention. Attention he didn't want to give it. He was disgusted, abhorred and sickened by what he had seen. If the scene at the base of the pillar was in fact real, then some of what he had learned made sense, even if the whole situation made absolutely none.

Only El Che's face was visible in the darkness of his bedroom. This was of course because it was still night-time and daylight was still at least two hours away. The hands on the double bell alarm clock on his locker told him that it was just after four o'clock in the morning.

Damn. Still early and no chance of sleep coming back to him. Not just then anyway.

Once again the only sound to be heard was the sound of silence. It was like a continuous quiet whistling sound in his ears, and always at the same pitch. It was annoying, but also a little unnerving. If there was one thing he had learned since he moved out to Shayleigh, it was that silence did not actually exist. He understood it to be a state of mind or something other than just nothingness.

His senses were heightened and he could hear, smell and see everything clearer. He also felt differently. Inside, outside, everywhere. Martin touched and stroked his head and body, but everything seemed to be fine, but he still sensed a difference. Something was different. Should he get out of bed? That was the question rolling around in his brain. He wasn't getting any hints from the voices up there, good or bad, so he sure wasn't going to receive any intimation from his new found companion(s). He was warm and comfortable, even if his heart and lungs were still working faster than normal. He looked up at the wall.

"Well, El Che, should I stay here in bed?"

No reply.

"That settles it then", he replied to his own question, "I'll get up then. You're the best El Che." Smiling up at his hero,

The Blackthorn Legacy

he got out of bed. The floor was freezing cold and in this state of heightened sensitivity it felt as though he could have been standing barefoot on a block of Siberian ice. He put on a pair of socks and walked out to the kitchen and made his way to the Banker's Light and turned it on. The light emitted from the bulb, the same as always, but forced him to close his eyes tight for a moment to adapt to the brightness, as he perceived it. The creamy glow that was cast across the kitchen from the little light seemed to be pushing the darkness out, only allowing some of it to remain in some corners and under the table. Light is powerful, but not to the potency or intensity of the ever present darkness.

He walked to the sink, armed with his mug, and he turned on the cold water tap. Again it gurgled and immediately he turned it off. He stood back anxiously, his mind alerted to something. The dream, the stream in the dream came back to him as he stood there. He realised that the water from his pump-house was most definitely being provided by that waterway. The Ordnance Survey map showed it, his dream showed him. The pieces of the jigsaw were all there and now it was just a matter of him properly connecting them, and not just making them fit together. If you want a drink, he told himself, get some milk.

"Warm milk", he said aloud. Then he smiled, a large face changing smile, as though he was the proud discoverer of some new way of life. Something life changing, maybe. Martin had just escaped the biggest life changing experience of all – death.

Placing the saucepan on the hob with half a pint of milk in it, he turned it on to a low heat. It was going to take a few minutes for it to come to the boil, so he decided to take a look in the shaving mirror which still stood on the window board of the kitchen window, just over the back of the hob.

Numbness overtook his entire physical body. He stood there motionless for what seemed like an eternity. The reflection that bounced back to him was not Martin Carey, it couldn't have been. The man looking back at him from the

The Blackthorn Legacy

glass had a head of hair that was completely grey, almost silver. His face was somewhat weather beaten, to boot.

How could that have happened?

What had happened?

Was it really him?

Martin looked into the mirror again and caressed his face, up and down with the palms and backs of his hands. It certainly felt like his own skin. His hair also felt like it belonged to him. The image did however look exactly as he did. Because it was him.

"What happened to me?" He asked his reflection. The likeness in the glass moved out of sync with Martin's movements. It was a little slower, but not by much. It was probably his imagination, he told himself. After all it was just after four in the morning. He got a dose of the jitters. His insides seemed to move of their own accord. Fear was setting in and he knew only too well what that felt like. He anxiously, fearfully looked around the room. There was nobody else in there with him playing a trick with the light, or darkness for that matter.

"Who am I?"

There was no reply, as expected.

The milk in the saucepan began to boil and it took his concentration away from the creepy mirror reflection. Surely is had to be a distortion, a trick of light. Something else. It had to be, surely.

He tipped the milk into the mug and sipped at the sizzling white liquid. That certainly felt much better. His insides were coming back to life after the jolt he had suffered standing before the little mirror. He sipped again and everything seemed to improve infinitely.

"Let's take another look." He had thought his mind was alert but it could have been his sleepy mushy brain convincing him he was awake. That could have been the reason he had mixed up the image on the reflecting glass. He doubted it however. One more sip and then he readied

The Blackthorn Legacy

himself for a second look. He moved slowly towards the mirror, as if that was going to change the result.

Not a chance. The identical image looked right back at him.

"Who am I?" He asked again. It was going to be difficult to accept this new appearance. He wasn't one to worry about how he looked, or what people thought about him, but this was...

"You are me, you know you are" replied the image from the mirror. Martin's mug fell from his hand. The mirror had spoken to him. In the same dark, deep voice that had been annoying to him all along. Telling him what to do.

"No", he screamed, "you didn't talk to me." He felt like he wanted to cry in shock, but he wasn't able to. His whole system was stunned and his muscles were turning to jelly. As he collapsed forward, he caught the edge of the counter in front of the hob with his hands and managed to hold himself up.

"Yes Marty, you are me, you know you are. I live here, I've always lived here and you're just using my house. I own Rahaduff. I am Rahaduff." The deep voice spoke to Martin firmly, but without any malice. "I am the person you wanted to be. And yes, it was your body that was found at the top of the lane all that time ago", it continued.

"What?" Screamed Martin. He didn't know what else to say. It was a reflex scream. "What the hell does that mean? Who am I?" Begging for answers that he probably didn't really want to hear. He stopped and tears began rolling from the corners of his eyes. "I don't understand – any of this." Snuffling, sobbing now. "The body parts I saw at the pillar. Why – was my head – there? Why am – I – still here if – I'm – dead?" He was sobbing more now. Wiping his tears and nose, both running as much as each other.

"Is it not true, Marty, that you are always looking for clarity, fairness and equality?"

"What?" The disbelief in his voice was stronger than the sobbing.

The Blackthorn Legacy

"Take Detective Walsh and Jimmy Jones for instance. Both of those are bad eggs. They alone ruined more lives in this area, than any others. You took them out, saving the balance, the natural balance. You should be proud of yourself."

"You did that, I saw you. You went through the window or some shit. Don't put that on me."

"No Marty, I just told you how to do it, you carried it out."

"I can't...I don't...Why? How?" Confusion had set in.

"Like I said Marty, you are who you always wanted to be, to do what you always wanted to do. I am just the provider."

"How – do – I get rid of this? How did – I get – it?" The sobbing continued but the conversation was over. There was no more from the mirror.

There was a noise over at the table. The sound of falling and rustling. Slowly, he moved he jelly-like limbs, struggling to his feet. He stumbled to the far side of the table and there he saw his notebook lying face down on the floor, open on a page.

Martin spent the next hour wading through his notes. The fairy fort removal and the distorted photo, the stream flowing only to his house and probably his well. URME UNO UR. You are me, you know you are. And finally well done, now let's clear it up. Of course, the *well* had been constructed.

He was who the mirror said he was. Now he was who he needed to be. Sorting out the rest had to be dealt with. Oh yes, that bitch Deirdre King was going to be next. The feeling of acquired power was starting to seep in. Martin would have his advisor with him at all times.

The Blackthorn Legacy

CHAPTER FORTY THREE:

THE SECRET ENVELOPE

LATER on that morning, the Dunphy sisters, The Humpy Dunphys called to Martin. The kitchen floor had been cleaned to a spotless finish, as always. He opened his front door to see two witch like creatures standing there.

Both had shocks of grey curly hair sticking out of their heads in all directions. Like spent springs. Something a comb or brush would easily have fixed. They wore long ill-fitting flowery dresses, making them look bigger, in every way, than they actually were. The black ankle boots of the one on the right gave her a granny witch look, whilst her sister wore light brown pointy shoes, much like those sported by one of the wicked witches in The Wizard of Oz. The shoddily applied make-up consisting of strange pink lipstick and red blush which seemed to have been heavily applied in places. They had obviously been looking for the porcelain doll blush look, but the rough edges in their attempt at round cheeks blush, was nothing short of atrocious.

"Mr Carey", said the one on the left began. Her soft but strong voice was not what he had expected to come from the wild looking woman. "We just want to thank you and your cat for helping us out."

"Excuse me?" Martin was totally at a loss. He had no idea what they were talking about.

The Blackthorn Legacy

"Your cat", said the other one. "He attacked and caught a fox the other night. That fox that killed three of our hens."

"We love our hens." The sisters looked at each other and smiled. It was an eerie smile, strange looking. But that just could have been the weird make-up and its terrible attempt at application. "We have, sorry had, ten hens. Now there are only seven left."

"But there could have been many less, but for you cat", continued her sister.

"Yes, Mr Carey. The balance has been restored. Thanks to you and your cat."

Balance, that's what the voice, the man in the mirror kept saying, Martin thought to himself.

"I didn't, I didn't do anything. I mean it was my cat. I'll give him something, a present from the two of you. Extra food or something." He had been totally flabbergasted and it was very obvious to the Dunphys as the words just fell out of Martin's mouth with absolutely no thought process behind them.

"Oh Mr Carey, don't play that game with us. We know you; we know you understand the balance of nature. It's always been here in Rahaduff. It has always been in that secret envelope you hid away up there", she said pointing to his head.

"It's just a shame our money grabbing Uncle Tom and his council cronies could not have understood what was at stake."

"Or how important the BlackFort was."

Martin fell back a step, dumbfounded. The two women turned on the step to go begin their walk back up the lane. There was no sign of any car or means of transport of any sort. It seemed that these two old women had walked the whole way down the lane to see him. They didn't look capable of making it out to his road entrance, let alone walk another mile or so. One of them turned back as she shuffled down the driveway.

"I think the grey hair suits you, Marty."

The Blackthorn Legacy

*****

Two week later, Mason recommenced the investigations into the murders in Fellowmore. His new partner, Detective Joey Thornsberry had been appointed by Morahan more for his own personal sake than because of his perceived ability or otherwise of Thornsberry. They reached a *behind the scenes agreement* that Joey would no longer search out information relating to him or Ed Walsh who was still awaiting trial for the murder of Jimmy Jones.

The investigation would eventually lead to nothing regarding the detective's investigation; however the public's perception of Superintendent Morahan had improved no end following his handing over and finger pointing his own detective as a criminal. Walsh had been seen taking the life of a man, a despicable man, but a man all the same, in broad daylight. Questions were also raised concerning the possibility of his involvement in the killing of the three hoodlums in Shayleigh. There was an obvious connection between the slain men and Jones was that connection, in many people's eyes, thus inferring Walsh's involvement – in the public court of the media, in any case.

Martin Carey however, was still hearing voices inside his head, but he was accepting their orders. He no longer feared the sounds of others where others were not present. His dream no longer visited him because he had solved that mystery and had dealt with what needed to be done.

-THE END-

The Blackthorn Legacy

Made in the USA
Charleston, SC
03 April 2015